CW00486993

BLACK GIRL FROM PYONGYANG

In Search of my Identity

BLACK GIRL FROM PYONGYANG

In Search of my Identity

Monica Macias

With Becky Branford

First published in the United Kingdom by Duckworth,
an imprint of Duckworth Books Ltd, in 2023

Duckworth, an imprint of Duckworth Books Ltd
1 Golden Court, Richmond, TW9 1EU, United Kingdom
www.duckworthbooks.co.uk

For bulk and special sales please contact
info@duckworthbooks.com

Copyright © Monica Macias, 2023

No part of this publication may be reproduced, stored in a
retrieval system, or transmitted in any form by any means
electronic, mechanical, photocopying, recording or otherwise,
without the prior permission of the publisher.

The right of Monica Macias to be identified as the Author
of this Work has been asserted by her in accordance with
the Copyright, Designs and Patents Act 1988.

A CIP catalogue record for this book is available
from the British Library.

1 3 5 7 9 10 8 6 4 2

Text design and typesetting by Danny Lyle.
Printed and bound in Great Britain by Clays.

Hardback ISBN: 9780715654309
Trade paperback ISBN: 9780715654316
eISBN: 9780715654323

To my parents

CONTENTS

Part 3: Consolidation

Preface

The story I want to share with you in this book is an unusual one. Why? It is uncommon because I was born the fourth child of Francisco Macias, the first legitimate president of independent Equatorial Guinea, a small country and former Spanish colony in West Africa, but I was raised by Kim Il Sung, the former president of the Democratic People's Republic of Korea (DPRK), otherwise known as North Korea.

Now, you might wonder why my father would choose to send us – for it was not only me but two of my siblings too – to Pyongyang, North Korea. Well, to understand that I need to give you a bit of context; the full picture will emerge as you read the book.

This is where arguably the two most important processes in our modern history, which shook and shaped so many millions of lives, take centre stage: colonisation and decolonisation. Colonisation was characterised by the ruthless exploitation of the colonised by colonial powers. People from those colonised territories were considered subhuman, inferior to white people, with no rights whatsoever, including the right to education. As a consequence, in the aftermath of decolonisation there were no proper educational institutions in Equatorial Guinea. This prompted Macias's decision to send young Guineans, including us, his own children, to study abroad. And relations between Equatorial Guinea and its former coloniser, Spain, were so difficult that Kim Il Sung's offer of fraternal assistance was welcome. Moreover, deeply disillusioned by their relations with former colonial powers, many emerging independent African nations were open to offers of solidarity and support from Russia, China, Cuba and North Korea.

Not long after I moved to North Korea to study, my father was put on trial in Equatorial Guinea on 24 September 1979, accused of perpetrating atrocities during his time in office, along with other allegations. During the trial, he requested a thorough investigation. However, his voice was not heard and his version of events was not taken seriously. He was found guilty on 29 September 1979 and, with no right of appeal, executed by firing squad on the same day. I was seven years old, and I hadn't seen my father since arriving in North Korea. At the time, what was happening back in Guinea was mysterious to me, and it would remain so for many years to come.

When, in 1994, I left Pyongyang and came to experience life in Europe and West Africa, I was plunged into an identity crisis that finally pushed me to research Macias and his time in office. I learned about the killings and violence that took place in Equatorial Guinea during his rule and what precipitated those events, as well as Macias's self-proclamation as president for life. The popular depictions of both Macias and Kim were shattering to me. It was also a confusing process learning about and adapting to new cultures which – in theory – were mine, and in which my family was deeply implicated.

The truths that I had held as absolute as I grew up in Pyongyang started to teeter, replaced by a slew of questions. What is the truth? What is political discourse? Why is there a discrepancy between what I personally know and experienced of Kim Il Sung and the depiction of him in the West? Why is there a discrepancy between what I learned about Macias from Kim Il Sung and the depiction of him in the West? Who is lying? Are they biased? Why do Western narratives about Macias and Kim Il Sung differ from my own knowledge and personal experience? Why are these narratives accepted as truth? Do they tell the complete story?

I have now spent half my life researching and investigating Macias. During my research, I also encountered many discrepancies between the accounts of witnesses to events in Equatorial Guinea and the official narratives. The dominant narratives rightly highlight the horrors, debased living standards and economic recession that afflicted Equatorial Guinea during that period. These are facts and I do not dispute them. But what the narratives omit is the root cause of those horrors. Why? Are we being told the full story, or one that ignores the real forces at play?

I condemn any and all atrocities while also strongly believing that by telling a complete version of events we identify their true cause. In doing so, we accurately interpret the legacy of colonisation in the present: the authentic memorialisation of the past helps us to avoid repeating the same tragedy and acknowledges the historical obligations and responsibility that colonial rulers – in this case Spain – have towards their former colonies.

Finding the truth has been one of the strongest motivations of my life's journey.

But this book isn't about my 'two fathers', Francisco Macias and Kim Il Sung. They are just part of my story. This book is about me, Monica-Mening Macias Bindang. In it, I share my experience of growing up in Pyongyang and Western societies. I challenged my own prejudice and went to live in countries and societies that contrast ideologically and culturally with my host country, North Korea. So, I want to ask you to take a leap with me. Fasten your seatbelt – there will be emotional turbulence!

In 2013, I published the Korean version of my memoir. Before handing in the manuscript to my South Korean publisher, I was quite nervous that it would not be accepted, and even if it were, that it would not get a good reception.

These thoughts were in part a response to the antagonistic and fluctuating relations between North and South Korea. However, after accepting some restrictions on the usage of certain terminology, and making other concessions in light of national security laws governing representations of North Korea in the South, the memoir was published for South Korean readers.

To my surprise, the book was very well received; readers told me they chimed with the human face of North Korea that I presented. The book also piqued the interest of Western media outlets, and elicited demands for translated editions. So here, I share my story in English.

This book is based on the diaries I have kept throughout my life. The anecdotes that I choose to share here are selective, but chronological.

A few names are real, but in most cases I used pseudonyms, to protect the identities of those concerned. I used North Korean romanisation for North Korean names and South Korean romanisation for South Korean names.

I am painfully aware that had I been a gifted native English writer I could have relayed my story in a more sophisticated way. And the story was further complicated by the contradictions I have encountered throughout my life. Each time I sat down to write – on a piece of paper or in my diary app, aboard an aeroplane, bus or train, or sitting in a cafe in London, in a taxi in Malabo or on a Renfe train in Madrid – I found myself resisting a single narrative and obliged instead to give alternative perspectives based on personal experience and my honest reflections. This is because I believe there is a powerful public need to know the full picture of historical events, and to acknowledge social illnesses such as structural racism, fake news and so on. By acknowledging such issues, we take the first step towards tackling them.

I hoped to give an honest rendering of my experiences. Where possible I wanted to offer you a sense of what it is like to be raised by two of the most caricatured postcolonial leaders. I wanted to remind you that behind those cardboard cut-outs there are other human beings, their families, whose lives and reputations become mere collateral damage.

I wanted also to tell a personal story that might inspire those who are going through a difficult moment in their lives, those who are facing defamation or bullying, those who are struggling emotionally. I wanted to speak up, acknowledge and challenge the existing racism in our modern era. I might also offer insight to those studying International Relations, as I did, since colonialism, decolonisation and the Cold War are woven into the fabric of my story.

I want this book to be inclusive, for everyone and for all societies.

Part 1
In Pyongyang

Toasting with Kim Sŏng Ae, First Lady of North Korea, 1977

Broken Memories

I am very little, probably five years old. I am in a plantation. I am among rows of shrubs, but they tower over me like trees. Between them, I see weeds.

I also see a man. He is black. I am standing about a metre behind him. He is wearing a white shirt, and his hair is a salt-and-pepper blend of black and grey. He is attacking the weeds energetically with a machete. I can't see his face; everything is blurry. But I know that this man is my father. This is what comes to mind when I close my eyes and try to evoke Francisco Macias.

I need to check whether these blurry remembrances are real and not imagined, so I ring my sister, Maribel, who is six years older than me and remembers our father more clearly.

'It's not your imagination,' she assures me down the line. 'Papa used to work in the office Monday to Friday and then in his coffee plantation at weekends. He used to take the four of us – Teo, Fran, you and me – to the plantation. Then he would show us how to weed.' Teo is the oldest, then comes Maribel, and then Fran. I am the youngest.

'Papa would lead, followed by Teo, Fran and me. You used to stand and watch us weeding, and sometimes you would pull at the weeds with your small hands. Then Papa would say proudly, "That's the spirit!"

'Mama would sometimes object when Papa took us to the plantation. She said that Papa was a workaholic, that it was too much for him and we were too young to be working in a plantation. But Papa would respond that we needed to learn work and discipline. He was stubborn, just like you. You have his character as well as his looks!'

Everyone who sees Papa's photo says how alike we are, but only my mother, Teo, Maribel and Fran know me well enough to see that the similarity goes deeper. My curiosity grows.

'Tell me more about him,' I urge.

'When he came home after work, Papa would kiss our foreheads and ask whether we had eaten and done our homework. He didn't like us to neglect our studies or spend time unproductively. His favourite sermon was: "There is no future for Equatorial Guinea without study. You are the future." He always looked tired after his long days at work. He wasn't talkative at home. I suppose that was because of the long speeches he was always giving. He was quite disciplined, but attentive to both Mum and us. He treated all of us children equally. Mama had several miscarriages before you were born and her health was always delicate. He was always by her side, taking care of her.

'Sometimes he would invite us to watch films with him. But Fran and I found them boring, and we would sneak out. You were the only one who would stay to the end, sitting in his lap.'

* * *

Another memory. The year is 1977 and I am not much older. I am aboard a presidential plane, descending towards Sunan airport, Pyongyang, Democratic People's Republic of Korea. I hear the click of seatbelts being fastened around me and a rustle of activity.

I am sitting next to Fran.

'Fran, look, balloons! Look how many people!' I shout, excited. He looks out through the window as we come in to land. 'Wow.'

'I want a balloon!' I say to Fran.

'No, you can't have one,' he replies, with the officious air of the senior sibling.

Fran is a mischievous boy who has always been my ally. Since I was tiny, I've known how to persuade him to help me get what I want. But this time, it seems, it is different.

The plane touches down. My mother is gathering her things and my father, Francisco Macias Nguema, the first president of the independent African nation of Equatorial Guinea, has his head together with his ministers. I notice the aeroplane door is open. 'Now or never!' I say to myself as I skip nimbly down the aisle towards the door. Behind me my mother lets out a gasp. 'Catch her, catch her!'

I reach the aircraft door and step outside onto the stairs. Balloons are floating on the breeze, a crowd is shouting and waving flowers, and a red carpet runs from the foot of the stairs towards a group of people dressed in black suits. It all takes my breath away and I stand still, stunned. Suddenly, a black hand grabs me and leads me back into the plane. My brief adventure has been brought to an abrupt halt by one of my father's bodyguards.

'I told you that you couldn't have it,' Fran says, a triumphant smile on his face. After that, our nanny never lets go of my hand.

My parents lead the way out of the plane. An Asian man standing apart from the crowd greets my father, shaking his hand and talking to him animatedly. Photographers and onlookers gather round them before they get into an open-topped car at the head of a motorcade.

My siblings and I are escorted to a black car that follows my mother's for the drive into Pyongyang, along a motorway flanked by vivid green rice paddies. I notice that at regular intervals there are wooden boards lodged into the ground, bearing painted symbols that look like stickmen. 'Ms Park,' I ask our interpreter, 'what are those drawings?' She laughs, and then speaks in Korean to the driver, who chuckles. My siblings and I look at each other.

'Those are not drawings, they are Korean letters,' she explains.

'Letters?' They seem more like illustrations to me. One letter, '우', looks to me like a person standing with outstretched arms.

Our car enters Pyongyang city and there are more crowds on the street to welcome us, waving flowers and shouting. There is a sudden hush as my father's car at the front draws to a halt close to a statue of a winged horse.* Two children smartly dressed in red neckties and school uniforms greet my father and the Asian man with him, presenting them with a bouquet of flowers. '*Hangsang junbi!*', they chant in unison.** They are pioneer scouts, Ms Park explains. I gaze at them, fascinated.

The motorcade of black cars sets off again, snaking through wooded hills before finally arriving at our guesthouse. There is yet another welcoming committee to greet us as we emerge from

* The Chŏllima Thousand-Mile Horse, symbolising rapid modernisation.

** In Korean, 항상준비! – '*Always ready!*'

the cars to find a quiet, secluded house surrounded by mountains and near a huge lake.

The house is on two levels. Through the front door, there is a dining room on the right leading to a kitchen, and on the left a spiral staircase and an open-plan living room. On the second floor is a large seating area connected to three bedrooms and a study with a huge terrace. Everything is new to me – both the décor and the architectural style. It is beautiful. In the evening before going to sleep I chat to Maribel, and tell her how beautiful I find the house. Maribel is like our second mother. In fact, she looks like our mum: fair skin, a narrow nose and naturally wavy black hair. She is quiet, reserved and receptive. She is a reader, a listener, an observer and a helper. One of those kinds of people that wait behind you in silence, watching your step, ready to catch you if you fall. She never raises her voice to anyone. I ask her if this is our new home. 'For now, yes, until we go back home to Malabo. I like it too.'

We settle in for our stay. I enjoy spending time with my family, though I barely see my father, who is busy deal-making with Korean officials. My focus is different: there is to be a special gala at the Mansudae Arts Theatre, where I am expected to recite greetings and sing a song – 'The Song of General Kim Il Sung' – in Korean. Over the following day or two, my interpreter Ms Park and I rehearse the first verse, which she puts into a romanised script that I can read and learn by rote.

The morning of the gala arrives and our nerves start to fray. The house is busy with preparations, with people running up and down the stairs, while my mother lays out our clothes and selects my father's tie.

'Fran, Fran!' calls my mother. 'Have you seen him?' she asks me.

'No,' I say; but I know that he will be outside exploring the surroundings and trying to talk to the ground staff even though he speaks no Korean. Finally, someone dredges him up. Apparently he was rowing a boat he found out onto the lake. Fran is warm and incredibly easy to get on with. He has a natural ability to make friends and a curiosity that will leave no stone unturned. He seems to elude cultural and language barriers.

Meanwhile, my sister is busy combing her long hair in the cocoon of her own quietness. A Korean lady with an elegant beehive hairstyle comes to speak with Mum. She speaks fluent Spanish. She exudes a gentle kindness, and is constantly smiling.

It is time to get into the cars again, now heading for the Mansudae Art Theatre half an hour away in central Pyongyang, where the gala is taking place. When we arrive, I am once again wide-eyed with awe – this time at the beautiful, enormous, imposing building. It is long and rectangular, with tower-like structures at each end, one taller than the other. It has more than a hundred windows. On one façade hangs a giant Russian-style revolutionary painting. As we pass through the iron fence surrounding the theatre, I see white stone statues of women folk-dancers and numerous small fountains.

Once again, the red carpet is rolled out.

Proceeding down an elegant corridor, we enter a huge, opulent room dotted with tables facing a stage. Once everyone is seated, someone makes a speech from the stage. The big red curtain behind the speaker opens as he finishes, and the concert starts.

Female and male performers sing Korean songs and even two songs in Fang, one of Equatorial Guinea's five languages and that of my father's ethnic group. The large delegation of Guineans in the audience are delighted and applaud enthusiastically – including, I notice, my father.

Ten or twelve dancers in colourful *chosŏn-ot*, Korean traditional dress, perform the famous Korean fan dance, the *puchaechum*. With their beautifully painted fans, they mimic butterflies, a flower in full bloom and ocean waves in precise and graceful movements. No one is out of place. This kind of dance, which focuses on arm movements, is new to me. The Guinean dance I am familiar with is all about the torso and hip movements. The combination of the colourful *chosŏn-ot* and the elegant movements is captivating. The choreography begins with all dancers in stillness, their faces hidden by the fans. One dancer reveals her face, rising and moving her fan gracefully around her body. Gradually, the other dancers start to move their fans in the same fashion, as if a flower is blossoming. Later, I learn that the *puchaechum* has roots in shamanic religion and was used to entertain officials during Korea's centuries-long Chosŏn dynasty.

'You're next, are you ready?' asks Ms Park.

'Yes,' I say, excited.

I walk to the centre of the stage and someone comes to adjust the microphone to my height. All eyes are on me, yet I do not feel intimidated. I feel confident, like when I have done my homework. I recite my pre-scripted greeting and begin to sing the first three verses of 'The Song of General Kim Il Sung', a paean to his role in the resistance against Japanese colonial forces. The words are meaningless to me, but later I will come to know them well.

Annyŏnghi kyesipsio.

Traces of blood on the crags of Changpaek Mountain still gleam
The Amrok river still carries along, signs of blood in its stream
...
Annyŏnghasimnikka.

As I finish, people in the room start to laugh out loud. I am puzzled. I do not understand why they are laughing – including, after a few words from his interpreter, my father. I walk down the steps from the stage, and the man sitting next to my father beckons me to come. He sits me on his lap and starts to speak. Ms Park hurries over to translate. 'You really sang very well. But you got the greetings the wrong way around!' I had opened my performance by saying 'goodbye' (*annyŏnghi kyesipsio)* and ended with 'hello' (*annyŏnghasimnikka*).

At this moment I have no idea that this man, whose picture is so ubiquitous, will one day be my protector. This man is Kim Il Sung.

Me (front centre) with my family and the First Couple of North Korea

Orphaned

Our visit continued. My memories from the time are golden, suffused with a sense of family and togetherness, studded with daily delicacies of the novel and the alien.

Every day I discovered and experienced new things. As I had already found, the Korean script was utterly different from Spanish. I had never seen buildings such as those constructed in the traditional Korean Hanok style, with their flared roofs like wings. Compared to Malabo, the capital of Equatorial Guinea, Pyongyang was pristine. I began to fall in love with the city's leafy beauty, with the ubiquitous weeping willows, the forsythias, cherry blossoms, magnolias, roses and azaleas. Our friendly housekeepers and cooks taught me my first Korean words and introduced me to Korean food. I discovered *kimchi* (fermented spicy cabbage), *kimbap* (sticky rice with vegetables or meat in a roll of dry seaweed), *sinsŏllo* (a round hot pot with meat or vegetables in soup), and so on. All these new interesting dishes were unveiled before my eyes, though I was reluctant to actually taste them. I preferred the sweet red bean buns, custard buns and all kinds of rice cake. I noticed that the word for cucumber, pronounced *oi*, sounded like the word for 'today' (*hoy*) in Spanish. It was fascinating to learn that similar sounds could have different meanings in different languages.

But most of all I loved being with my parents and siblings. I was happy in my own little wonderland and I did not need anything else.

On a visit to Samji Lake, late 1970s

My affection for North Korea was rekindled on my return to Pyongyang in May 1979, when my father sent us to study in North Korea as wards of Kim Il Sung, as he had sent my older brother Teo to Cuba in 1975.

My mother came with us to have gallstone surgery in the city's Ponghwa hospital. We were given a spacious apartment on the top floor of one of the four red brick apartment blocks that mainly housed Workers' Party members and their families, in an upmarket district in the centre of Pyongyang. My siblings and I were enrolled at the elite Namsan High School.

We quickly adjusted to our new lives, adopting the rhythms of our fellow Pyongyang citizens. My mother was recovering from her surgery. We spent weekends in parks and amusement parks, just like many Pyongyang families. Pyongyang has many parks, which, more than simply an embellishment, feel like the real heart of the city. On the weekends, they were thronged with families eating beef or jellyfish barbecue and *kimbap* followed by watermelon, apple and pear, and drinking *sochu* (the potato-based alcoholic drink, colourless like vodka), *makkŏlli* (another traditional drink, a creamy rice-based wine) and Taedonggang, the most popular beer in the country. When the alcohol took effect, people started playing guitars, singing songs and dancing. The scent of the barbecuing beef made my mouth water.

Sometimes people would mark traditional festivals, like Dano, held on the fifth day of the fifth month of the lunar calendar, when the rice-planting was finished and farmers would hope for a good harvest year. Women would appear in their beautiful brightly coloured *choson-ŏt* and there would be raucous tournaments of *ssirŭm*, folk wrestling similar to Sumo in Japan.

Once, our hosts organised a week's trip to Chuŭl, a town in North Hamgyŏng about four hours' drive northeast of Pyongyang, famous since the Chosŏn dynasty for its hot springs.

We started intensive language classes. I enjoyed learning Korean and the words were coming thick and fast. I had the security of my siblings at school and my mother at home. I spent my afternoons watching *Clever Raccoon* on TV, which I loved. It was a cartoon with an educational purpose, incorporating elements of maths, science, road safety, physical fitness and so on through the adventures of three animal friends – a raccoon, a bear and a cat – who competed in challenges on behalf of their respective animal 'communities'. The slender cat and bear made fun of the tubby raccoon, but he always got the last laugh when he used his knowledge to outwit them. In one episode, the pals catch fish in the river and decide to make a stew. When they realise they don't have any salt, the raccoon goes off to fetch some. In his absence, the other two set a fire under the stew pot using gasoline, but then neglect it to go and play in the river, and nearby grass catches fire. Spotting the fire, the panicked pair try to put it out, but to no avail. The fire spreads. When the raccoon returns to the troubled scene, he thinks before acting. He creates a fire break by pulling up grass and then, bearing the wind direction in mind, sets a fire from the opposing direction – fighting fire with fire – and eventually it burns out without spreading further. The clever raccoon's lesson is etched on my mind.

My siblings and I focused on learning the language tools that would allow us to mingle and make friends in our new city. While I enjoyed studying Korean through watching TV, my sister spent her afternoons on language homework: writing Korean letters in her notebook, reading them aloud and memorising Korean numbers. But probably the most interesting method was my brother Fran's; he appeared to learn the language in a completely different way. Standing on the balcony one afternoon, I marvelled at him as he played with a group of Korean children in the apartment grounds below. He was able to make himself understood even without speaking the language, and his thick skin seemed impervious to any notion that he did not fit in.

It was the opposite for me. I had a burning sense of embarrassment about being different. I was not only black, but unusually large and tall for my age. Some of the children at school would touch my curly African hair and call me *yang ajumŏni* ('sheep wife') after a popular cartoon character. I would blush to my roots.

I had not heard from my father or Teo since we left Malabo. According to my sister – though I do not remember the moment – after a few months, my mother suddenly announced that she had to return to Equatorial Guinea. We were to be sent to the Mangyŏngdae Revolutionary Boarding School in the eponymous district of Pyongyang, some thirty minutes southwest by car of the city centre.

The school had been established after the colonial period to educate the children of Korean martyrs in the struggle against Japanese rule before the Second World War. In the late 1980s, the school began accepting the children of party members. The school then took a special step to accommodate my sister and me. On the order of Kim Il Sung, what was originally a boys' school became mixed gender. Ten additional girls were brought in to create a form for me, and about the same number for my sister, who was fourteen.

As our black car drew up in front of the main school building on that hot July day, an old man stood waiting for us in military

With my siblings Maribel and Fran at Mangyŏngdae Revolutionary Boarding School

dress. He was wearing an impeccably pressed khaki uniform, shiny black shoes and a khaki hat. He saluted and shook hands with each of us in turn. An excited Fran, now eleven years old, mimicked him behind his back.

This man, O Chae Won, was the school director. He led us to his office, a large room with a balcony leading off it. We sat down on a sofa near his large, neat desk and Director O began to address my sister, as the eldest of the three of us. By this time, we spoke good Korean.

'I am glad to tell you that you have the privilege of studying at the Mangyŏngdae Revolutionary Boarding School,' he said.

While Director O and my sister talked, Fran got up and walked out onto the balcony. I followed him. We gazed out over the sprawling grounds of the school, which was surrounded by a wooded park. From the balcony you could see five large buildings arranged around the school's playing fields, housing a clinic, library, theatre/cinema, gym, canteen, laboratory and dormitory. Outside the main building loomed a large statue of Kim Il Sung.

Suddenly a voice barked at us from inside. 'Fran, hold your sister's hand in case she tries to climb the balcony railing.' It was Director O, and it sounded like an order.

'Yes, sir!' said Fran, as if he too were a soldier. He took my hand.

We were taken to be introduced to our new classmates. They came from all over the country, mostly from lower-ranked social backgrounds. All of my new classmates were fatherless. In later years I realised that they had been deliberately selected on this basis.

Another fact about my classmates became immediately apparent: although they had been chosen to make up a cohort for me, all of them were two years older. As my age did not match the school year, my study schedule was slightly different. I joined them for their second-year primary school classes in the morning, and while they played in the afternoon, I attended first-year classes on my own to catch up.

Years later, just before I left the school, I learned that my classmates had been chosen in order to approximate my height; naturally that meant I would be the youngster of the class for the remainder of my time in the North Korean education system.

At the time, this did not surprise me in the slightest, but it

With my 'platoon', the platoon leader (behind my right shoulder) and the school director O Chae Won (front centre)

interests many Westerners when I tell them. I guess it is a cultural thing because it does not surprise South Koreans either.

Another problem – and a worse one – came with adapting to school discipline. Our class – or platoon, in the military terminology favoured by the school – had a platoon leader, a *sotaejang*, a pretty and surprisingly even-handed young woman whose job was to keep us in line according to the school's strict standards of discipline. I admired my new classmates for their energy and positive outlook, but they lacked spontaneity. They did nothing without asking permission. Everything, even going to the toilet, required permission. I was used to speaking on a whim, when the thought occurred to me, but this was frowned upon. I complained about that in the early days at school. 'Remember, you are a soldier!' my teacher responded. I could not understand how I could be a soldier in a foreign country.

I also found it difficult to relate to my new classmates because I could not read them well. When they spoke, they often seemed rigid and expressionless (until you got to know them). This is a trait that East Asians now remark upon in me. 'I feel like I'm speaking to an Asian,' a Japanese woman I met in the Netherlands once said to me as we became acquainted. But at the time, motherless, fatherless and wrenched from my home and the creature comforts of my early life in Korea, I found the lack of warmth and openness shattering, and I struggled to adapt.

Every night, I spent hours crying in bed. At six a.m. the morning routine came around like a wheel to crush me. The reveille would sound. We had to run around the playing fields before breakfast. Classes began at eight a.m.

After classes finished at two p.m., we went for lunch, along with Herve and Montan, the sons of Mathieu Kerekou, president of Benin, our friends and the only other black students in the school. We Guinean and Beninese children were served in a different room, with food cooked by a different chef as a courtesy to us. By this point I could not stand Korean food, and in particular *kimchi* and *tofu*. I had always been picky with food, even at home in Equatorial Guinea.

And I yearned for my mother, who had not returned. I did not know why.

My anguish drove me to refuse all food. For a month, nothing passed my lips but water. My weight plummeted, raising fears that I might die. I was taken to Ponghwa hospital, where I was put on a glucose drip that kept me alive. Even there, my nights were spent crying: 'I want my mum.'

A month later, when I had recovered, I went back to school. My classmates were relieved and happy to see me back. Some of the barriers between us dissolved. Special food was couriered from a hotel in central Pyongyang for me to eat. This made my day-to-day life easier, but no one could replace my mother. There was no news of her. I just had to accept that she was gone.

From this point onwards, my attitude changed, hardening from my natural ebullience into an overt rebellion against authority and hierarchy. I did not understand why I had to live in that boarding school under such strict discipline at only eight years old. I was one of three girls in my class who vied for dominance over the others. I spoke disrespectfully to others and showed little regard for Korean social ranking according to age, for which one of my sister's classmates took me to task.

'What's wrong with you? You know you cannot speak to me like that. I am older than you! You should respect those older than you,' she said.

I simply ignored her.

My feisty attitude masked an acute sense of social rejection. I wanted desperately to blend in with my classmates, but their unspoken message seemed to be: 'You are not Korean, you are not like us.' Biology and history classes seemed geared to accentuate my difference. In history, we studied ancient Korea, from the Three Kingdoms era to the Koryŏ dynasty, the Chosŏn era to Japanese occupation. For a moment, my interest in my adoptive country would be piqued, until I would suddenly notice one of my classmates giving me a sly look that said, unmistakably: 'This history has nothing to do with you.' It was true. While for them this was the story of their grandparents and great-grandparents, for me it was just a class.

Biology class also triggered personal questions about my differences. *Why am I brown when my friends are yellow?* I wanted to be like them, with yellow skin, straight black hair and almond eyes. I hated my brown skin, big eyes and curly hair. I used to tell myself, 'I am Korean, I am Korean,' while combing my hair to try to force it straight, but it never worked.

However, as an adult my sister showed me a letter that my father wrote to accompany us when we were sent to Pyongyang.

My dear children,

I send you to Pyongyang in the charge of my friend Kim Il Sung, whom I respect as a brother, to study. He will take care of you and put you into whichever school he considers is right for your education.

Do not ever forget who you are. You are African. You should go back to Guinea to build this country after your studies. Our country needs you. Never forget what Spanish colonists did to our country.

From your father who loves you,

Francisco Macias

In my mum's absence, Kim Il Sung was now my guardian, and I was effectively an orphan. I had lost my parents, my home, and the sense of security those things provided. I had to become prematurely independent and to grow up, fast. My sister, friends and my tutors filled the void left by my mother. My life became a structured one, dominated by discipline, in which loneliness was my bosom companion.

Fran with O Chae Won in the school parade ground

Escape

One day, when we were in third grade,* our teacher asked us, 'What is life? What does it mean to you?' and invited each student to respond.

'Friendship, because it's the most important thing in life,' one student opined. 'Love, my mum's love,' said another. My immediate urge was to blurt out, 'Solitude! Life is all about becoming more and more alone as time goes by. That's it.' I had become an expert on loneliness, though I was still very young. But I stifled the urge and kept my mouth shut.

By this time, one after the other, my siblings Maribel and Fran, and then Herve and Montan had all left the boarding school. Following the course their father had set out for them, Herve and Montan had joined the Kim Il Sung Military University in order to become

* The students were twelve or thirteen years old, but because I had skipped first grade and been placed in a class with older students, as detailed above, I was younger. In addition, Koreans count ages differently: they are one year old when born and then turn a year older on the New Year. Since I still counted my age according to the Western norm, on paper I was significantly younger – only ten.

military officers. This, one of the prominent military academies in North Korea, was also located in the Mangyŏngdae district, and shared a boundary with our boarding school. Meanwhile, Maribel was now attending Pyongyang Medical University, while Fran was at Pyongyang University of Architecture. My siblings were now living in Haebangsan Hotel, in the centre of Pyongyang, which had become a kind of hall of residence for foreign students in Pyongyang. There were Syrian students who were studying engineering at Kim Ch'aek University of Technology, and Chinese students attending various Pyongyang institutions such as the Pyongyang Law College, Pyongyang University of Light Industry, Pyongyang University of Music and Dance, and so on.

I was suddenly alone. It was unbearable. For a long period, once again I had swollen eyes every morning after crying the whole night. It was Maribel in particular whom I yearned for. I even looked back fondly on Fran, Herve and Montan rebuffing my attempts to play with them. 'Leave us alone!' they would say. 'This is boy stuff, go and find Maribel!' But I would have my threat ready: 'If you don't let me play with you guys, I will tell the deputy director that some Thursday nights you escape to the centre to meet girls in Potongang Hotel.'

'OK, you win! Don't say a word to anyone, even Maribel.'

'I promise!'

'No, you must swear!' Herve would insist.

'What does "swear" mean?'

'Never mind! Just don't tell anyone, you chubby little strategist!' Fran would harrumph.

The lonelier and more nostalgic I felt, the more intolerable school life was – above all, the monotony of the military routine.

I devised a plan to run away. I put on casual civilian clothes under my sleepwear and pretended to be ready for bed as usual for the nine p.m. check. After lights-out, I sneaked out of the room and went to the toilet, where I put on my uniform over the casual clothes. I headed to the school's West Gate, a plastic bag in my hands. Across the street there was the Chŏnsŏk restaurant, known for its delicious menu of delicacies such as Korean barbecue, noodles, pancakes, red bean buns and *kimbap*. Sometimes at lunchtime I used to leave school to buy red bean buns, so the gate security staff knew me.

'Monica, is that you? You're supposed to be in bed by now!' said the guard.

'Please, I'm so hungry. I've been starving all day today. Please let me just go and buy red bean buns – please, please, please! Just a few minutes.'

'No, it's too late!'

'I'm hungry and I can't sleep. This is killing me. Please, let me just go for a few minutes, please?'

After a long back-and-forth, he gave up and let me go, saying I should return as soon as I bought them.

'Hurry up! The restaurant is going to close soon, so you'll have to run.'

I crossed the road and crept into the grove of pine trees next to the restaurant, where I took off my uniform, stuffed it into the plastic bag, and set off walking down the road. This was a national highway connecting Pyongyang and the port city of Nampo. It took about half an hour to reach Pyongyang city centre from the school by car, but I did not know how long it would take me on foot.

It was a quiet night, and I passed only a few people and cars as I walked.

The stars were shining in the sky as I walked and walked into the night.

'Maribel and Fran will be so happy to see me!' I thought, my excitement dulling the throbbing in my feet.

I later found out that while I was on my peaceful quest, uproar had spread throughout the school as my disappearance was discovered and a state of emergency was declared. From the school's director to my classmates, everybody was employed on 'Operation Find Monica'.

It was about four a.m. when I got to Haebangsan Hotel. I had finally made it! But my footsteps faltered when I saw Maribel and Fran sitting on the sofa in the lobby.

She stood up as I approached.

'Why are you so serious? Aren't you happy to see me?' I asked, my voice quavering.

'I am, but not like this,' said Maribel, in a tone both puzzled and severe. 'You know you can't leave the school just like that! How did you manage to find the hotel?'

'I know, but I missed you so much! I just wanted to see you and then go back to school! I knew the way, more or less. I found out from Fran, Herve and Montan one day,' I said, nearly crying.

My sister hugged me and broke into tears.

'Monica, I understand that, but you shouldn't leave the school that way. Everyone in the school is looking for you. They called me here to ask.'

My sister called the school and they sent the driver to pick me up. I did not say a word during the journey back to school.

Kim Il Sung's nephew, the deputy director of the school, who was usually always smiling, was waiting for me, grim-faced, in his office.

'The discipline of the military is directly linked to life and death. Do you not know what punishment you will face if you desert from the army? This school is like an army. You have committed a very serious error. Besides, a girl alone going out at night on her own!'

The deputy director pounded his desk with his fist as he shouted.

From that day on, I realised that I had no choice but to accept the order and discipline of the school, and finally embraced the rigours of the life I had been given. Even now, as an adult, structure is threaded through my daily habits. This lifestyle has helped me to focus on my tasks and goals, to be productive and manage stress successfully. As one of my teachers would say, 'Your habits reflect your state of mind. If your room is a mess, your mind is too.'

On the same highway I had previously used to make my escape from school

Obiang's Envoy

'Monica, we must go to meet someone tomorrow.'

It was Maribel, her voice serious and cold. She was not one to hang up first, but that day she did.

Something's going on, I thought. What could it be? I've been behaving really well since Operation Find Monica! Uh-oh, maybe she knows about my Spanish class rebellion!

I had been sent a Spanish teacher by Kim Il Sung, who was keen for me to keep up my native language. Ri Kyŏng Mu was twenty-four years old and had just graduated from Pyongyang University of Foreign Studies. His major was Spanish and he also spoke English. He was handsome: tall, with flawless skin. Nevertheless, I was not disposed to reacquaint myself with Spanish; instead, my objective was to erase anything that represented my origins, or even reminded me of them, in the process of reaching my ultimate goal of becoming a 'true Korean'. In my mind, I was not of mixed African and European heritage but an Asian, like my friends. Learning Spanish was not part of this plan, and I was hell-bent on sabotaging it. I made Mr Ri's job impossible.

'Do you have a girlfriend? How old is she? Is she pretty like you? Do you love her? Are you going to marry her? How many children do you plan to have? Did you meet her through a matchmaker or were you classmates on campus?' These were the sort of impertinent questions I posed in class. But Mr Ri was persistent. He spoke to me in Spanish on topics relevant to the lessons, while I spoke to him in Korean on irrelevant matters.

We spent three months locked in this futile dynamic before he finally gave up. This time, he addressed me in Korean. 'Before being assigned this job, I was briefed about your background. I know, and I understand. You are going through a difficult time in your life. And now you are an adolescent of twelve years old. Your mum left, your sister left the school and on top of that the school discipline is not easy. But you will overcome this. You are intelligent and strong.' Before I realised, my eyes were wet and I was choked with emotion. I could only murmur, 'No, you don't know me.' But he had seen the truth, and we both knew it.

He sent a report to Kim Il Sung saying that it was impossible for him to teach me Spanish at this stage of my life. He said the reasons were psychological: above all, trauma caused by my mother leaving. Kim Il Sung agreed. Ri became instead my supervisor, a kind of older brother whom I could talk to if I needed anything.

He never spoke to me in Spanish again. My childish rebellion had worked.

I continued to comb through the reasons why I might be in trouble with Maribel.

Maybe it's the homework. I have let some homework slide. I am supposed to be studying two grades at once and catching up with my classmates. It's too much!

I was faced with the constant temptation of seeing my classmates at play while I was supposed to be working in the afternoons. Our games included hide-and-seek, rubber-band games or *chagal nori* (known as *gonggi nori* in the South), also known as Korean jackstones. *Chagal nori* was my favourite, and was both a physically and mentally demanding game. You threw five stones on the floor. Then you picked one up, threw it in the air, grabbed another stone from the floor (without touching the others), and then caught the airborne pebble. You repeated the operation while gradually catching pebbles from the floor, scoring points when you caught the stones successfully. Until, all being well, you had five stones in your hand. (If you touched any stones on the floor or failed to catch the stones, play passed to the next player.) In the last stage – the *kkokki*, or break – you threw them all in the air at once and tried to catch them on the back of your hand. The player with most accumulated points won, and we often played in teams. It was a gripping game, tense at times, and its lure often meant my homework did not stand a chance.

Why doesn't she understand? No one understands me! But despite racking my brains, I could not fathom why Maribel was calling this meeting under such apparently grave circumstances.

The next morning, there was a knock at the classroom door. Maribel and Fran had come to pick me up. I got into the sleek black car and sat next to Maribel. Fran, as usual, was next to the driver, his favourite spot. Often, he helped the driver change gears, but not today. Even Fran looked serious. I took courage and addressed Maribel.

A rare photo of me catching up on homework

'Are you angry because I didn't do my homework? I'm so sorry. It's just too much. It won't happen again. Please don't be angry with me,' I said.

At that Maribel turned to me with concern, while Fran laughed at my easily surrendered confession.

'Are you not doing your homework, then? How many times do I have to tell you how important it is to study and do your homework?' she replied.

Our car passed over Moran Hill and stopped in front of a hybrid of a modern concrete building with a traditional Korean roof. We were led to a spacious reception room presided over by a black guard in a suit, his face expressionless. I sat between Maribel and Fran. The awkward silence and tension in the air were oppressive. I felt I was going to faint.

A door opened suddenly and a black man came in. Smiling,

he approached Maribel and tried to kiss and hug her. She brusquely refused and would not allow him to hug us either. His expression changed. Then Maribel said something in Spanish – the language I no longer understood and refused to re-learn, but still recognised. Although I could not understand what they were saying, I was struck by how clearly their body language communicated their feelings.

The man seemed puzzled and at a loss for words.

I was familiar with Korean chess *(changki)* thanks to our driver, who loved the game and had explained the rules to me. It seemed to me that my sister, the Queen, had put this man, the rival King, into checkmate. He had no way out and he was embarrassed.

'*Kaja*!' said Maribel in Korean – let's go! It sounded like an order. She grabbed us by our wrists and we swept out.

'Get into the car. We are done here. Driver, please take us back to our place. Thank you.'

My heart was thumping wildly in my chest. Why would Maribel behave like this? Why was she so angry? I could not bear not knowing any longer.

'Maribel, who is he? Did he hurt you?'

'Not me, us!'

'You're so stupid!' said Fran. 'Don't you realise? The president of Equatorial Guinea, the person who killed our father, sent that person. And he wants to take us back. Do you understand?'

It was as if I had been hit with a club. A bomb went off in my head; I went deaf; my ears rang.

Dad was *killed*?

Having fatherless classmates, until then I had had a vague idea that my father was dead. I believed – or rather, I had told myself – that my father had passed away from natural causes. Now I knew that my father had been killed, and by the incumbent president of Equatorial Guinea, Obiang Nguema, my father's own nephew! That moment, that day, I received the deepest wound of my life. Why, how, could relatives kill each other?

The envoy was leaving Pyongyang the next day and asked to see us again before leaving. He handed Maribel an envelope of banknotes. She looked straight at him and tore the envelope to pieces. That was all I saw.

Years later, when I was an undergraduate at Pyongyang University of Light Industry, I dared to ask my sister about it.

'What did you tell that guy that day?'

I did not need to explain what guy or what day I was referring to. She knew.

'I asked him why they killed our father. I didn't want to meet him but Kim Il Sung asked me to do it for him and he reassured me that he wouldn't let us go back. According to my supervisor at medical school, he told the envoy that we were the children of his late friend Macias, who had left us in his charge. He informed him that we would stay to study, and when grown up could decide whether to leave or stay. But not then.'

Unlike Fidel Castro, into whose care my elder brother, Teo, had been entrusted and who nonetheless allowed Teo to return to the uncertain and dangerous territory that was Equatorial Guinea at the time, Kim Il Sung kept his promise, even after my father's death. I later learned that Kim Il Sung knew about the coup d'état in Equatorial Guinea when it happened. He waited until my mother had recovered from her operation to tell her the sad news about my father and Teo's return to Equatorial Guinea. He offered her a house in Pyongyang where she could stay with us. My mother rejected the safety and comfort offered by Kim Il Sung and took the risk of returning to Equatorial Guinea – a dangerous place for our family at that time. She went back to protect Teo, who was only eighteen. Following the Fang tradition, she did *akus*, which consists of cutting off one's hair, sleeping on the floor for three days and bathing in the river on the fourth day, and wearing black clothes for months in mourning for the deceased husband. Also, during *akus*, the sisters-in-law of the widow can curse the widow. Fang people are convinced that these curses have real power. Some households take *akus* to the extreme of forcing the widow to sleep alongside the husband's corpse on the floor. Such practices have a negative psychological impact on the widow, who is already in emotional pain. Yet these kinds of traditions that increase emotional suffering are strongly ingrained in Guinean society.

It was because of my father's assassination and my brother's return to Equatorial Guinea that my mother suddenly disappeared from my life in 1979. As a result, I suffered from a kind of traumatic amnesia throughout my youth. It is like a malfunctioning computer file that paralyses the machine and turns the screen black. But this 'black screen' protected me from depression while growing up.

In my spare time at university I read a lot of world literature, which I loved, spurred on by Maribel's passion for books and in particular classical literature. *War and Peace* and *Anna Karenina* by Leo Tolstoy, *Les Misérables* by Victor Hugo, and *Romeo and Juliet* and *Hamlet* by Shakespeare all made me think about human life and society in past centuries and the present.

I devoured all those classics – except one, *Hamlet*. As soon as I opened the first page and started to read, I felt my eyes become wet, my heart start to thud. I have never been able to finish reading it or to watch dramatic adaptations of it. It is too painful. The details differ slightly, but it is as if Shakespeare were telling my own story.

My family tragedy is not the first, nor will it be the last. Centuries separate my story and Hamlet's, and yet it resonates with me strongly. Mine is just one more tragedy in the story of human society.

Survival Test

After the envoy's visit, my class was sent on a month-long camp in the hills surrounding our school. This was a one-time event that all students participated in before graduation. We spent a month living in tents, receiving military field training.

We learned to shoot. Initially, this was on a range using the sort of replica weapons you might find in an amusement park, but as we progressed, we were introduced to real firearms. By the end, we could dismantle and reassemble the gun with our eyes closed.

Everything was unfamiliar to me. Of course, the Mangyŏngdae Revolutionary Boarding School was a military boarding school, where the students wore uniforms and followed strict, army-style discipline. The majority of graduates enrolled at the Kim Il Sung Military University afterwards, or joined the armed forces, so naturally everyone received military training, but I was getting more and more sceptical. Why did I need this kind of education?

When I was young, I just followed instructions, but as I got older I began to question more and my personality slowly began

With Director O and my weapon during training camp

to assert itself. I had a different attitude to military training from the other children. During the military games, the class was divided into two sides – allies and enemies, identified by a red or blue cap. One day I wandered off to buy red bean buns at the Chŏnsŏk restaurant. In my absence, our team was defeated, and when I returned the children gathered round to berate me.

'Because of you! Because of you, we lost!' one shouted.

'You leave your friends and allies for red bean buns? Traitor!' yelled another.

In a collective society, teamwork is very important. For the military, it is critical, along with hierarchical respect and obedience to authority. Deserting your fellow soldiers or officers is unacceptable unless you have an overriding reason to do so. You must stick together, share and submit to power, because together we all win. No one is left behind. You achieve things by helping each other. This collective mindset and obedience to authority is rooted in Confucianism and embedded in every aspect of Korean society. Confucius believed that harmony between the universe and human beings was achieved when everyone understood their status in society and behaved accordingly, and that the failure of a person to act according to their prescribed role would threaten the social order.

I apologised repeatedly, but inside I was wondering why they wanted to win so badly. I was still resistant to the military training. I trudged up the hill with my comrades, all the while shaking my head.

During field training, we were put into smaller groups and learned how to survive on our own. We woke at five in the morning and splashed our faces with cold water from the stream. After breakfast, we gathered together to study military strategies; a variety of firearms, from pistols to Kalashnikovs; and hands-on training. None of it was easy, but I found shooting pistols one of the most difficult things to learn.

In the movies, pistols look small and light, but in reality, they are really heavy. I found it difficult to hold the weapon with one hand and keep precise aim at the target – the gun kept dropping because of the weight. Behind me, the instructor shouted: 'Raise your arm up, up, after shooting!'

But every time I fired a shot, the weight of the pistol would drag my arm down as I pulled the trigger. The bullet would reach just a few paces in front of me, prompting more shouting from behind.

'What are you doing? Are you kidding me? Do you want to injure yourself?' the instructor said.

I was made to spend all day in the tent alone as punishment. Had I been a real soldier, it would have been much worse.

A month felt like a year when you were field training. Day after day there were drills – pitching tents, marching, tackling obstacles and scaling walls. It was even tougher than shooting practice. The other children ran over the walls like squirrels, but I was much heavier and floundered every time. Sometimes I even felt I was drowning in the muddy water that collected at the bottom after it rained.

But the most painful thing – to say the least – was the hunger. When the field training started, we were given food rations calculated to last one week and ordered to manage them accordingly. At first, rather than taking the order seriously, we simply acted on the urge to eat. Without much thought, we prepared a fire, cooked and ate – and our weekly ration lasted only three or four days. Then we were, quite literally, starving. It was forbidden to ask for more food until the next supplies arrived. It was not only the daily hunger pangs of the classroom as lunchtime approached; it was the unimaginable pain of being continuously hungry while engaged in intense physical activity. It was then I realised that the depictions of soldiers eating snakes or mice in movies and TV shows were not exaggerated. As I starved over two or three days, my anger and hostility grew and grew. Only my animal instincts were left. I hated the instructors to the point of wanting them to die. We learned why senior students called this 'training for hell'.

After training all day, my body became, as they say in Korean, a 'fingernail': enervated, exhausted, but too hungry to sleep. Every night I heard whispering voices everywhere. The instructor came into our tent and told us: 'You must learn to overcome this. When you are in trouble because of mistakes or unexpected problems, when you are in crisis, you will analyse the situation based on your emotional judgement rather than reason, but this will only make the situation worse. You must learn to judge, to analyse the situation properly and rationally, even at a difficult moment.'

After the instructor left, one by one the children stopped crying and fell asleep. And the following week we learned to dispense our food rations prudently.

One month later we went back to school. Something had changed. We were no longer the weak and immature adolescents we had been; we were more bonded to each other, and returning to the disciplined school regime seemed as easy as pie.

My brother Fran with his classmates during military school training

Mother Tongue, the Betrayal of Memory

It might have been on the fringes of a capital city, but Mangyŏngdae Revolutionary Boarding School was isolated, 'an island within an island'. And I was even more cut off from outside than the other children. When on occasion a Chongryŏn* delegation would visit the school from Japan, the pupils would crowd round and receive an armful of Japanese-made school supplies as gifts. But I was not allowed. When I asked the teacher, 'Why am I the only one who can't meet them?' the answer was always, 'Because you're a special child.' Only a tiny minority of very high-level officials at the school knew about my father, and the reality that I was under the simultaneous monitoring and protection of Kim Il Sung. No matter how well I got on with the other children, there was always a gap between us. Being 'special' meant receiving special privileges, but it also meant living a life of special restrictions.

---

* The General Association of Korean Residents in Japan, also known as ChōsenSōren.

And then one day someone came and knocked on my door. When I opened it, my best friend Sŏn Hwa was standing there, holding a giant bag in each hand. I was startled.

'Sŏn Hwa, are you going somewhere?' I asked.

'Yes, from now on I have to bunk with you,' she replied.

'Really?'

Of course, allocating roommates at the school was mostly done for monitoring purposes, but giving me Sŏn Hwa as my partner was an extremely generous concession. Being able to live with my best friend made me happy. From then on, we would lie awake each night hugging our pillows, giggling and chattering ceaselessly. Thanks to that happy time after evening roll call, I was able to withstand the daily grind from morning to evening. But I was alone from Saturday afternoon, when visiting hours began and Sŏn Hwa left the school, to the time she returned on Sunday. While everybody else looked forward to the weekend, to me it felt like a punishment.

It was a Saturday, a few weeks after Sŏn Hwa and I became roommates. Visiting hours began as usual at three p.m. My friends were all busy changing their clothes and getting ready to go out. Sŏn Hwa came up to me.

'Monica, do you want to go with me to the visiting room?'

'Visiting room? Me?'

'Yeah. I'm going to see my mum, and I want you to come with me.'

When we arrived at the visiting room, a nice-looking woman dressed in a beautiful *chosŏn-ot* caught my eye. I could tell immediately that it was Sŏn Hwa's mother. Now I understood why Sŏn Hwa was so pretty. They looked exactly like one another.

'Mum, this is Monica.'

'So, you're Monica,' Sŏn Hwa's mother responded. She threw her arms around me and embraced me lovingly and unhurriedly, just as she greeted her own daughter. For the first time in my life – or the life I could consciously remember – I felt a mother's embrace. I could not stop sudden tears from flowing. Sŏn Hwa's mother cried with me, patting me on the back.

That night I told Sŏn Hwa, 'I want to go and visit your house in Kaesŏng. And I want to meet your family and your friends too.'

Until that point, I had never been to a 'friend's house'. I had been in Pyongyang more than five years, and in all that time I had stayed inside the track permitted to foreigners: the school, Haebangsan Hotel, Changgwangwŏn Health Complex. I hadn't once entered the life of a real Pyongyang citizen, even though it was possible, after applying for the bureaucratic paperwork and permissions, to visit a friend's house. While I could tolerate that, I couldn't help but wonder about the home life of my most beloved friend. But Sŏn Hwa's face hardened at the suggestion.

'I'm sorry, Monica. But there's a limit to what I can do for you.'

What Sŏn Hwa went on to say next made me very sad. Even though we were friends, as a native Korean and a foreigner there was an indelible line drawn between us. Not only was it difficult to visit Sŏn Hwa's house, but after finishing school, even meeting as friends would no longer be possible. The relationship that Sŏn Hwa and I shared was confined to 'friendship as monitoring' and was only permitted within the boarding school. I couldn't be content with that, but I had to accept it. We were friends who could not share a future.

Sometime after that, there was a change to my school routine: I too received permission to go out at the weekends. I wasn't allowed out in the company of Korean children, and I was forbidden from meeting Koreans privately outside the school without prior permission. But now, at almost fourteen years old, I was allowed leisure time with Maribel and Fran, as well as Herve and Montan Kerekou and other foreigners, and for that I was grateful.

Only now do I realise how persistent Sŏn Hwa must have been in lobbying to gain permission for my weekend excursions. I only found out much later that her request finally reached President Kim Il Sung, who then gave a specific order to allow me to leave the school on weekends.

From that time on, every Saturday I would dash to meet my brother, sister and the Kerekou boys at the Haebangsan Hotel – the base for our weekend pursuits. The place we went most often was the Changgwangwŏn Health Complex, which opened in the 1980s. It was one of Pyongyang's largest leisure centres, offering swimming pools, large public baths, saunas and a gymnasium. Right in front of Changgwangwŏn there was Pingsangkwan, a huge indoor ice rink.

At Changgwangwŏn I saw white foreigners for the first time in my life. They must have been from Russia, Cuba, or perhaps an Eastern European country, but they looked very strange and scary, with their bulbous noses, blue eyes, white skin and blonde hair. They in turn were shocked to see a group of black children speaking fluent Korean. Each weekend we made a circuit from Changgwangwŏn and Pingsangkwan to the Potongang Hotel and the banks of the Taedong river. In the evenings, the buildings on the river would turn on their decorative lights, while street lamps guided lovers on their dates. I especially loved these glimpses of night-time Pyongyang reflected in the clean waters of the river. I drew great contentment from this new routine. And by now, I had forgotten about my mother.

One day, we were messing about on the riverbank when Maribel came running up to me and said: 'Monica, quickly, get dressed! We have to go to the airport.'

'To the airport? Why?'

'Mum's coming. We have to go to meet her.'

When Maribel said 'Mum', I couldn't at that moment immediately connect my real mother to the conceptual 'mother' in my head. Since the year of the coup d'état in Equatorial Guinea, when my mother left Pyongyang in a hurry, she had become vaguer and vaguer in my memory, and now, like my father, she felt like an ethereal being who did not actually exist on earth.

'Maribel, I can't remember our mother. What does she look like?' Maribel pulled out a photo from her purse and handed it to me. It showed her with our mother. I stared for a long time at the woman in the picture.

'She's so pretty.'

That afternoon, when we met our mother at Sunan airport, even then all I could think was 'she's a very pretty lady'. Maribel and Fran flew to her like arrows, hugging her tightly and chattering excitedly in Spanish, but I stood apart with a blank expression, staring at them like a sightseer. At that moment my eyes met my mother's. She flung her arms wide and gestured for me to come. I approached her hesitantly, and she clutched me to her bosom and cried. Then she started speaking to me but I couldn't understand anything she was saying because I had forgotten all my Spanish. Now, I couldn't speak any language but Korean.

'Mum, I can't speak Spanish. I don't know what you're saying,' I kept mumbling in Korean, but my mother couldn't understand anything I said either. After a while, her smile faded, and she started muttering at me.

I asked Maribel to interpret for me.

'Monica, she thinks you're not talking because you resent her.'

'That's not true! Maribel, you know that's not true! Mum, it's because I can't speak Spanish. Honestly!'

I kept shouting in Korean. I felt misjudged and disheartened at the same time. The phrase 'mother tongue' was the wrong term for me. I didn't know my mother's language, and my mother didn't know mine. Mother and daughter looked at each other and spoke a foreign language that the other could not understand at all. Then Maribel said, trying to calm me, 'Yes, I know. It's because Mum doesn't know. Try to understand.'

But I knew that in my heart, a deep cut was already being made.

During the time I spent with our mother, I could not hold a proper conversation with her without Maribel or Fran acting as interpreter. When the two of us happened to be alone, we had to spend that time in uncomfortable silence. My mother could not accept the fact that I was no longer able to speak Spanish when she had known me as a child who spoke it fluently. This terrible situation in which a mother and her youngest daughter couldn't talk to each other created an emotional chasm between us.

After two or three months in Pyongyang, Mum went back to Equatorial Guinea. Even on the day she departed, I could only

My mother with Fran and Maribel during her visit to Pyongyang

offer a silent embrace. Looking at my mother as she walked to the plane, as she turned at every step to wave back at us, I felt very melancholy. After the plane took off with our mother in it, Maribel turned to me and said, 'Mum is farming plantain in the countryside of Equatorial Guinea. She came here to see us with the money she earned selling fried plantain.'

I now know that my mother had been through a physically and psychologically horrendous and painful experience in Equatorial Guinea. She had lost her husband, had no money and had suffered physical abuse – even having her leg broken – at the hands of members of my father's family who had never accepted her. As I look back, I understand the strength of character that must have been required for her survival, and I marvel.

At the time, it stung to realise that my mother was a stranger to me.

With Maribel, Fran, his classmate and my mother during her visit to Pyongyang

At Last, a College Student

In late 1987, at fifteen years old, I graduated from Mangyŏngdae Revolutionary Boarding School. On the day of our graduation ceremony, we took a souvenir photo on the sports field and shared heartfelt farewells and embraces. With that graduation, the girls' class I had belonged to evaporated and the school became single-sex again. That special system had only been set up for me and Maribel, and with my departure there was no longer any reason for it to exist. The experience I had shared with the other girls in the school would never be repeated.

Almost all of the foreign students in Pyongyang lived at the Haebangsan Hotel, a name that for me held magical promise. The reason I wanted so much to become a university student was because I longed to leave the cloying confines of the boarding school and join my siblings, who had been living at the hotel for some years. I was over the moon: no more military discipline for me! As it turned out, the discipline had been hard-boiled into me, but becoming a college student still spelled a dizzying new freedom. I could go to the Ch'anggwangsan or Koryŏ hotels, or even just out for a walk, whenever I wanted.

On the first day of university, I jumped out of bed at five a.m., full of excitement and expectation. After showering, instead of mechanically donning my tired school uniform, I picked out an outfit of street fashion with the veneration appropriate to a sacred ceremony. Being able to wear what I wanted was another privilege of being a university student. At seven a.m., I went downstairs and ate breakfast with the other foreign students in the hotel, who were mostly from Syria and China.

After a brief breakfast, the students left the hotel for class. Those who went to school nearby walked, and the rest took a university shuttle bus. I got on the bus with the Chinese students and headed for the Pyongyang University of Light Industry.

With two slightly older university classmates who had already completed their military service

As we crossed the Taedong Bridge, through the bus windows I could see flowers – forsythia, rose of Sharon and morning glory – waving in the wind as if applauding. Pyongyang was truly a city of flowers, especially in spring, when there were blossoms and trees wherever the eye wandered. It was as if the houses were among the flowers, and the streets were paved between the trees. It was dreamlike to be able to enjoy this view, not just on weekends, but on weekday mornings. Back at boarding school, I would have been marching past the main building to the classrooms at this time.

As the bus stopped outside the front gate, we saw our supervising teacher waiting for us. She came towards us with a smile. In general, at every university in Pyongyang, a supervising teacher and two roommates were assigned to every five foreign students. Their purported role was to assist foreign students with any difficulties or problems, but their duties also included keeping an eye on the foreigners and reporting on every aspect of their lives. Duties and roles were one thing, but according to Maribel and Fran, as happens when people get to know each other, after a while the dormitory roommates ended up as friends or even co-conspirators. They initially intended to keep watch on us but ended up more on the side of their fellow students than on that of the authorities. They wrote the right things in their reports to their superiors while simultaneously safeguarding the foreign students' freedoms.

Our supervising teacher gathered us together in a group. 'Ladies and gentlemen, welcome. If you have any difficulties during your time at our university, let me know through your Korean dormitory roommates.'

Our roommates introduced themselves. As we followed them onto campus, I looked around eagerly, like a country bumpkin in the big city for the first time. The main building was five storeys high, with lecture theatres and laboratories, and behind that there was a two-storey building with a library; workshop spaces, such as sewing rooms; and a large sports field. 'Wow, so this is university.'

Finally, we entered a classroom by the back door. The students, who had been talking away, suddenly turned and looked at us in silence. I scanned their faces, and my heart sang as I discovered among the strange expressionless faces three friendly ones from boarding school: Chin Suk, Su Ryŏn, and my special friend Sŏn Hwa.

The head of department came into the classroom and began to explain the semester timetable and curriculum.

'Here in the textile department, after taking a preparatory course, you will take revolutionary theory, mathematics, physics and chemistry as general education subjects during your first and second years. In your third year you will begin your major specialisation, and from around the middle of that year you will learn textile factory management techniques and other mainly practical studies.'

Unlike in the design department, in the textile department students learned garment construction, how to operate machines and manage garment factories. The head of department explained that after four-and-a-half years of studies, students were required to write and defend a thesis and take a national exam. He began to write lecture times and the subjects that we were to take on thc board in a mixed script of Korean and

Chinese characters, and I quickly jotted it all down. A student sitting next to me stared over my shoulder at my handwriting with a surprised look on her face.

'You write Korean really well!' she exclaimed.

At recess, the students gathered around me in a pack. I had quickly become a spectacle. Behind me, I heard voices whispering. 'Her skin is really black'; 'She's big, too'; 'Look at her hair.' At the boarding school, I had long ceased to be an object of interest on account of my ethnicity, but this was a different world. I would have to start afresh.

The dormitory roommate responsible for me tried to intervene, but at that moment Sŏn Hwa stood up and, with the approval of the roommate, turned to address the class.

'Listen, you can't say that Monica is a foreign student. She has lived in Pyongyang since she was little, so she might look different on the outside but on the inside she is just as Korean as the rest of us. So, from now on I hope you don't treat her any differently or as some kind of circus exhibit.'

Her eyes twinkling, she mouthed, 'Good one, right?' Thanks to her, by the end of the first day I had quickly grown close to the new students in the textile department. I had the largest frame of any of them, despite also being the youngest. Strictly speaking, they were all seventeen or eighteen, thus, *ŏnni** to me, but they didn't worry about that and we simply became friends.

I also made new friends at the Haebangsan Hotel. Of course, it was still forbidden to meet North Koreans in private outside school, so most of my friends were other foreign students at the

---

* *Ŏnni* means 'older sister' and implies a senior social status.

hotel. On the fourth floor there were mainly Chinese students studying on national scholarships. From about 1981 China began sending students en masse to study in North Korea, and each year China would send its best students from all areas – Beijing, Shandong, Heilongjiang, Szechuan, Jilin, and so on – to study at the Pyongyang University of Architecture, Kim Il Sung University, Pyongyang University of Light Industry, Kim Ch'aek University of Technology, and Pyongyang University of Music and Dance. A considerable number of these students later ended up in Seoul and other major world cities, on the fast track to success.

With my classmates at an outdoor drawing lesson in springtime

There were Chinese students in the textile department at Pyongyang University of Light Industry too. I became very close friends with Wang Tien Mou and Guo Xu Gun. They had both been studying at the university before I arrived, but because I was a big, tall girl who seemed older than my years, they became my friends. We became the 'three musketeers' of Pyongyang. Every Saturday we would go to the discotheque on the eighteenth floor of Ch'anggwangsan Hotel, primarily a haunt of foreign students, diplomats and other outsiders. Known simply as 'the eighteenth floor', it served up a menu of eighties Western pop. I especially loved Madonna's 'La Isla Bonita' and Desireless's 'Voyage, Voyage'. In the 'Voyage, Voyage' music video, the singer wears a black shirt, black suit with high-waisted, cropped balloon-leg trousers, and chunky black boots. Her hair was short, boyish and punky, and she wore red lipstick. Her style was revolutionary to me.

'I want the same outfit and hairstyle,' I said to Tien Mou and Xu Gun.

They looked at each other and said in chorus: 'Yes!'

We all seemed to agree that Desireless's style fitted a part of my personality, and I ordered a completely new wardrobe from Pyongyang Diplomat Store's tailor. It was not until a few years later, when I started taking piano lessons and got immersed in classical music, that I changed to a more feminine style. I discovered that what we wear can reflect our state of mind – our feelings, passions and emotions – and can thus communicate them. Self-articulation through fashion.

The three of us would watch TV together on Sunday afternoons, when foreign films were shown; we saw Chinese, Romanian, Cuban and Russian films such as *Anna Karenina* and *War and Peace*, among others.

Often our supervisor at university would organise a picnic in one of Pyongyang's parks so that my classmates and I could

Wearing my Desireless-inspired black suit, late 1980s

get to know each other better. Everyone would bring large amounts of food to share. My classmates would bring *kimbap*, *kimchi*, rice cakes and other Korean dishes. Sometimes it felt like a cooking contest. My food of choice was the simplest – red bean buns – and whenever these picnics took place the director of the Haebangsan Hotel would order the kitchen to turn out a batch of them for me.

One thing was for sure: college life offered me more freedom and fun than boarding school.

'You Are Korean!'

'Could we too choose to lead our own lives?' asked Sŏn Hwa. Her question resonated in my head. Although no one else expressed it in words, we all had similar thoughts as we watched Lim Su Kyung on television. Lim Su Kyung, a South Korean activist, had defied the South Korean government to travel from Seoul to Pyongyang (via a circuitous route that took her through Japan and Germany) to participate in the 13th World Festival of Youth and Students held in Pyongyang from 1–8 July 1989. She became an icon in North Korean society, receiving the nickname 'the flower of reunification', and was admired for her spirit – and her hairstyle. Many of my classmates cut their hair like hers: straight, medium length with a fringe, in a style that became known as the 'Lim Su Kyung cut'.

If the situation was reversed, and a North Korean student travelled to Seoul, gave a speech and returned to Pyongyang via Panmunjom, what kind of punishment would they receive? None of us talked about that hypothetical situation. The same was true of what kind of punishment Lim Su Kyung would receive upon going back to South Korea. But inside we were all pondering it.

Since coming to live in Pyongyang I had never once made my own choice about anything at all, so I was afraid of Sŏn Hwa's words. To be honest, until this point I had never even entertained such a thought. Even in my second year at university I was still enjoying the benefits of my status as an international student, with special privileges, who was studying in North Korea. I didn't yet want to make my own decisions.

Around this time, Fran suggested that we go to Beijing to visit our cousin Lino, who was Equatorial Guinea's ambassador to China. 'Maribel can't take time off because of her studies, but I want to go. How about you?'

I hesitated. Apparently, all I had to do was to make a choice to experience something new, but this choice was still overshadowed by fear. On top of that, I was having plenty of fun as I was and felt safe. It wasn't worth the risk.

My everyday life was rolling happily along. Every Saturday, after drinking tea at the place we referred to as the Kimchi Bar, we foreign students invariably made our way to Changgwangwŏn Health Complex. There we would have a swim and sauna and relax, after which I would sally to the Rakwŏn Department store in a happy mood. In the clothing department, I would survey the newly imported fashions from Japan, which I justified as market research. Looking at the pretty designs made me dream of graduating university quickly and designing my own clothes. Around sunset, we would pile back into my Syrian friend Ali's old used car and go back to 'the eighteenth floor' at the Ch'anggwangsan Hotel to socialise.

Maribel and me with saleswomen at the department store

One day I was waiting in front of the hotel entrance for another Syrian student, Al Waleed, to park his car. Suddenly a serious-looking Korean man appeared in front of me.

'Would you come with me for a moment, please?' he asked in Korean.

'Where?' I answered cockily.

'Follow me, while I am still asking you nicely,' he demanded.

'First tell me what this is about.'

At that point his expression darkened. I immediately thought of a rumour I had heard going around – that security officers in plain clothes were watching everybody. Until then, I had dismissed it. I had never imagined I would experience it.

'Look, comrade! Don't you know that it is not allowed for our people to go out with foreigners?' he said, raising his voice. I was seized by fear.

'What? Our people? Did I hear you all right? Do I look Korean to you? Are you perhaps blind?'

As soon as I said that, a little voice within me hissed, *You coward, Monica!* I recalled all the times in the past when I had resolved to become a true Korean; when I had refused to learn Spanish at boarding school; when I had insisted with a raised voice that I was a Korean. At the same time, I resented this situation. I had tried so hard to live like a Korean only to be excluded, and now suddenly I was one of 'our people' and they wanted to punish me?

'Enough! Let's go!' He finally became angry and took my arm with a steel grip.

'No! I won't go. I am not Korean!'

'If you are not Korean, how can you speak Korean so fluently? You only speak Korean, don't you? Let's go!'

At that moment Al Waleed appeared and rushed towards me.

'Monica, what's the matter?'

'This man says I am Korean, and he is trying to take me somewhere.'

'This woman is not Korean,' Al Waleed said to the man, puzzled.

'What do you mean she is not Korean? If she were a foreigner, she would have an accent like you, wouldn't she? But this woman speaks Korean perfectly!'

Al Waleed went into the hotel and called a manager he knew well. Only after the manager and the security officer had exchanged words could I escape the charge of being Korean.

The story did the rounds among the international students as a funny anecdote. But that funny anecdote was like a bomb that woke a long-slumbering awareness within me that those surveillance agents did exist and we were under scrutiny.

Because You Grew Up in Pyongyang

It wasn't long before all my certainties were blown apart again, this time by another outsider.

Each day, we went into college for lectures in the morning and returned to the hotel for lunch. In the afternoon, we could choose either to return to the university to study or to remain at home.

One afternoon, I chose to stay in the hotel, and once I had finished my studies I joined Ali, who was watching TV in our communal lounge. We were talking about the drama we were watching when he stood up and then sat down on a coffee table in front of the television. The table was where the daily newspapers were placed, each one bearing Kim Il Sung's portrait, which was (and continues to be) regarded as sacrosanct. Ali sat on a copy of *Rutong Sinmun*, the official Workers' Party newspaper – right on President Kim's face. I could not believe my eyes.

'You can't sit on that!' I said, aghast.

'Why not?' Ali responded.

'Because Kim Il Sung's picture is there!'

'I don't care. He is not my father; he isn't feeding me; I'm here on my own account, and I don't care.'

'You can't, you can't,' I bleated helplessly, and began to preach to him about respecting our leaders and authorities. Respect for authority seemed a natural thing to me. Ali laughed. 'Oh, that's because you grew up in Pyongyang,' he sniggered, and walked out, leaving my mind reeling with puzzlement and anger.

What bothered me about Ali's action was not so much the disrespect he was showing to President Kim. It was more his easy confidence in throwing away the rulebook I had been trained to follow mechanically since childhood. A thousand questions pulsed through my mind. *What's wrong with growing up here? How dare he sit there like that? Why doesn't he understand?*

I was suddenly painfully aware of a certain parochialism in my outlook. I saw fences in my mind that until then had been invisible to me; and with that perception came a new, uncomfortable feeling of being trapped. The old certainties were invaded by a new doubt. Walking around Pyongyang, I looked at its hotels, shops and streets with new eyes.

I would often frequent a store for Koreans situated near our hotel. Strictly speaking, they should not have served me as I was a foreigner, but they did because they knew me. But now when I visited the shop, a critical, insistent inner voice piped up. *These people don't care about the service they are providing. They don't care if they sell goods or not! It doesn't matter to them whether or not their customers are happy.*

All night those words of Ali's swirled around in my head. And the next day, and the day after that. I couldn't shake them from my mind.

With my foreign student friends at the hotel

Even in the past I had heard many times that I was too naive. I had a habit of assuming that any person I met was a 'good person', unconditionally. I believed that everyone was innocent and truthful until they demonstrated the contrary. On the other hand, if it was proven that someone was a 'bad person' I remained steadfast and stubborn in that assessment, to the point that I wouldn't dream of meeting them again. (Years later, living in Europe, some of the episodes of culture shock I experienced were related to this mental habit. Most Europeans seem to think that people need to prove they are trustworthy, rather than the other way round. They are reluctant to trust a stranger at first sight.) Having that kind of personality, everything that I had learned at the Mangyŏngdae Revolutionary School stuck with me as the gospel truth. Just like the other children in Pyongyang, I called President Kim Il

Sung 'the Great Leader', due utter respect. Besides, had I not personally received his kindness?

History, philosophy, politics – everything that I had learned at school I had believed was unquestionable fact. America was to be cursed and treated as untrustworthy, and South Koreans were American puppets. 'America you shall hate, due to the Korean War, but South Korea you shall pity', was the everyday message disguised in the books, films and songs that I had grown up with.

In everyone's life there comes a time to break the invisible shell and emerge from it, but in order to do that, you must recognise that you are in a shell to begin with. Growing up in Pyongyang, without my even being aware of it, my beliefs had grown into a thick, hard carapace. Thanks to the single sentence Ali said to me that day, a hairline crack began to appear in that thick shell. Until then, it hadn't even occurred to me that I might be feeling trapped. I mulled over his words many times.

'Because you grew up in Pyongyang... Because you grew up in Pyongyang...'

Towards Beijing

What is it like, the other world, out there? Even asking the question felt strange. *How do people in other countries live? What is their culture?* I began to wonder.

I decided that when the summer holidays came, I would go to see what the outside world looked like for myself. It was 1989 and I was in my second year of university. It was a strange feeling, that moment, as if I had woken up from a deep dream and all my senses had come alive. As soon as I embraced the idea of going away, new sensations began sprouting all over my body like spring shoots. It was as if a wanderlust that had been hibernating inside me for years suddenly started to break out.

At that time China was the only country I could choose for my experiment. A month earlier, when Fran had asked me to go with him to Beijing, I had declined. But now there was only one thing on my mind: Beijing!

That's it, it's decided. I'm going to Beijing. Now another feeling invaded me; this time it was fear. Since arriving in Pyongyang, I had never visited another country; I had never even travelled alone. The fear was understandable. But in the end, my curiosity outweighed it.

I prepared for the trip, applying for my Chinese visa and a North Korean permit to leave. I was still using a passport from Equatorial Guinea – a country that had brought my father a cruel death. To me, it was a faraway land. I had succeeded in erasing every memory from that country but ironically was still forced to travel as an Equatorial Guinean. I could speak neither Fang, my father's tribal language, nor Spanish, the country's official tongue. I was a strange traveller: one who couldn't speak the language on her own passport; a black girl on the outside and a Korean inside. It made me realise how important identity was to human beings; I began to see that I needed to know more about my roots. I also realised that courage was more important than material goods. After two weeks of preparation, on a hot summer's morning I walked towards Pyongyang Central Station carrying only one bag. Maribel came with me.

'Are you sure you want to go alone?' she asked, anxious.

'Yes, I'll be fine, stop worrying.' As I spoke, I heard someone calling my name. I looked back and it was Sŏn Hwa. She was wearing an immaculate university uniform with not a single wrinkle, her short hairstyle perfect. She bowed to my sister.

'Take this.' Sŏn Hwa handed me a plastic bag.

'What's this?' I asked.

'It's *songp'yŏn*,' she told me, a variety of Korean rice cake. 'You're travelling a long way. You might feel hungry.' Sŏn Hwa knew how much I loved *songp'yŏn* and often woke early in the morning to prepare it for me. I embraced her; my gaze locked on to the sky to try to stop the tears falling down my cheeks.

I boarded the train and sat in my seat. I watched my sister and Sŏn Hwa waving through the window. I kept looking until the train moved off and they disappeared from view.

Our carriage was in the middle of the train. It had bunks and a small table under the window. There was a middle-aged white lady sitting in front of me. She had blue eyes, blonde hair, pale skin and symmetrical features that to me suggested kindness. I could tell she was Russian. The plastic bag she was carrying bore Cyrillic writing. I was able to read Russian, although I didn't know what it meant. At school I had studied Russian until I dropped it for English.

The lady smiled at me and I smiled back, leaning against the window. The train started to speed up as we left central Pyongyang behind. We sped past big modern buildings, and others which included aspects of the traditional Korean style, like the famous restaurant Ch'ongryukwan and the people's grand library, an icon of the city. 'Neo-Korean' style, perhaps.

The lush scenery caught my eye. A huge green rice plantation outside the city was dancing to Tchaikovsky's 'Waltz of the Flowers', orchestrated by the hot wind and directed by the beautiful blue sky. My trip to Beijing had officially begun!

But as the journey wore on and the train passed through other cities, my mental demons were still plaguing me. I thought back to conversations with my friends in breaks between lessons at university.

'I heard that China is opening up! That means there is going to be chaos, and a lot of gangs. Are you going to be OK?'

'I am not sure if it's a good idea to go to Beijing,' another friend had said.

They all worried about me and couldn't understand my desire to travel, to see beyond the borders of North Korea. I had smiled and ignored their concerns – but now I was wondering if they were right.

These thoughts going round and round were dizzying, and I slumped forwards with a hand to my forehead. The Russian woman sitting opposite suddenly held out a white tablet: it was an aspirin – she must have thought I had a headache. The lady smiled and gave me a bottle of Sindŏk spring water that she had with her.

'Thank you.'

I reluctantly smiled and popped the pill in my mouth.

'Did you come to Pyongyang for a visit?' the Russian lady asked in English. I could understand her curiosity, but I didn't know how to answer that question without raising another one.

'No speak English,' I said.

I was a curious case for everyone. In fact, I had studied English at school and university, and used to practise with Charles and Luis – American soldiers who had crossed the 38th parallel in the Korean War and now lived in Pyongyang. They had become celebrities after starring in a famous movie, *Unsung Heroes*. Luis, indeed, was referred to by the name of his movie character. But despite all this practice, my English wasn't good enough to answer all the questions that might be asked – and I didn't know if I even knew the answers. Nor could I speak Spanish like a person from Equatorial Guinea. And to say 'Korean is my first language' would lead to so many questions that needed explanation. For the first time, I came to think I really needed to be fluent in a language that matched my external appearance.

After about six hours, the train pulled into a new city. Workers bustled here and there, weighed down by bags and parcels. Many were on bicycles. The city was in a busy mood. The station was surrounded by factories and chimneys. I realised it was Sinuiju, whose sister city, Dandong, was just across the Chinese border. I had reached the northern edge of the Korean peninsula.

A policeman came into our carriage. Despite the heat, he was wearing a khaki uniform that left only his hands and face uncovered. I felt as though I was inside the sauna in Changgwangwŏn.

'Passport and ticket, please,' he asked the Russian lady in English, before directing the same to me. Having completed his inspection, the border guard said:

'Have a nice trip.'

He returned our passports and saluted.

The train moved on to Dandong. Once again, it was passport control – with another overdressed policeman, this time Chinese.

Dandong station was a blur of people. The air was just as thick with humidity. I went out to stretch my legs, but only for a moment because, just like in Pyongyang, everyone was looking at me. Back in our carriage, the Russian lady was already asleep. I lay down on my berth looking at the sky through the streaked windowpane.

Emotions of fear and excitement welled in my chest; I couldn't sleep. The stars followed me as the train barrelled its way towards Beijing.

Twenty-four hours had passed since we left Pyongyang. The train was slowly drawing into Beijing.

I was excited – and yet afraid. Hustled along by the mass of people pushing into the city from the station, I emerged onto the street. I looked around, befuddled. Beijing station was huge, and swarming with people going in and out. It seemed to me that they all were talking at the same time. Many people were on bicycle taxis, which, unlike in Pyongyang, you could hail. The air was grey. Everything was new to me. I remembered my teacher's words in geography class: 'China is the country with the largest population in the world.'

My teacher was right!

I stopped in front of a huge building. The advertising hoarding on the front took my breath away. It was a huge picture of a beautiful lady's eyes. I felt like she was gazing straight down at me and saying *Buy this mascara and your eyes will become as beautiful as mine.* The picture was so charming that I stayed there a while just looking at it. It was the first time I had seen such an enormous image promoting a product. What a wonderful idea, I thought. All we had in Pyongyang was revolutionaries and movie posters.

After wandering around for about an hour, I decided to go to my cousin Lino's place. Lino was expecting me. When I had spoken to him on the phone a month earlier, I had told him that I was coming to visit him in Beijing, and would find my way on my own. I didn't want him to pick me up. It was my first trip outside North Korea, and I wanted to prove to myself that I could manage alone.

'Excuse me? Excuse me!'

I started trying to ask the way, brandishing a piece of paper bearing Lino's address. I couldn't speak Chinese, and no one would understand Korean, but I assumed at least someone would understand English. But my luck was out!

I spent another thirty minutes trying to find someone who could tell me the way, but no one seemed willing to stop and help. It was maddening and demoralising. I should have learned Chinese from my Chinese friends in Pyongyang.

I started to lose hope and slumped onto the floor watching the streams of people passing by. Suddenly a white man carrying a huge backpack came into view. *He must speak English!* I thought. *Maybe he's a student who lives here and knows the city.* I stood up and walked towards him.

'Do you speak English?' I asked brightly.

'Yes.'

'Thank God,' I whispered to myself, and thrust forward the address. 'Do you happen to know this street and how to get there by bus?'

'You're in luck! I am going that way myself. Follow me.'

But as I listened, I froze. A thousand thoughts crowded my mind.

He was American! I knew the difference between British and American accents thanks to an English teacher in the language college in Pyongyang who was British.

No, no, no, no… I must run! I began to back away. He pressed towards me, looking concerned. 'What's wrong with you? Are you all right?' he asked, catching my hand. 'God, your hands are cold!'

I snatched my hand away, turned and started to run, with all the force I could muster. I would have won any race, even though I was always last at school.

Eventually, I gave in and took a taxi to Lino's place. And like that, my plan to find the way myself was ruined by a kind American.

Lino was frantic.

'Where you have been? I was worried! I've been calling your sister in Pyongyang!'

I ignored what he was saying and tried to explain in my bad English what had happened, as I could not speak Spanish. As he listened, his face began to change and eventually he erupted in guffaws.

'What's so funny?' I could not understand why he was laughing.

'He was American!'

'So what?'

'America is scary!' I blurted.

Images swam into my mind – canvasses from the Pyongyang war museum and Sinch'ŏn Museum of American War Atrocities, and Picasso's depiction of the Sinch'ŏn Massacre.

'You feel that way because you grew up in Pyongyang!'

That again! What did he mean?

'What's wrong with growing up in Pyongyang?'

'You need to open your mind.'

The next day Lino took me out and introduced me to some of his friends and acquaintances. Most were diplomats. They were all very curious, asking what it was like to live in Pyongyang as an African. Some asked about the education system, others about the people. How did I spend my time and how was I treated? There were so many questions. Sometimes I felt I was being interrogated by detectives. I had never experienced this level of fascination in Pyongyang.

Lino also took me to visit the city's historical sites: the Forbidden City, the Temple of Heaven, the Great Wall, *Beihai Gongyuan* and the *hutong*. We ended our tour at the street-food market in Wangfujing in the evening when the city came alive. Visiting the Forbidden City brought the 1987 TV adaptation of *Hong Lu Meng* (*Dream of the Red Chamber*) to mind. *Hong Lu Meng* is one of four classical Chinese masterpieces written by Cao Xue Qin in the eighteenth century and the story is still very popular in Pyongyang. Growing up, I used to watch the TV series, as well as adaptations of other classical novels such as *Journey to the West*, arguably the most popular novel in East Asia. *Hong Lu Meng* is about a love triangle against the backdrop of a noble family that falls from grace. It is believed that the author based it on the story of his own family and the woman he loved. It reflects the social, cultural and spiritual life of that era in great detail, featuring almost 700 characters. I could picture *Hong Lu Meng* characters in their beautiful ancient Chinese costumes as I walked the alleys of the Forbidden City.

One day Lino and I went to the Beijing Lido Hotel for a delicious lunch at the hotel's fancy restaurant. We were walking out through the lobby when we passed a group of people talking. I turned my head towards them.

'Korean?' asked Lino.

I nodded. My language and my people, I thought. I missed speaking in Korean.

'Why don't you go over there and talk to them?'

'I'd like to, but they're from the South.'

'So? Just go and talk.'

I was torn. Of course, in North Korea South Koreans were considered puppets of the Americans, but at the same time I wanted to speak my language.

'Go and talk to them. North or South, we're all human. Plus, it's the same language. Just go!'

Coyly I approached them.

'Hello, you're South Korean, right?'

'Oh my, you scared me! If I wasn't looking at you, I'd think you were Korean!' said one of the group. All eyes were on me. Again, the interrogation began.

'How come you speak my language so perfectly?'

'Are you half-Korean?'

The reaction was all too familiar. I elicited the same response from Koreans, whether from North or South, every time they heard me speaking their tongue.

The Koreans gave me their contact details and invited me out for a long dinner that ended with karaoke. We sang well-known South Korean eighties pop songs. They were, inevitably, surprised that I knew all the words.

It was a lovely evening, full of warmth and good cheer. The mental barricade I had nurtured against South Koreans for so long crumpled in a second. When people interact in good faith and get to know each other, without the intervention of ideology and politics, respect and mutual learning flourish.

Singing karaoke with South Korean friends

Doubt

When I returned to Pyongyang, summer was almost over and the next semester due to begin. The shocks to my system that I had experienced in Beijing had already died down a bit. As usual, I got up each morning and went to classes at college. During the break, when my friends gathered around me and asked, 'How was Beijing?' I would answer briefly, 'Oh, it was good. China seems like a really big country and very dynamic.'

On the outside, it seemed as if nothing had changed. Autumn flowers had started to bloom in the hills behind the school, and the red bean buns from the Chŏnsŏk restaurant still tasted great. I was suddenly struck by the quiet and cleanliness of Haebangsan Street, the paths along the banks of the Taedong river, and Changgwang Street. I had become somewhat frazzled by the endless hustle and bustle of Beijing, and coming back to my serene hometown felt good. Even so, within me a change had already begun to take place.

The biggest change was that Pyongyang did, in some ways, look different from before. The city's streets, which felt so orderly and safe compared to confusing and complex Beijing, nonetheless took on an unnatural air. Even when I sat on the lawns of the university campus chatting with my friends, I felt trapped. It was almost as if I had walked onto a giant movie set and was reciting my lines of dialogue from an approved script. Our perceptions and judgements of the world and of people were the same yesterday and today, and conversation did not go beyond that framework. My encounters with Americans and South Koreans in Beijing had suddenly cast the everyday judgements and pronouncements made about them in a new light. I saw now that they were based not on direct experience but on received knowledge, and so, naturally, they felt empty.

Within me, a chaotic transformation began. Until now I had believed – believed one hundred per cent, unwaveringly, without a doubt; nobody had been as steadfast as I – but now cracks were appearing in that belief. Of course, I still loved Pyongyang – I always will. It is the city I grew up in. But as much as I loved it, I also had questions, and they were increasing day by day. *Is this all there is? Is there no more than what is seen with the eyes?* This idea was at the core of all my questions.

Maribel once told me a story about when I was young. One day, my mother came back to the house and when she saw me, she nearly jumped out of her skin. There was her three-year-old daughter sitting at her make-up table, having shaved off her own eyebrows, and even cut off her eyelashes. Mum became very angry and scolded my brother and sister for not looking after the baby. Recalling that episode, Maribel said, 'When I asked you that night why on earth you had done that, you just mumbled, "I'm curious, I'm curious". That's how impossible a child you were.'

Maribel told me that since my early youth, I had been compelled to try whatever came into my head or I would not be satisfied. No matter what anybody said to me, I had to experience and understand things myself before becoming convinced of them. If what she said was true, then I had lived for a long time with that nature deeply suppressed. From the time I went to school until I was at university, I believed everything I learned without question. But from the moment I first left North Korean soil, my original personality was reawakened and reared its head. I had begun to question the familiar.

My curiosity and questioning soon led to a full-frontal confrontation with university authorities. I was in a philosophy class. As always, the students were holding their tongues, taking everything down or simply listening to the professor's words. That was when I shot my hand up and raised objections that had not been raised before.

'Sir, are the principles of the public distribution system really ideal? I often go to a shop near where I live, and other shops too, and every time I go there the women managers are just passing the time knitting. If a customer comes to the shop, they don't look pleased to see them, nor do they work hard to sell them anything. The customer service is very poor. And this is because the manager will receive her portion of public distribution every month whether she sells or not. And if our society pursues much more collective wellbeing compared to a capitalist society, then why does the level of happiness or wealth vary so much from person to person? The students' faces at this school speak for themselves.' The philosophy teacher asked me, 'So, Monica, do you believe that capitalism is better?'

'Yes, to some extent. Communism is a beautiful idea, but we can't achieve it due to selfish human nature. It's a utopia.'

It was an answer that took courage to voice, but I had no choice but to play devil's advocate, recklessly if need be, to keep the conversation going. Since an ideological dispute threatened to break out, the professor decided to continue the debate with me after class, one on one. He explained point by point how inhumane capitalism was, while I stubbornly raised objections. After a time, the professor shook his head. 'Oh, Monica! You wouldn't believe me if I told you that you'll break your legs by jumping out of a tree. You'd have to jump and break your legs first before you admitted it. You stubborn mule.'

I had begun to view the society and environment that I lived in with more objective eyes, and little by little my life was changing. I had stuffed my bag with tapes of American and Korean movies before returning from Beijing. What I wanted to see, more than an interesting storyline or glamorous stars, were the settings and scenery. South Korea, Europe and America – what kind of places were they? And the people of those countries – what kind of facial expressions did they have, what kind of conversations, how did they interact?

I may have been sheltered, but the window on the outside world that these tapes gave me were in fact another example of my privilege, one not afforded to my Korean friends in Pyongyang. I could not talk to them about this other world – not even Sŏn Hwa.

The only people with whom I could have an open and honest discussion on these matters were my foreign friends at the Haebangsan Hotel. I began to meet the international students one by one and cautiously ask them questions I'd never asked before.

Trips to the Kimchi Bar, the discotheque and Changgwangwŏn became infrequent. Instead, I stayed in my room to reflect on what they told me, confronting a number of inconvenient truths. I cannot forget the shocks – and the sadness – of the successive challenges to my beliefs at that time.

'It's natural that you think like that because you've only lived in Pyongyang,' Ali had said. From this one pronouncement, an incipient disbelief started to undermine my faith in everything: the country and culture I lived in, and the supreme leader of North Korea who had looked after me.

The Farewells

From my third year of university until the time I graduated was a time of conflict and partings. It was something I had to deal with by myself, and a lonely experience. I do not remember when it started, but I would often go to the site of an old palace at the foot of Mount Taesŏng and spend half a day just watching people coming and going. Children holding onto their mother's or father's hand as they climbed the mountain, affectionate lovers, young women carrying parasols and old people walking with their hands behind their backs... these were what I loved to see the most. Ever since I was young, my feet would instinctively halt at the sight of a family all gathered in one place and I would simply stand there, looking at them. If you ask what happiness is, people will beat about the bush trying to give an impressive-sounding answer, but to me it was only this: 'Living together with the people I love.'

Everybody needs some alone time, but a person who is always alone is an emotional cripple. From the autumn of that third college year, I spent more time alone than anybody else I knew.

Each year at vacation time all my school friends would go back to their hometowns. When that happened, I thought long and hard about that word, 'hometown'. When Koreans talk about their hometown, they picture bucolic rice paddies or green fields of barley, or the sound of cattle lowing from afar, but I had nothing to be reminded of. The feeling of emptiness I felt was beyond words. And so, every time a vacation came around, I would set off with Fran, Herve and Montan for Wŏnsan, a port city in North Kangwŏn province on the eastern side of the peninsula, where we took a boat off the coast. From Wŏnsan we would travel all the way to the Kŭmgang mountains, mythologised by Koreans, ranging along the east coast from Tongcheon county in Kangwŏn province in North Korea to Inje county of Gangwŏn province in South Korea. The beauty of Paltam, a series of eight ponds above Kuryong Falls at Mount Kŭmgang, struck me as if someone had thrown eight emeralds from the sky. At Paltam we heard the tale of the woodcutter and the fairies.

Once upon a time, a woodcutter lived with his mother in Mount Kŭmgang. One day, while cutting the trees he found a deer in the mountain. A hunter was chasing it. The woodcutter hid the deer and saved his life. In gratitude the deer asked the woodcutter what he could do to compensate. The woodcutter asked for a wife.

'Go to the ponds where the fairies bathe,' said the deer. 'Hide the wings of one fairy. She won't be able to fly back to heaven without her wing dress. She will become your wife. You must never return her wing dress until you have three children with her.'

Following the deer's advice, the woodcutter went to the pond and took a winged dress. The eight fairies were bathing and playing in the ponds, and when they finished they put on their winged dresses to ascend to heaven – except one, who could not find her wings.

She became the woodcutter's wife. After some time, she bore two children, but she missed her home in heaven. The woodcutter, who felt very sorry, confessed what he had done to stop her flying back home. The disappointed wife demanded her wings and, her children in her arms, ascended to heaven.

The deer came to visit the desperate woodcutter and said to him: 'On the fifteenth of this month, there will be a bucket coming from heaven. Get into that bucket to ascend to heaven and you will meet them there.' Indeed, a bucket appeared from heaven on the night of the full moon, and the woodcutter ascended to heaven and met his family. He lived happily with them in heaven, but his happiness was marred by worry about his mother. His wife gave him a flying heaven horse to visit his mother on earth. She warned him never to get off the horse.

The happy woodcutter descended to earth riding the heavenly horse. His mother gave him a dish of hot red bean porridge. The woodcutter spilt the hot porridge on the back of the horse. The frightened horse reared and the woodcutter fell off. The horse ascended to heaven without him and he became a rooster. That is why roosters still go up onto the roof and cry sadly while looking up at the sky.

This ancient tale reflects the deep class divide in classical Korean society – the earth-dwelling woodcutter can seek marriage with a heavenly fairy, but eventually their union is broken because of their differences.

At Mount Paektu, a volcanic mountain located in the north of the peninsula, on the border between North Korea and China, the erratic and sometimes severe weather would constantly change, catching us off guard. In North Korea, if a person was capricious we would say they were 'like Mount Paektu'. You did not need to visit all the mountains in the world to know that Mount Paektu was of an exceedingly rare beauty. Koreans say that the flowers that bloom in each of its foothills cannot be seen on any other mountain; they belong only to Mount Paektu. In summer, if you were lucky, the mountain's Heaven Lake would show you its beautiful turquoise face – though for eight months of the year it is frozen.

On those vacations, I went to Hamhung city, capital of South Hamgyŏng province, the country's second largest city by population, on the northeast coast and tried local Hamhung cold noodles.

While in Wŏnsan, I sat near the hiking trails at Wŏnsan Beach and drank alcohol with my 'older brothers'. I do not have the physical constitution to tolerate alcohol, but my brothers drank with the Pyongyang university students and there was no alcohol they could not imbibe, from Taedonggang beer to blueberry liquor, *sochu* and even *makkŏlli*. Once I gave in to mischievous Fran's entreaties and drank some strong whisky, almost passing out. Those three wicked musketeers would seize any chance to tease me, and I would once again be fooled into drinking. Even so, thanks to their being there, my vacations were somewhat less lonely. Eventually, even that period of my life came to an end, because they all graduated from university and went back to their home countries. Herve and Montan departed for Benin and Fran went to Equatorial Guinea.

When he was due to leave, I held on to Fran like grim death.

'Fran, why do you want to go? It's still dangerous there! Stay here with us, OK?'

Fran, Maribel and the Kerekou brothers on an excursion to Nam Po with our North Korean friends

But Fran had long ago made up his mind.

'Did you forget why Father sent us to Pyongyang? He sent us so that we could study and go back to Equatorial Guinea and be of some use to our country. I studied architecture, so I'm going to go to back and construct. I will build a city!'

I had always thought he was just a child who played around and chased after girls, but it turned out that Fran was a man with a plan of his own. I had no choice but to let him go. At least Maribel was still at my side. It takes such a long time to study to be a doctor that she had to stay on in Pyongyang.

Waving off Fran, Herve and Montan at almost the same time, I couldn't help but feel desolate. But there was one more farewell looming, one that I could not see coming: Sŏn Hwa, who had been my bosom buddy since childhood, suddenly had to drop out of college.

When I first heard the news from a friend named Kyŏng Mi, I did not believe it. Kyŏng Mi was like college radio: whenever there was a rumour, it started with her. Any news coming from outside the university was also first heard by Kyŏng Mi, who then passed it on to us. Even when there was no interesting news to tell, she would find some tiny hint of a rumour and blow it up like a balloon.

Since coming back from Beijing, I had set a kind of principle for myself to believe nothing I did not see with my own eyes or hear with my own ears. So, on this occasion, I simply made myself scarce when it seemed as if fantastic stories about Sŏn Hwa were doing the rounds. And after class, I didn't catch the shuttle bus back to the hotel but instead waited for Sŏn Hwa at the gate. She lived in a dormitory ten minutes' walk from school, so she always walked. As soon as I saw Sŏn Hwa, I rushed to her.

'Hey, Monica! Why aren't you on the bus?'

'I wanted to talk to you.'

And then Sŏn Hwa shook her head slowly and said, 'Have you heard the rumour too?'

'I heard you were dropping out of school. I want to hear the rest from you. Can you tell me?'

Sŏn Hwa linked arms with me and we set off walking.

'Listen. I'm pregnant.'

'What?'

That was when I noticed that Sŏn Hwa's belly had grown a bit.

'For a while I tried to hide the bump by tying a belt inside my uniform, but the sports teacher caught me. That's why, according to the rules, I can't attend any more.'

'Who is it? The baby's father?'

'An older boy I love. We're going to get married. Even if it's not right away.'

'Aren't you scared?'

'Of what? Of the rumours? Or of having a baby?'

'Both. There'll be all sorts of crazy rumours soon. Doesn't that make you worry? And what about giving birth?'

'Rumours are just stupid things spread by people who have a lot of time to spare and like to poke their noses into other people's business. Bringing a new life into this world is a good thing. What's wrong with having a baby with the one I love? As long as I'm happy. I can continue my studies after having the baby, through the Open University.* I'll just be having a family early. The happiest family on earth.'

When the word 'family' came out of Sŏn Hwa's mouth, I shut my own mouth. I was always struck dumb when I heard that word.

'Monica, I'm choosing to live my own life now.'

After that, it became hard to see Sŏn Hwa. A rumour went around that she had had an abortion, but it was nonsense. Sŏn Hwa showed up at college again about a fortnight later.

'Monica, I'm leaving now. I came to see your face one more time.'

Sŏn Hwa said that after she went down to her hometown of Kaesŏng and had her baby, she'd think about marriage. Now it is really time to say goodbye, I thought, and suddenly I remembered how at night, in our room at boarding school, we would whisper by candlelight. How, whenever I was starving, Sŏn Hwa

* Similar to distance learning programmes in the West, in the 1950s the North Korean government created a scheme called the 'learning while working system' to target illiteracy among working adults in the country. Students studied university lectures in the evening after work, via print and radio, and corresponded with their teachers by letter.

would sneak out to Chŏnsŏk restaurant and bring me red bean buns. And how, when my face got dirty from splashing through muddy puddles during night-time military training, she would tenderly wipe me clean. The girl who back then had dreamed of being a film star was now having a baby with someone she loved.

'Monica, there's something I must tell you.'

'What is it?'

'When things in life don't go your way, don't grumble or get angry, just focus on trying to solve the problem. If you get angry, you'll develop wrinkles and your face won't be nice to look at. And then you'll give people a bad impression. You're much more beautiful when you smile than when you frown. Got it?'

I wondered why she picked the moment she was leaving to say this kind of thing, but maybe that is precisely why I have never forgotten those words. Sŏn Hwa was someone who always smiled. She never raised her voice, and although she was always gentle and quiet, she had a confident personality and she said what needed to be said. I never wanted to leave her side.

'Monica, let's not cry. They say that a meeting is completed by a parting. You and I, let's live happy lives whatever it takes.'

Sŏn Hwa wiped away her tears with her handkerchief, and left for ever, while I crouched down, there by the college fence, and cried like a baby. That was the last time I saw Sŏn Hwa.

Even after all these years, whenever I think about 'the most beautiful thing in Korea', without fail Sŏn Hwa's face is what comes to mind. Even though we had no future together, and could not share our lives with each other, that unfinished connection was enough to keep Sŏn Hwa engraved on my heart.

After Sŏn Hwa left, more partings followed. My Syrian friends left Pyongyang, and Wang Tien Mou and Guo Xu Gun went back to China. One by one, I saw them off, and then one day I caught myself in the mirror, sitting in the Kimchi Bar, alone, fiddling with my beer glass. I had to accept the fact that my turn was approaching.

Leaving Pyongyang

After Sŏn Hwa left, the only friend who stayed with me until I graduated was my university friend Yun Mi. Because she was the daughter of a diplomat and had been born overseas, she knew the outside world better than anyone. Her bookishness and experience overseas made her think and speak a little differently than my other Pyongyang friends, which meant she had to be careful about what she said.

One day Yun Mi told me something of great significance.

'Monica, as you know, I lived abroad when I was young. That's why I know what a closed world Pyongyang is. But now my thinking has changed a bit. Is it really only we who lived trapped inside a world? You'll find out if you go out there and experience it, but even in the so-called free world there are lots of people who live their whole lives shut off. Wherever you go, the people of that country have their own fences constructed of self-made prejudices and stereotypes. If we're trapped, those people are trapped too. The only difference is that they have a few more things they can enjoy. Monica, once you determine to live a new life, you'll always have to think about what living freely really is.'

I embedded Yun Mi's words deep in my heart. Actually, in that moment it was hard to understand completely what she meant. But in the decades since, I have not forgotten it.

In 1992, I graduated. It was a lonely ceremony. The first thing I did after that was to enrol in a Spanish course at the University of Foreign Studies.

'Excuse me, where is the Spanish classroom?' I asked some students I met at Pyongyang University of Foreign Studies. Confused, they replied in English, pointing towards the end of the corridor.

'Go straight and turn right at the corner.'

It was a somewhat comical situation. A black student asks for directions in Korean, and Korean students answer in English.

'Aren't we allowed to use Korean at this school?' I said in English. Indeed, it turned out that the school rules banned the use of Korean inside the school building. But it felt awkward, given that we all shared the same native language. So I added 'thank you' in Korean.

'You're welcome!' they said in English.

The students smiled politely and walked on. I heard them chatting among themselves. 'That's weird. I guess a Korean-speaking foreign woman came to this school to learn another language.'

Deciding to learn Spanish again was entirely my own choice. It was a tool that I needed in order to be able to live the life I had in mind. I did not want to be an obedient 'victim of fate' any longer. I wanted to reject a passive life where I only thought and felt what was given to me, in a place that was prepared for me. The world was bigger than Pyongyang, and I needed to see it. I wanted to witness it, with my own eyes and ears. Most importantly, I was looking for the identity I had lost. At that moment, I was unable to define myself – and that had to be more important than how others might define me. Of course, on the surface I knew I was of mixed African and European heritage. But my knowledge of those two cultures that were part of my make-up was superficial. I lacked the fundamental awareness that might help me to know who I really was, where I fitted, and what I wanted out of life.

In his letter to us, sent from Equatorial Guinea to Pyongyang, my father had told us not to forget we were African. What did he mean? Who was my father, really? Who was my mother?

I needed to embark on a backward journey in search of my roots. To take the first step, I had to learn Spanish.

As it turned out, learning Spanish was as easy as pie. I thought that there were no traces of the Spanish language left in my brain, but I was wrong. If the teacher said a word or gave me a sentence to complete, without thinking other related words would pop into my head. I was surprised and the teacher was too.

After about six months, I was ready to speak Spanish. My teacher chuckled and said, 'This is less like giving a lesson and more like pushing the play button on a cassette machine.' He asked me why I wanted to learn Spanish again, and I replied, 'To go to Spain.' In fact, when my siblings and I first came to Pyongyang, our stay was only supposed to last until we graduated from university. Our father had asked President Kim Il Sung to host us until we finished our studies. So when Fran was graduating, he was asked by Kim Il Sung's aide what his intentions were:

'What do you want to do now? If you want to stay, then stay. If you want to go, then go. You decide what you want to do.'

Fran said that he would leave, and the secretary sent him a small sum to cover travel expenses. Just before I graduated, I was asked the same question. I replied that I wanted to build a life for myself in Spain. Through his aide, Kim Il Sung replied: 'Monica, are you strong enough to live in that harsh capitalist world?' It was the question that I had been asking myself for the last two or three years. It would be hard to make a living in Spain with the skills that I had learned at university because the system was different. Frankly speaking, in the fifteen years I had lived in Pyongyang I had never worried about money: all necessary living expenses were provided for by the state. On top of that, because I was a special ward of the state, I couldn't be safer. Leaving Pyongyang meant that the secure system that had kept me going for all those years, that had looked after me and given me economic stability, would abruptly disappear. It was a choice: a sheltered, counterfeit existence, or a real life, my own life, with the attendant adventure and risk.

I had to leave. I wanted to live in a bigger world; I wanted to live a life I chose for myself in a world different from the one I had lived in until now. I gave the aide my response, and he sent me enough money to get to Madrid. Later, when Maribel had finished medical school in Pyongyang and said she wanted to go to China, she was also provided with travel expenses. With that, President Kim Il Sung's promise to my father was fulfilled.

By the time I graduated from university, I had no idea what the outside world thought of North Korea and Pyongyang, or about Kim Il Sung as a person. President Kim Il Sung was always a person whom I was and am thankful to – not on a political level, but on a personal level. If it had not been for him, I and perhaps my whole family might no longer be here on earth. Politics apart, the Kim Il Sung of my memory is a man who kept a promise to his dead friend for twenty years.

Maribel's reaction to my plan to go to Spain was matter of fact: 'Sure, that's where your starting point has to be.'

Maribel never asked me why I was going to Spain rather than Equatorial Guinea because she knew what a fearful place Equatorial Guinea was to me. At that time my mother, Fran and my elder brother Teo were all living there. Except for me, my sister, and our father, who had already left this world, all my relatives were living there, but it was still a country I feared and hated. That is why I chose Spain, the country of one half of my lineage. But that was not my final destination. I had planned a tour with many stops – beginning in Spain, then America and South Korea – and then, when I judged that I was strong enough, I would seek out my ultimate destination: Equatorial Guinea. It was to be a meandering journey to a faraway final place.

One day when I was rushing around, preparing for my departure, I received a letter from Teo. He was opposed to my going to Spain.

> Why Spain? Why choose that country of all places? Don't you know how Spaniards perceive women from Equatorial Guinea? They think Guinean women are prostitutes who go to Spain looking for white men. I am afraid that you'll go to that country and be treated like such a woman. Please, reconsider.

I could barely even remember Teo's face, but I was disappointed in him. Did he really think that I might end up setting foot in that world? Did he really not know what kind of country I had grown up in and what kind of education I had received? But in all honesty, I could not be certain what kind of place Spain would turn out to be. I only knew that it would be a completely different world from Pyongyang. My Pyongyang friends described a nation of *Carmen* and bullfighting, a nation where gypsy grandmothers wearing black shawls carried baskets while begging, the poorest nation in Europe, where the ETA terrorist organisation killed people on a monthly basis. But nobody I knew had ever been to Spain themselves, so I decided to shut my ears. Until I saw it for myself, I was not going to make any judgements – not about Spain, not about any place.

Before leaving Pyongyang, I sent one last letter to Sŏn Hwa in Kaesŏng.

'Sŏn Hwa, I'm going far away now. I don't know when we'll be able to meet again, but I hope you will always be happy.'

On the day before my departure, after I had done all that I needed to do, I got up early and walked slowly through the streets of Pyongyang for a long time. I wandered past Mangyŏngdae Boarding School and Chŏnsŏk restaurant and along the Taedong river from Okryu Bridge to Yongkwang Street. There I turned around and followed Changgwang Street to Moranbong Street, and then on to Mansudae Art Theatre. I walked until my legs were sore, but something inside kept pushing me to walk on.

The sun hasn't set yet. I'll keep filling my eyes a little longer.

That day I could not fight the tears as I watched the sun go down over the Taedong river.

In the spring of 1994, I boarded a plane from Pyongyang to Madrid, via Beijing. On board, a group of young Spaniards returning from a trip to China chatted loudly, as if in their own living rooms. I gazed out of the tiny window, immersed in my own sorrow. I was clutching a sheet of paper in my hand. It was a letter from Sŏn Hwa, and it had arrived that same morning. It was long, around ten pages, and at the end was this: 'Monica, always stay confident and be brave! Keep going, you must complete your journey no matter how far you roam, detour, or wander off the path.'

What will Spain be like? The only way to know was to experience it.

Part 2
In the West

On the steps of the Capitol, Washington DC

Madrid

On the twelve-hour flight out of Pyongyang, I crossed not only several time zones but also the frontiers between two different worlds: ideological and sociocultural. I did not know what to expect in Madrid. Long before the plane came into land, my heart was pounding, and when I had passed through the airport and finally faced the immigration desk, I felt I might faint. As I stood in line I gulped in breaths, trying to adjust to the air of a strange world. All the staff and security personnel seemed to be looking at me.

When my turn came, the immigration official's expression was grave. He looked at my passport with a keen eye.

I prayed: *Let me through, quickly!* There was nothing wrong, but I could feel a cold sweat prickling me. Then came a blunt and chilly question.

'Why are you coming to Spain?'

A routine question for most, but for me the answer was a long story. I couldn't say, *I'm here to learn who I am.*

So, I just answered simply, 'I have come to live here.'

'Aha!'

The immigration officer pressed a button on his desk, his sombre gaze fixed on me. I had no idea what was going on. A short time later, a security guard approached. As I followed him to an immigration office, I felt like everyone was staring at me.

As soon as I sat down, I took courage and asked in English, 'Why are you bringing me here?'

'Hey, speak Spanish. We don't know English,' the security guard scolded.

'I'm not good at Spanish yet.'

'Can't speak Spanish and you are an Equatorial Guinean? Are you kidding me?'

'No. It's a long story.'

Of course, I was able to understand them, and I could speak, more or less. But my Spanish was not good enough to explain my purposes. And the fear and turmoil that had invaded me as I entered this uncharted territory had frozen my tongue.

The 'classroom Spanish' I had learned at the Pyongyang Foreign Study University and the real Spanish I was encountering now were quite different in accent and speed of delivery. Surrounded by two or three security personnel, I felt as if I were in custody, under suspicion like a drug trafficker or terrorist. I had never been so frightened. They kept speaking to me in Spanish, but I couldn't answer.

After about ten minutes of insisting on speaking to me in Spanish, they finally gave up.

'I think I need an interpreter,' said the immigration official.

They wanted someone to translate English to Spanish, but what I needed was someone who could speak Korean.

'Please call a Korean interpreter.'

'Korean? This is odd. A Guinean who doesn't speak Spanish but Korean. Who *are* you?'

Then someone opened the door, looked at my passport, and spoke slowly in English.

'Hello, young lady. I'm Jose. Your name is… Monica?'

'Yes, that is correct. But why have I been arrested?'

'Oh, you haven't been arrested. We have brought you here to ask a few questions. According to the stamp on your passport you have come via Beijing.'

'Yes, but I departed from Pyongyang, and then caught a connection from Beijing.'

'Pyongyang? Pyongyang in North Korea?'

'Yes. Pyongyang. Is something wrong?' I noticed my tone become defensive.

'Let me see if I understand properly. So, you are a Guinean who doesn't speak Spanish coming from Pyongyang. That's interesting.'

The guards in the room began to talk between themselves about North Korea and Equatorial Guinea. I caught a few whispered words: 'The dictator's country'.

The moment I heard that, I stared at them angrily. Then the interpreter asked me, 'What is Pyongyang like? According to the news, it's a harsh place to live.'

'I will not answer that question.'

'It's OK. This is a free country. You can say whatever you want, you won't go to jail. There are lots of Cubans living here and they all talk about Cuba, mostly cursing their own country.'

'So you mean I must curse the place I have lived in since I was young, just for the sake of cursing it?'

'We mean you can talk freely here. Honestly.' And then they started bad-mouthing North Korea and the former 'dictator' of Equatorial Guinea.

'Stop it!'

The guards looked at me, perplexed. 'But you're Guinean!' The interrogation resumed.

'I will ask again. Why are you coming to Madrid?'

'As I said, I came here to live.'

'Monica, you can only stay here for a few days with your transit visa. If you want to live here you need a different visa, a residence visa from your country of origin. Your passport says you are Guinean, so you need to go there and get a residence visa. We will give you a visa for ten days, then you must leave. You can go now.'

I was already exhausted. Even more distressing was the fact that I would eventually have to go to Equatorial Guinea.

As I walked towards the exit, my mind churned with what those guards were whispering about North Korea, and about my father; the dictator of dictators, a despicable human being. Kim Il Sung had always told us that our father was a good friend, a good person. I had always imagined him as a hero who fought for the independence of our country.

Why are these people bad-mouthing my father? What kind of person was my father, Francisco Macias? If all these comments are true, what about me? Am I the daughter of evil?

Zaragoza

After nearly five hours of interrogation and background searches in the immigration office of Terminal 1 of Madrid's Barajas International Airport, I was finally allowed to cross the invisible line dividing immigration from arrivals.

Everywhere there were happy people hugging and kissing. I looked around. Alicia, my mother's friend, was supposed to meet me and she would have had a long wait. All I knew about her was that she was Guinean but had been living in Spain a long time. I did not even know what she looked like.

I saw someone holding up a sheet of paper with my name on it. I walked towards her and greeted her in the Korean way, with a bow.

'In this country we hug and kiss both cheeks,' said Alicia, demonstrating as she talked. It made me uncomfortable, especially the kissing. Where I had grown up, making bodily contact in public was unusual. It is a custom I still struggle with. I feel awkward when an acquaintance tries to kiss me on the cheeks.

'Oh my god, they took so long!' said Alicia. 'You must be exhausted. Let's go to my sister's house to have lunch and then we'll hit the road for Zaragoza.'

I nodded. I was too tired to speak.

After an hour we were on the way to Zaragoza, the capital of Spain's northeastern region of Aragon. During the three-hour journey I did not say a word. My mind was busy processing my emotions and absorbing the scenery that was unfolding before me, an arid landscape that seemed an expression of the uncertainty and fear that pervaded me.

At last, we arrived in one of the city's residential neighbourhoods, stopping on Santander Street, where Alicia owned two flats. I looked around me. The buildings looked so different from the ones in Pyongyang.

'OK, here we are,' said Alicia, opening the door. 'It's the first floor.' I hefted my suitcase inside and followed her. I was surprised when she summoned the lift. In North Korea, the first floor is the ground floor. But when the doors opened, sure enough there was a '1' on the wall.

I bent down to take off my shoes, and Alicia smiled. 'You don't need to take those off. Here in Spain you can wear shoes in the house.'

There were people to greet us: Alicia's husband, Mariano; her granddaughter, Julia; and other relatives.

'I live here, but you will be staying in a room in the other flat. Come, I will show you.'

Alicia led me to where I would be staying. Unlike Alicia's flat, this one had only two rooms and a bathroom. She opened a door, and I saw two bunk beds inside, and four black women sleeping. I assumed they all were Guinean.

'Let's leave them to sleep. They've been working all night.'

She closed the door and opened another one to a slightly smaller room, with a single bed and a built-in wardrobe. 'This is your room. Put your stuff down, get some rest and come to my flat for dinner later.' Then Alicia left.

I dropped my suitcase and sat on the bed. I felt my eyes begin to pour with tears like a waterfall. I cried in silence. I felt so lonely among all these people, and the language barrier only contributed to my sense of isolation. I started to doubt my decision to come to Spain to learn about my origins and my identity.

I want to go back to Pyongyang, I thought. I had a very comfortable life and friends there.

Then there was another voice. *It was comfortable on the surface, but how can you overcome the discomfort of not knowing where you come from or who you are? That would be a hollow life.*

There was a knock at the door. 'May I come in?'

'Yes,' I said, wiping my eyes.

The door opened. It was Julia, Alicia's granddaughter. She said something quickly in Spanish.

'Sorry Julia, my Spanish is very bad. Can you repeat it slowly for me please?'

She spoke again, pronouncing each word clearly.

'Oh, sorry. I was saying that I don't know much about Asian countries. North Korea must be different to here.'

'Yes, very different.'

'Anyway, Grandma is calling you for dinner.'

It was a hearty dinner. All the dishes were new to me and some had a very distinctive smell. Unlike a Korean table, which presents a variety of communal dishes in small portions, with rice and soup as the mainstays, in Guinean culture each person is given a generous portion on their own plate, and most of the dishes are oily.

'Sit down,' said Alicia. I sat next to Julia, who was the same age as me, twenty-two. We were also both mixed-race with the same brown skin tone.

'Are you used to a knife and fork? I understand that Asians use chopsticks but we haven't got any.'

'That's fine. In Korea we use them too, in hotels.'

'This is *yuca*,' said Alicia, pointing to a dish with a pungent smell. 'This is called *nfugowon*, chicken with peanut sauce. This is *mansaa*, meat and spinach with palm oil. This is fried plantain, and this is *fufu*. This is *modicca* sauce with fish. Now, eat. Try all of them.'

'Well, Granny, she can try what she can, maybe not all of them. It's just too much food!' I shot Julia a look of gratitude. I have always found new foods difficult, and I was missing Korean dishes. But the fried plantain smelled delicious. There was plenty of it and I helped myself to some.

'That's not a main dish, it's a side dish. Try some of the main dishes with some sauce,' admonished Alicia.

I felt like a child learning how to eat. But the truth was I didn't like any of the main dishes.

'This is OK for me. Thank you.'

The fried plantain was really delicious: sweet despite being oily. I had another helping and then drank a lot of water to fill my stomach.

Mariano, Alicia's Spanish husband, seemed well acquainted with all these dishes and he enjoyed them. He did not say a word during the dinner. I waited for the others to finish, and then took my plate to the kitchen to wash.

'Leave it. I'll do it,' said a girl who was in the kitchen, eating her dinner alone.

'Thank you, but I'll wash mine.'

I returned to the other flat, shut myself in my room and lay down on the bed. I closed my eyes and tried to sleep, but I found myself fighting the demons in my mind that summoned terror of the looming forced journey to Equatorial Guinea. They would not go away.

I racked my brain for childhood recollections of Guinea as I tried to imagine what lay in store, but my memory box was black. Nor did I have any objects that could act as aide-memoires and transport me back to that place. Instead, grim images surfaced. I saw black children of about six or seven years old. They were severely undernourished; so fragile they could not stand. They lay in beds that looked very uncomfortable, in dirty surroundings. Flies and mosquitoes landed on them but they did not react. The next image was a brownish landscape, dry and cracked, with no trees or plants, strewn with animal skulls. Then, a long queue of people, some sitting, some lying on the ground. Adding to the bleak atmosphere, a solemn North Korean voice described the 1980s Ethiopian famine. He said people were dying and called for solidarity. These images from North Korean TV were the only ones that came to mind when I thought of Africa, and they made my heart sink. Once again, my eyes became moist. Was this what Equatorial Guinea was like? What would happen to me there? Would the presidential incumbent kill me like he did my father? Having grown up in a quasi-hermetic society under the protection of Kim Il Sung, I did not know how Guinea would receive me. The sky turned black. I was shrouded in clouds. No one was there. I was alone, lost and trailing aimlessly. I felt I was walking in a nightmare, not knowing where I was going. My pulse raced.

These feelings of trepidation and foreboding stayed with me, multiplying, as the day of my departure approached.

To Malabo

A few days later, I was on the plane to Malabo, tense and fearful. I wished the plane would turn and head for Pyongyang instead. My doubts about having left North Korea were still strongly present. I missed Sŏn Hwa and Yun Mi. I thought back to when I was at boarding school and we would visit Chŏnsŏk restaurant to buy red bean buns and *songp'yŏn*, and sit on the grass, talking and laughing.

Impervious to my inner anguish, the plane continued on its five-hour journey, and as it landed on the island of Bioko (the site of the capital, more than 200 kilometres northwest of the mainland) I caught a glimpse of bright green vegetation outside. Just as on my descent into Madrid a few days earlier, my heart began to beat so fast that I felt it might explode. I felt awkward, disassociated, as if I did not belong to that place. Panicked thoughts invaded me once again. *What's going to become of me? Do all Guineans hate my father? Will they hate me as well?*

Stepping out of the plane, hot, dry heat hit my face. I couldn't breathe; my body wasn't used to this kind of climate. Once again, it brought Pyongyang to mind – this time, the contrast with Pyongyang's humidity.

This was the land where I was born, the land where my father was buried. But it felt like a strange and unfamiliar place. Nature was exuberant here. The airstrip was surrounded by impressive green jungle and a small shack served as the airport. People were waiting for their family or friends and I scanned their faces to find Fran and my mother.

Suddenly I heard 'Here, here!' in Korean. It was Fran. His height and light brown skin made him stand out from the crowd. Next to him there was someone else with a similar skin tone. It must be Teo, my elder brother, who had studied in Havana, Cuba, and of whom I had no memory. He was serious, unsmiling. Was he happy to see me? Fran ran forward and hugged me.

'Are you all right?' I gabbled in Korean. 'You are alive! They didn't kill you! I am so scared!' I clasped Fran's hands tightly and would not let him go.

'No, don't worry. It's all right. You'll be fine!' he said. 'This is Teo,' he added. 'Here we hug or shake hands. We don't bow like in Korea,' he said when he saw me trying to bow towards Teo.

Teo was very cold. Following Fran's instruction, I hugged him, but he was stiff and unresponsive.

Does he hate me? I couldn't help wondering.

'Come, Mum is waiting in there.' Holding my hand, Fran led me to the shack.

I recognised my mother immediately. She hurried to hug and kiss me. It was the first time I had seen her since her visit to Korea, years earlier.

'Are you able to speak Spanish now?'

'Yes, a little bit,' I replied. 'But I have more to learn and need to practise.'

We got into the car and headed to the house in Malabo city. The dirt road was lined with very tall trees.

When we arrived, about twenty minutes later, there were people waiting.

'Who are all these people?' I asked Fran.

'Family members and neighbours. Cousins, uncles, aunts, et cetera.'

'Do you know all of them?' I asked.

'Of course not! Not even half of them.'

They were singing, dancing and speaking loudly – even more loudly than the group of young Spaniards I had encountered on the Beijing–Madrid flight.

I appreciated the welcome, but I wanted to escape to my room and be alone. My mind was overwhelmed with thoughts about my father and the succession of new cultures, Spanish and then Guinean, that I had been exposed to. I needed time to process it all.

'Dinner is ready, come along,' said my mum happily. Another parade of dishes awaited me, accompanied with rice or fried plantain. The only thing I was familiar with, from my stay in Zaragoza, was the fried plantain.

'Can I have some fried plantain?'

'Of course! This is your home. I made plantain because I remember you loved it when you were young,' Mum said.

I took some plantain and started to eat, but I found the other dishes very oily.

After dinner, I locked myself in my room and lay down. I tried to sleep but couldn't. I had a pounding headache and was still plagued by uncertainty and fear.

The next day, Fran took me to the Spanish embassy to apply for a student visa. 'Why don't you stay with us in Malabo?' asked my mum, hoping to persuade me.

'I need to go back to learn Spanish properly and I don't feel ready to live here.' Even I could hear the determination in my voice.

'I understand, but remember, all that is in the past now. Besides, there won't be anyone to take care of you in Spain.'

'Mum, I lived under protection for all those years in Pyongyang. Now is the time to live by myself.'

'Why do you think you can't live your life in Equatorial Guinea? I would like you to meet a nice man, get married and live with us here. You are just like your father – stubborn!'

I had so many questions for my mum, but I didn't know where to start.

'What was my father like? Why is he known as a killer? Why is his reputation so bad?' I blurted out.

My mother took a long pause. 'Your father wasn't what they say. The Spanish government and press of that era organised a campaign to discredit him. They even claimed that I escaped to Switzerland with the country's money, because they didn't know where I was when the coup took place. I have never been to Switzerland or Ethiopia as they claim. I will give you the number of your father's lawyer, Antonio Garcia-Trevijano, in Madrid. Go and meet him, and he will be able to clarify all this.'

But I did not feel that my mum's answers were enough. I needed to dig deeper. I needed to meet more people who knew him.

'Thank you, Mum. I need to know where I came from and understand my two cultures, Guinean and Spanish. I need to find the answers to my questions myself. My mind is like a blank sheet of paper that I need to fill out. I have to do this by myself.'

A week later, I received my Spanish student visa. Relieved, I started to prepare for the trip to Spain.

'Monica, open up!' It was Fran knocking at my door. 'He passed away!'

'Who?' I asked, worried.

'Kim Il Sung.'

It felt as though someone had plunged a knife into my heart. Tears fell from my eyes. We went straight to the North Korean embassy, where we attended a ceremony of mourning. After an hour we returned home. I locked myself in my room. After arriving in Pyongyang in 1979, my biological father died, and after arriving in Guinea my adopted father died. Was this a cruel joke?

Memories of Kim Il Sung came back to me. I could see his charismatic face, always with a smile. I could hear his voice.

It was the autumn of 1986. I was outside the office of the boarding school's deputy director, Kim Il Sung's nephew, waiting to be sent in. He was very tall for a Korean, with dark hair half covering his forehead. He had a kindly face and used to invite us to picnics of barbecued meat, shellfish and *kimbap*. After lunch, we would play cards.

His house was located next to the library on campus. One day, his beautiful daughter played the piano as her parents and I listened. She was in her twenties, with dark hair and pale skin, slim and tall like her father. Her performance took our breath away, and the three of us applauded as she finished.

'What song is that?' I asked her. 'It's so beautiful. You play like an angel.'

'It's "Für Elise" by Beethoven. Have you heard of him?'

'No.'

'He was a famous German composer of the eighteenth century,' she explained. I was so excited to hear her play, and dazzled by her elegance, the way she talked and moved.

'How did you learn to play like that? I wish I could play the piano like you. All I know about music is what I learned in elementary school: how to read sheet music and sing.'

She smiled.

'I've been studying music since I was a little girl at the Pyongyang University of Music and Dance. Anyone can play the piano; you just need to be committed and practise a lot. Besides, you already know how to read sheet music.'

At that moment, I decided I would learn to play the piano.

A few weeks later, I was in the deputy director's office. His large desk was covered with important-looking papers, and an impressive Korean landscape painting hung on the wall.

'So, you will graduate soon,' he said in a friendly tone, gesturing for me to take a seat on a sofa, while he sat in an armchair beside it.

'Yes, I know what I...' But before I had finished the sentence the phone rang.

'That's for you,' he said. 'Go ahead and answer it.'

I knew who was calling.

Kim Il Sung asked me in a deep voice, 'How are you? Did you enjoy your holiday in Wŏnsan and Mount Kŭmgang?'

'Yes, I loved it. I especially loved the spa at Kŭmgang. And I had a nice time at Wŏnsan beach. I came back to Pyongyang with new energy.'

'Good! I know you are graduating next year, have you thought about the future and what you want to study?'

Is today 'future-thinking day' or something? I thought to myself, as I smiled towards Kim Il Sung's nephew.

'I want to be a pianist, and enrol in the University of Music and Dance,' I answered happily.

'A pianist? Mm,' he said. There was silence for a moment before he continued. 'I know you love music and you sing very well. But I think you should learn a skill. Besides, the piano students in that university are already professionals – they started learning piano when they were young. You wouldn't be at the same level...'

'But anyone can make it. It's just a question of practising every day. It is my dream. Please, please!'

I was desperate to convince him.

'My point here is that you need to learn a skill that is in immediate demand in Equatorial Guinea. Look, I suggest textile engineering. Learn about textiles, their production, how to manage a textile factory and how to make cloth. That way, you can open a textile factory in Guinea, create jobs, and Guinea would have its own textile production. That's what your father wanted. Study for Guinea.'

I could not muster enough arguments to persuade him. He was repeating my father's wishes – I was in Pyongyang to study for my homeland.

'You're right,' I conceded sadly. 'I'll do that.'

I said goodbye, hung up and looked at his nephew.

'So, you wanted to be a pianist? It's not a bad idea, it's just not practical for you at the moment. What did he tell you?'

'He said I should learn some technical skills and suggested I study textile engineering and how to make cloth.'

'I think that's a good idea. You have an eye for combining colours and creating styles.'

Years later, I registered for piano classes at Taedonggang Diplomatic Club each Saturday, behind Kim Il Sung's back. But my main programme of study was textile engineering at the University of Light Industry. Now I was in Malabo I didn't feel ready to use my knowledge for Equatorial Guinea. I just wanted to leave.

'The best weapon you have is education. Study a lot and never stop learning.' That was one of Kim's numerous sermons that had resounded in my head since leaving Pyongyang.

Just like my father, Kim was known in the West as a bad person, a dictator. My head was full of confusion, grief and memories of him in Pyongyang.

Days later, I left Malabo and arrived back in Zaragoza. This time I was a little more ready to find out about my roots. I decided to do it properly, and began by studying the language and culture.

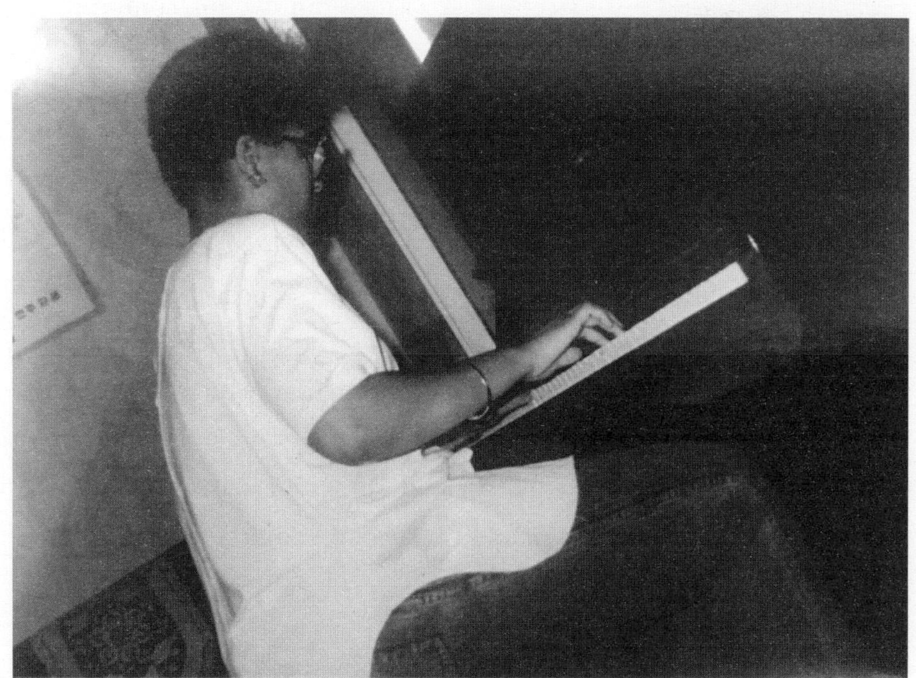

Illicit piano lessons at Taedonggang Diplomatic Club

Homesick

A week had passed since I had got back to Zaragoza from Equatorial Guinea. I was in my tiny room at Alicia's, swimming alone in a dark ocean of new emotions I struggled to understand. The women who lived in my flat would disappear every night and return in the morning, when they would chat noisily.

'Where are you all going every night so dressed up?' I asked one of the girls as she came out of the bathroom.

'To work.'

'Ah, it must be a very glamorous job, given how dressed up you are,' I said, thinking privately that their style was too provocative for my taste.

'Glamorous? Not really! Hang on, do you even know what we do?'

'No, I don't know.'

'We work at a nightclub.'

'And what's a nightclub?' I had never heard the word before.

'Really? Are you joking?'

'No, genuinely, I don't know.'

She laughed loudly. 'Seriously? What planet do you come from?' she said with a mystified look. 'A nightclub is where prostitutes work. Do you even know what a prostitute is, or that Alicia is a madam?'

I heard the word 'prostitute' and ran to lock myself in my room. My brother Teo's warning came to my mind. 'Why Spain? Don't you know how Spaniards perceive women from Equatorial Guinea?' Until then my only encounter with prostitutes had been through the centuries-old Korean folk tale, *The Tale of Ch'unhyang*, the story of the daughter of a *kisaeng* (a woman who dedicates her life to the traditional arts in order to entertain men, a concept similar to the Japanese geisha) who falls in love with the son of a government official. In conservative Korean society, quite aside from the illegality of prostitution, *kisaeng* are seen as shameful.

Once again, I was crying. *What have I come into? People are going to think I am a prostitute too! What shame! I could never consider doing this to myself! How can they do what they do, and so shamelessly?*

I wanted to run far away. But where I would go? I had no money; my Spanish was not good enough to get a job. I felt I was drowning, unable to breathe. Tears streamed down my cheeks. My spirit was crushed, my energy lost.

Then I heard a strange voice coming from the girls' room. I went to see what was going on. Their door was slightly open, and I peeked inside. One of the girls was sitting on the bed, producing a strange voice while her body shook, and her eyes rolled. Standing before her, another girl asked, 'Who are you?'

'I am your father's spirit.' The girl was speaking, but a man's voice came out! I was truly petrified. I ran, locked myself in my room and threw myself under my duvet, shaking.

I must go back to Pyongyang; I can't stay here any more. This is too much! I had endured one surprise after the other with no time to digest. I had no guidance. What to do? I wanted to go home.

Until then, I had only ever encountered such communion with the dead in the 1990 Hollywood movie *Ghost*, which I had watched in Pyongyang. I'd enjoyed Whoopi Goldberg's acting in the movie, and never felt any fear of spirits. But this was a real-life *Ghost*, and it was frightening.

Over the following weeks, the only thought that sustained me was *if I survived today, I can survive tomorrow.* I felt so very lonely. The language barrier, the intense culture shock and the unfamiliar foods kept me isolated from my surroundings and from other people. I became visibly thinner and depressed; I was full of self-loathing. My father was evil, I was living with prostitutes, I couldn't stand the food of my native country. I rejected everything, unable to open my heart and mind to new knowledge and cultures, and to accept them.

Three months passed as I grappled with my feelings, until finally I told myself that I needed to change my mindset, to try to understand these new cultures, Guinean and Spanish, that were part of me. I unlocked the door to my room and something inside me opened too. I went out on the street to breathe fresh air. I saw an Asian face in the crowd. 'My people,' I said to myself gladly. As we approached each other I addressed him in Korean:

'*Annyŏnghasimnikka*? You are Korean, right?' I was very excited to speak Korean after such a long time. He could have been Chinese or Japanese, but I did not care, my words just came naturally. The man stopped, looked around and shook his head, as if he were saying to himself: 'It must be a mistake. I must have misheard.' And he moved to walk past me.

'Here, here!' I said in Korean, waving my hand.

'Oh my god! You speak my language? And perfectly! You could have given me a heart attack.'

'I am so happy to see you! You can't even imagine!'

'Are you half-Korean?'

'No. But I grew up on the peninsula.'

'Where?'

'In Pyongyang.'

'Really? Wow! Incredible! I didn't think there were any foreigners in Pyongyang.'

'Are there many Koreans living here in Zaragoza?'

'There is a small community and we have a Korean church as well. Come to visit us on Sunday. We serve free Korean meals.' He handed me his business card, offering it in the Korean style with both hands. I received it with both hands and we bowed and went our separate ways.

Having had an atheist upbringing in Pyongyang, going to church was not really my thing. But my desire to be among 'my people', to speak Korean and eat Korean food, overpowered any other impulse. So that Sunday I went to the Korean church. Everyone was amazed by my Korean, while I, for the first time since arriving in Zaragoza, felt joy. I even happily ate the same soup I had once rejected in Pyongyang. All the Korean food seemed refreshingly delicious and took me straight home.

On my way home, I rang my sister, who was studying for her Master's degree in Shenyang Medical College, China. 'I ate plain white rice and Korean miso soup. I ate them!' I blurted out excitedly as soon as my sister answered the phone with a sleepy 'hello' in Korean.

'Do you have any idea what time it is here?'

'Midnight, I know, but I ate their soup!'

'You? No way! How come?'

'I met some South Koreans here and they invited me to their church where they serve free meals.'

'You needed to go that far to be able to eat a Korean miso soup? You know what that is? You're homesick! Are you OK? How are you coping alone?'

'I'm OK. Don't worry. Go back to sleep.' I didn't want to worry my sister by telling her what I had been going through.

I later realised that those three months locked away in my room were part of the process of adjusting to my surroundings and opening my mind to different ways of living. No matter how difficult an experience we encounter in life, there is always a positive and a valuable side to appreciate if only we can give ourselves time and space to see it.

Silvia

After meeting some fellow Koreans, my life in Zaragoza started to change for the better. I decided to take a general education course, with modules in Spanish and maths. It helped me to feel more confident and able to communicate.

One day after class, I walked into the city centre, which I had never visited, to explore. I was astonished. A small but majestic city unfolded before my eyes. Its historical buildings and monuments told of all who had conquered the city, Arabs and Romans among others. The Aljafería Palace, an example of Islamic architecture in Aragon known as Mudejar style, was beautifully preserved. La Catedral-basílica de Nuestra Señora del Pilar (the Cathedral-Basilica of our Lady of Pilar) took my breath away. It features the magnificent ceiling fresco *La Gloria* by Francisco de Goya, probably the city's most famous son.

I walked on until I arrived at a shopping mall formally called *La Independencia* but commonly known as *El Caracol* or The Snail, due to the shape of the building. I made my way up to the top floor, where an elegant black dress in a shop window caught my eye. It had been so long since I had last designed and made a dress. I missed it.

'*Hola*.' A girl came out and greeted me. She had a kind, beautiful smile and porcelain skin.

'*Hola*,' I replied.

'Do you like it?'

'Yes, but I can't afford it. I was just admiring the design.'

'That's fine. Come in and have a look. You seem to have a good eye for style.'

'Thank you.'

'My name is Silvia, by the way.'

'Monica.'

'Nice to meet you.'

'Nice to meet you too.'

We spent the next hour chatting.

Silvia became my first Spanish friend. She invited me to her house, where for the first time I tried Spanish food. I was introduced to dishes like *borrajas con patatas* (borage with potatoes), *ternasco de Aragon* (Aragonese lamb) and *migas aragonesas* (Aragonese breadcrumbs). The tastes were completely different from Korean and Guinean food. I was discovering new flavours, and they were delicious! Her mother, also called Maribel, treated me like her own. 'You are my African daughter,' she would proudly say. Every time she hugged me I felt the warmth of a mother.

Silvia and I grew closer and closer, and she became my guide. She introduced me to tapas, the delicious Spanish appetisers that reminded me of Korean side dishes, and thanks to her, I was once again able to enjoy good times with friends. We snacked on tapas while strolling from bar to bar, chatting and drinking wine

With Silvia in la Plaza de Santa Ana on a later visit to Madrid

or beer. She also introduced me to Spanish dating and flirting culture. While Korean men are generally shy about approaching women, Spanish men seemed very forward. The first time two handsome Zaragozanos approached us in a bar, I tensed up. But Silvia, who seemed used to it, handled the moment naturally and elegantly while I surreptitiously took note of her flirting technique.

'You look nervous!' said the man who approached me.

'Oh, that's because my Spanish isn't good yet,' I said.

'Relax! I am not here to judge your Spanish. I can help you to improve, though. Your eyes are very beautiful. And your skin tone is amazing! I love it!' he said, smiling while putting his hands on top of mine. He seemed so confident, while I could not even hold his gaze. My heart was beating fast.

'And your skin is so soft. I heard that black people have very soft skin but I've never touched it before.'

I just smiled as I listened to those kind words.

Compared to Koreans, the Spanish seemed to have mastered the art of flirting and giving compliments that made you feel over the moon. In Pyongyang, I had found that middle-aged men and women were more confident in talking about sex and giving compliments than young men. A male classmate of mine in college had taken aeons to confess his love to a female classmate, only to be rejected. Korean women, meanwhile, usually expected men to approach and 'conquer' them. Most would respond with a shy smile, blushing cheeks and eyes turned downward. This dynamic is very much embedded in Korean courtship culture: the woman is considered a passive flower awaiting a butterfly to land on her petals.

But Spaniards seemed spontaneous, natural and easy-going when it came to relationships and sex. This Spanish guy was confident; he knew how to make a woman feel like a queen, as they say in Spain. It was not just men – Silvia too seemed at ease, and more broadly women took a proactive role in flirting; they seemed just as passionate and outspoken as the men.

Talking about sex in Korean society is not strictly taboo but it is very much a private subject. Although the Socialist Women's Union of Korea, founded in 1945, had campaigned for and achieved some important milestones in gender equality, such as equal pay legislation, government-funded prenatal services and maternity leave, in other areas – such as dating culture – North Korea remained patriarchal. Having grown up in this conservative culture, my knowledge of sex, dating and flirting was naturally rather limited. And so on this 'first date' with a Westerner, I was self-conscious and lacked confidence. Daunted, I refused his kiss.

My new routine became studying in the morning and spending the afternoon with Silvia at *El Caracol.* Our conversation spanned dating, religion, spirituality and the meaning of life. When we argued, we were both so stubborn, but we were also able to reflect, apologise and laugh when we realised we were wrong. We became as close as sisters.

Out of the blue one day she said, 'I am going to call you Monique. You are chic in every sense, and Monique suits you. You are *una cosita rara*, a curious little thing,' she told me.

I laughed, and decided to take it as a compliment. I had never had a nickname before, except in boarding school when Fran had called me the 'chubby strategist'.

Silvia took me to her hometown, near the province of Teruel, Aragon. It had only fifty-two inhabitants, none of whom had seen a black person in their lives. Some of the neighbours used the excuse of visiting Silvia's uncle to catch sight of me. They would stare, making Silvia and me laugh.

In my dark emotional ocean, Silvia became a lighthouse. With that beam of light to guide me, I began to reflect on my attitude towards the girls with whom I lived. Who was I to judge them? What did I really know about them? I hadn't even asked their names. How selfish was I to judge and jump to conclusions?

Walking home one evening after seeing Silvia, as I turned a corner that led to Santander Street, I could sense someone rushing towards me. I turned around to face a black man.

'I know you. You are Macias's daughter. I am going to kill you. I am watching you.'

I ran to the gate of my house a few metres away. Hurrying indoors, I went straight to Alicia and told her what happened.

'In the Guinean community we all know each other. There are mixed political feelings about your father, those who liked him and those who didn't. That is normal, but he should not have attacked you. It's late. Tomorrow we'll go to the police and report it. Go to bed.'

But I could not sleep. Someone wanted me dead out of hatred for my father. Who was my father? What really happened during his era in office? The latent fear that seemed to have been assuaged by Silvia's presence in my life was surfacing again, and a lot of questions along with it.

Another evening soon afterwards, Alicia invited a guest to dinner. There were only four of us – Alicia, Mariano, a white Spanish guy, and me.

'Wow, Alicia, I didn't know you were hiding such a beauty in your home,' said the man, stroking my buttocks.

I threw a glass of water at him and slapped his face forcefully.

'This girl is fierce!' The man got up to leave, furious.

'I am very sorry,' said Alicia to the man. 'She isn't like the others.'

Alicia was very upset with me. I found out later that the man worked in the police force and would help Alicia with her girls' legal papers. For Alicia he was a very important client. But it did not matter how important he was – he did not have the right to touch me without my permission.

Two days later Alicia called me to her room.

'The other night was an unfortunate incident. And there was the stalker incident as well. Since you've been here, I have been living with my heart in my mouth. I'm worried. I would like you to leave. I can't have you here any more.'

A chill ran down my spine. I always knew that one day I would have to leave, but I did not expect to be told to go.

'I understand. I'll go. I'm sorry for causing you problems and worries. Despite everything, I appreciate your help during my stay here. Thank you very much.'

I sincerely meant what I said. During my stay in Alicia's house I had learned to accept people just as they were, without moral judgement. I had learned about both Spanish and Guinean culture, my Spanish had improved, I had even made a best friend in Silvia. I had gained the confidence to go to Madrid and pursue my goal.

One More Step Towards Capitalism

'Silvica, I will soon leave Zaragoza,' I said to Silvia, using my pet name for her.

'Where are you going?'

'To Madrid. The madam asked me to leave the house. Anyway, Zaragoza was beginning to feel small and I was thinking it was time to go to the capital. As you know, I have so many questions and some of the answers are in Madrid. We will keep in touch!'

'Of course, my dear friend Monique, *cosita rara*! I will miss you so much. It's been a pleasure knowing you, and especially having our conversations. But our friendship is for ever.'

'Yes, for ever! You don't know how much you mean to me. You helped me to survive and overcome my fears during my stay here in Zaragoza. You helped me make the best of this experience. You helped me to regain confidence. You have been my lighthouse. Thank you.' I embraced her, a lump in my throat.

My next home was in Torrejón de Ardoz, a satellite town on the outskirts of Madrid where my cousin Mary lived. Mary, the daughter of my mother's sister, had grown up in Spain. Her house was more spacious than Alicia's but, rather than having my own room, I shared a room with her eldest son, Oliver, who was nineteen.

'Monica, what kind of music do you like?' asked Oliver one day. I was struck by the way he addressed me, as if I were his friend and peer. If we had been in Korea, he would be expected to call me Auntie Monica, and to use a respectful tone. I soon realised that almost all young Spaniards addressed older people in this casual manner. At boarding school, I had been taken to task for my lack of respect towards my older sister's classmates, but the rules were different in Spain.

'I like classical music, opera; that kind of music helps me to relax. But occasionally I listen to eighties pop music and Kassav'* as well.'

'Wow! I didn't think you would be familiar with all those kinds of music.'

'Yes, I am. In fact, early on I wanted to be a pianist. North Korea was heavily influenced by Russian classical music and art. Do you know who Tchaikovsky was?'

'No, no idea. A pianist? Why didn't you – what happened?'

'Oh, it's a long story!'

Many people, not just Oliver, would ask me about my musical preferences and every time I replied they were bewildered. They seemed to struggle to connect North Korea, a black girl and classical music.

The first thing I did when I got to Madrid was to try to find a way to validate my North Korean undergraduate certificate. I paid a visit to the ministry of education.

---

* A French Caribbean group.

'I am afraid we cannot. Spain and North Korea do not have an agreement on that matter,' said the woman official, who was surprised to see my university diploma. 'I'm so sorry. What we can do is validate some individual modules, like physics, maths and chemistry, and you can study for some other modules again.'

'I see. Is the education system free here?'

'No, you will need to pay for it.'

I left the ministry frustrated and demoralised. It felt like my four-and-a-half years of studies in Pyongyang had gone out of the window. I could not afford to pay to study. Education is key to creating the skilled labour needed for the construction of a fairer society; and if higher education becomes subject to fees, wealthy families tend to benefit, driving social inequality and unrest. North Korea provides free education from elementary school up to university level, while in Spain those who want to be educated to a higher level must pay tuition fees.

On the train back to Torrejón de Ardoz, I wondered what to do. My immediate need was for money to survive, so I had to look for a job – I did not care what kind.

After several days combing newspaper advertisements and calling around, I found a job in Pozuelo de Alarcón, known as one of the wealthiest municipalities in Spain. I was to be a live-in nanny for a two-year-old boy. In the beginning it was hard; I had no experience of looking after an infant. Luckily, Curro was an angel baby who hardly cried, loved playing with me and was well used to his routines. I learned that raising a little human being is rewarding. Babies have their own language, they know who loves them and who does not, and they reward you with unconditional affection and acquiescence. Their love is a pure love. We liked each other and that made his parents happy with me. As a live-in employee I was also able to improve my everyday Spanish and learn more about Spanish culture and food in a traditional family setting. This experience sometimes prompted me to wonder what it would have been like to live with my parents.

I stayed in that job for a couple of years, but eventually the time came to leave. Curro's young mother cried when I said I was going, but I could not remain. I wanted new experiences, and living and working in that house had started to make me feel trapped, like the days when I first arrived in Spain.

My cousin Mary helped me to find another, similar job. This time I would look after a five-year-old girl, Natalie, from five p.m. to nine p.m. every day at her home in the centre of Madrid. Her mother, Solange – known as Sol – was from Argentina and worked in advertising. We hit it off right from the day of my interview, and she was intrigued by my North Korean background.

Soon, Natalie and I found we also got along well. She was a lovely little girl.

'No, Moni, don't go, don't go, please! Stay, stay!' she said every night, crying desperately as I tried to leave for home. In her mind, only today existed and there was no such thing as tomorrow. It was difficult to explain the concept of time to a five-year-old. Sol and I had to think up all kinds of tricks to distract her while I would sneak out of the house. And I could still hear 'Moni, Moni' from the lift. Did I do the same thing when my mum left me all those years ago? I sometimes wondered, but the hard truth was that I could not remember her leaving Pyongyang.

Some nights I stayed and would sing her North Korean lullabies, and she would fall asleep, looking cherubic.

With Natalie, all grown up, in Madrid, 2016

Another few years passed. When Natalie was old enough to stay at home alone, I found a job as a sales assistant in Leroy Merlin in San Sebastián de los Reyes on the outskirts of Madrid. I was getting used to my new life; I was happier. I had also found a flat in Alcalá de Henares, another town on the outskirts of Madrid and the birthplace of the famous writer Miguel de Cervantes. Leroy Merlin is a large French furniture and home décor retailer, a competitor to Ikea. I worked as a sales assistant in the interior décor and soft furnishings department. It was a great opportunity for me to learn about how corporations – the motor of capitalist economies – were run. In North Korea all companies were either one hundred per cent state-owned or joint ventures (mostly with Korean-run Japanese companies). In contrast, Leroy Merlin was part-owned by its employees, meaning I was a shareholder in the company. I had never come across that concept before. That boosted my morale and motivated me at work. I also came across several interesting commercial strategies.

'Listen up,' said Ronald, our section manager. 'We will launch our sale next week. This week we need to focus on preparing to make sure things go smoothly. Also, we have a shop-dressing competition. I want everyone to come up with an idea for the competition that will attract more customers. I know it will be a hectic week, but I trust you all. We can do it.'

I felt lost. When everyone had dispersed, I approached my colleague, who was also called Monica. 'What does he mean by "sale"?'

'Come on, stop pulling my leg! Are you seriously telling me you don't know what a sale is?' Monica did not know my background. I was not yet comfortable enough with her to let her know my story.

'I really don't know! I'm serious.'

'I sometimes think that you come from a different planet. I thought everyone knew what a sale was. It is a period when a shop or dealer sells things at reduced prices. In other words, it is a crazy time for us, when people go consumption-mad! I have already booked leave so I won't be serving them. Good luck!'

'Hmm. I want to experience that,' I said. If you only knew which planet I came from, I thought privately.

I worked hard on the shop-display competition, and came up with a Korean theme. I wrote simple Korean letters and sentences like *ŏso oseyo*, which means 'welcome' in Korean, and hung them at strategic points around the entrance.

I overheard Korean customers speaking to each other in happy surprise. 'Oh, that's our language! Who wrote this? How nice!'

That month we saw an increase of Asian customers in our store. My manager loved the display and I won the competition.

But not all of my experiences in the job were as pleasant.

'I want to return this curtain.'

The Korean-themed merchandising display that won Asian customers' hearts

'Good afternoon, madam. Yes, let me have a look at the curtain and receipt please. Could you please tell me the reason why you are returning it? It will help us to improve our product for you.'

'I realised that I just don't like it.'

As I opened the packaging a strong smell of fabric conditioner hit my nose. It appeared that she had washed the curtain without following the care instructions and it had shrunk.

'Madam, I am afraid I cannot take back this product. It's not resalable.'

'Who you think you are? You, *negra* [nigger], who came to my country in a boat from Africa to steal our jobs, dare to refuse me a refund? Go back to Africa!'

Her words hurt deeply.

Do not fall into this trap. Do not cry. Do not show her you are hurt, I repeated to myself again and again. It was not the word *negra* itself that upset me. It was the intention behind the word that was offensive.

'I want to speak to your manager right now!' she said, raising her voice.

'Of course, madam. I will call him,' I said, trying to keep my voice normal and feeling a lump in my throat.

Our department manager had witnessed the scene from the balcony above the shop floor.

'Are you OK? Take your break now and try to calm down. I will deal with her. It's unbelievable that racist people like this woman still exist.'

He did not accept the return and the woman left the store fuming.

At that time, in the late 1990s and early 2000s, there was quite a lot of unrest and negative sentiment against immigrants among many Spaniards. Back then, Spanish society was less multicultural than other countries in Europe such as the UK or France, where there was a longer history of immigration and more acceptance of different cultures.

I observed racism at several different levels. There were those who would bluntly vent their feelings about immigrants, like that woman who told me to go back to Africa, and there were those who would veneer their racism with elegant and apparently educated phrases. These people, with their internalised superiority, would never treat you as an equal. There existed an invisible line separating 'them' and 'us', where they occupied a superior intellectual position and would feel a duty to preach from on high. Blunt racism was more common in people with lower-class backgrounds (although some middle-class people also demonstrated it) while the middle and upper classes were more likely to deploy the disguised or undercover racism.

I also came across what I call the *confundidos*, the confused. My sister had moved to Madrid after working as a gynaecologist in Equatorial Guinea, and when my second niece, Cristina, was born in 2000, I went to the hospital to meet her. When I got there, I asked the nurse: 'Where is the maternity ward, please? I am looking for my sister who has just given birth.'

'Give me her name, I will find her in the register.'

'Maribel Macias.'

'Oh, yeah, the lady who had a baby of colour. She is in—'

'What "colour"?'

'I mean…' She was unable to continue.

'Do you feel offended if I call you white?'

'No,' she said, an uncomfortable smile on her face.

'So why are you calling us "of colour"? Clearly, I am brown. And I am sure my niece will be brown, since her father is black, and my sister is white. You don't offend us by calling us black or brown because that is what we are. Now, if you have a patronising intention behind the word "black" or use it with a disparaging tone, *that* is offensive. To be honest, we are all a different colour, aren't we? You are white, I'm brown, some are black, and some are yellow. There is nothing wrong with it as long as we respect each other and have good intentions.'

'I agree! Your lovely brown niece and white sister are in room four on the fifth floor.' I smiled and continued on my way.

These experiences showed me that structural racism is very much alive, concealed behind euphemism and the culture of 'niceness'. I do not mean being nice is a bad thing. On the contrary, we should be nice and respectful towards each other. However, 'niceness' should not conceal discrimination. Due to the ideology of colour blindness, the usage of euphemism and the culture of niceness, the majority of white people avoid acknowledging race or describing a racist situation accurately. While I can name their colour, white, they cannot name my colour, brown, without immediately adding 'I don't want to offend you'. Blackness is not a shameful thing or a taboo that should not be named.

The powerful can ban the word 'nigger' and say 'N-word', they could even ban the word 'black' and say 'B-word'. Meanwhile, structural racism brilliantly persists, hidden behind this euphemistic language. The lives of brown, black and yellow people are still strongly and deeply affected by structural racism that white people don't experience thanks to their skin tone.

Who benefits when we do not acknowledge racism or play the game of euphemism? Who benefits when we avoid uncomfortable and inconvenient dialogue? The avoidance and inaccurate depiction of our problems perpetuate and benefit the status quo of structural racism and, broadly, all our societal illness.

Despite the racial incidents, I enjoyed my time at Leroy Merlin. Although customer service was sometimes tough, it was also rewarding when people recognised and appreciated your service. I particularly remember one older lady, originally from Galicia in northwest Spain, who would often ask for me specifically, and called me *amor* ('love') or *cielo* ('heaven'). In Northeast Asia, such terms of endearment are strictly reserved for close family members, so it was a pleasant surprise to hear them from a relative stranger. Working as a customer service assistant gave me a wealth of insights into the people and culture of this part of the world that I was still striving to understand.

With my colleague on the shop floor at Leroy Merlin

Ruthless

Through this time, I kept hearing hostile comments about my father. One morning, I woke at five a.m., although it was my day off, to make the lengthy journey to the Civil Registry Office in the centre of Madrid. I had decided to apply for Spanish nationality, and I hoped that my application process would be smooth and quick. But when I arrived there was already a long queue of immigrants, mostly from Spain's former colonies in Latin America and Equatorial Guinea.

'Is this the queue for Spanish nationality?' I asked.

'Yes. A very long one!' said a lady with a strong Mexican accent.

'Thanks. So, you are also applying for nationality, I see.'

'Well, yes. There used to be a scheme that allowed people of Spanish descent to claim nationality. Apparently, it was a fast way of getting it. But now I have to do it through the regular scheme. What about you? Where are you from?' We chatted for a while about Equatorial Guinea, a Spanish colony she had never heard of, and our experiences of living in Spain as immigrants.

At last it was my turn and I was ushered into the registry office, where three women and a man were waiting.

'Have a seat,' said the man. 'Can I have your passport, please? Oh, Equatorial Guinea!' He opened the first page which bore my photo. 'A beautiful, small country. But Macias destroyed it and killed thousands of people, and he kicked us out. A ruthless dictator.'

As the man continued his tirade, his co-worker noticed my eyes welling with tears. She looked carefully at my passport and took note of my surname.

'Shut up, shut up,' she whispered urgently, but her colleague seemed not to realise what was going on. He continued to rant as he filled in the paperwork. As soon as he had finished, I snatched up my passport and ran out.

At around this time, I went to a bar near my home in Alcalá de Henares with Martina. I had met Martina shortly after arriving in Madrid when I worked for her as a domestic cleaner. Now she was trying to start a new business exporting luxury bedding and was carrying out market research. I offered to find her possible customers in Malabo so she could expand her business into Equatorial Guinea. Malabo was going through a petrodollar boom and it seemed that everyone there was looking for luxury goods. Over cups of tea we were discussing prospective customers when, out of nowhere, she said, 'Your father eliminated all of the intellectuals. And he had a Swiss bank account full of public money.' She made the claim as if she were in Guinea, witnessing it for herself.

I was calm but perplexed.

'Oh? Who told you that?'

'Well, I have a friend whose father studied at university in Equatorial Guinea.'

'University in Guinea in the Macias era? Just after decolonisation? No way! I've never heard of it.' It was said that the Spanish colonisers had not founded any universities in Guinea because they didn't want the natives to be educated. 'Can you give me the name of that university? I'll ask Guineans who were there at the time.'

I knew her claim was absurd, but I needed to be sure.

'I will ask my friend and tell you.'

'And the claim that Macias had an account in Switzerland, what proof do you have for it?'

'Well, I can't prove it, but all African dictators have them. Obiang has them.'

'So, your reasoning is that if everyone else has them my father must have had one too. If that were true, would I have had to work as your cleaner?'

'Maybe he didn't tell your mother?'

I looked at her in shock, trying to understand how people can be so easily manipulated into believing what they hear without question.

After some years in Spain, these and countless other encounters with strangers who had an opinion on my father's actions and legacy gave me the push to dig more deeply for the truth. I began looking for people, both Guinean and Spanish, who had experienced life under Macias to interview. Since leaving North Korea, I have interviewed more than 3,000 people. But, due to the sensitive nature of the political situation in Equatorial Guinea, only Don Antonio Garcia-Trevijano, Dr Pipa and Daniel Mba Oyono consented to the use of their names in public. Wanting to avoid political bias, I made sure to interview a range of people whose views spanned the political spectrum. All my witnesses were between the ages of forty and seventy, and experienced the Macias era either directly or indirectly through the testimony of their parents.

I also went into the archives to seek out official documents. There was a big gap in the Guinean-Spanish scholarship and history of that era of decolonisation. The more I dug, the more inconsistencies I found. My thorough research into Macias began to draw an utterly different picture of him, and of historical events of the aftermath of decolonisation, when he was president of Equatorial Guinea. It was a shock to see how far the official account differed from that picture that was emerging from personal testimonies and the archives.

My father with Manuel Fraga, Spain's former Minister of Information and Tourism and founder of the Partido Popular, *late 1960s*

The Daughter of Evil?

'Hey, I have a friend who belongs to the *Movimiento de Ciudadanos hacia la República Constitucional* [Movement of Citizens Towards a Constitutional Republic – MCRC], founded by Don Antonio Garcia-Trevijano. He probably has Don Antonio's private phone number,' said my friend Benito Arranz, whom I had met while working at Leroy Merlin and who was aware of my research into my father. The whole time I had been working, I had also been conducting research and interviews into what had happened in Equatorial Guinea. Benito was a retired economist who ran his own business from an office in the centre of Madrid.

'Really? Please do ask your friend,' I said with enthusiasm. Benito made the call and then wrote a number down on a sticky note that he placed in front of me. 'Call him,' he said.

I could not believe I finally had Don Antonio's number. The one my mother had given me in Malabo was no longer in operation. I had been struggling all year to locate him, while also trying to summon the courage to make contact. It was about a decade since my mother first told me about him.

After so many half-truths and rumours from strangers, I was ready to hear from someone who knew my father, whatever that truth might be. Was he a liberator from our colonisers, the mass murderer depicted by the Spanish media, or both? I was overcome by emotion; my heart was hammering and my hands were shaking. Benito saw all of this.

'Do you want me to ring him for you?'

'Yes. Please.'

He picked up the phone. 'Hello? My name is Benito Arranz and I am calling on behalf of Monica Macias who—'

I could clearly hear a voice at the other end of the line. 'Monica Macias? The younger daughter of Francisco Macias?'

'Yes, sir.'

'Is she with you now? Pass her the phone,' the voice instructed.

Benito looked at me inquiringly and I nodded my head.

'Hello?' I tried to keep my voice steady.

'How are you?'

'I am very well, thank you, sir. I would like to meet you.'

'Of course, of course! Any time you want. My door is always open to you.'

'Thank you very much, sir.' Tears dampened my face as I hung up.

Although my mother had told me a little about Don Antonio, I had also done my own research into him. He was a republican, a political realist and one of the most prestigious and best-known lawyers of his era, a political activist who fought against the regime of Generalissimo Franco, the dictator who ruled Spain from 1939 to 1975. Don Antonio faced repression for his work on behalf of political freedom during Franco's lifetime. He had advised my father's circle to push for a truly independent Equatorial Guinea, in contrast to the nominal independence backed by Spanish colonisers keen to protect their economic interests in the country. For that reason, the Spanish government took him to the Court of Public Order (Marshal of Ghent), accusing him of high treason. He became the subject of a defamation campaign organised by Madrid and the mainstream media.

Don Antonio drafted a constitution for the new country, but the Spanish government enforced its own, a copy-and-paste of the French constitution. He opposed this constitution on the grounds that it meant imposing a European paradigm on a tribal state, and was thus a form of neo-colonialism, arguing that a Guinean constitution should reflect Guinea's socio-political make-up rather than serving Spanish interests. The Spanish government dismissed this argument and tried to discredit him morally by claiming, falsely, that he was motivated by his own economic interests in Guinea. More than five decades after independence, the current situation in the country suggests that Don Antonio may have been right.

Don Antonio had five passports cancelled, was arrested three times and fined twice. In the late 1970s, he was the victim of a serious attack by unknown assailants for his statements to the BBC when Franco was dying, and was prosecuted by the Court of Public Order (Gómez Chaparro) for an offence against the State and imprisoned for four months by order of Manuel Fraga Iribarne, the founder of the *Partido Popular* (People's Party – PP). He never stopped fighting. Even as an elderly man he continued his struggle for political collective freedom in Spain, a country he described as an oligarchy.

After my phone conversation with Don Antonio, I took up his invitation and finally visited him.

'You are the living image of your father!' he said in his strong, steady voice, which was unusual for a person of his eighty-six years. He was waiting for me, leaning on a walking stick, at the entrance to his mansion. I later learned that his limp was the result of the injuries he sustained during Franco's era.

He led me to a reception room decorated with antiques and paintings from past centuries. The mansion and adornments

With Don Antonio at his home in Somosaguas

reflected the wealth he had acquired from his work as a lawyer in Europe and America.

'I am guessing you want to know about your father.'

'Yes. Please tell me, was he… like they say?'

He laughed. 'That question is not an easy one to ask. It takes a lot of courage to find out the truth. Not many young people are able to do that.'

'Thank you, but was he a killer?' I asked more boldly.

'Don't be impatient. The path to finding the truth about your father is a long one. I'll begin with the conclusion, and we will then go through each accusation against him in turn and examine the falsehoods and rumours that have grown up around him. I will also give you original documents as proof of what I am talking about.

'Your father was not a killer. I read the International Court of Justice [ICJ] report about his trial, prepared by Alejandro Artucio, and I can assure you that I never read such a sloppy report in my entire career as a lawyer and jurist. We can look at that report once you understand the background.

'There is a thing in the legal world called the presumption of innocence. It is the legal principle that one is considered innocent until proven guilty. The prosecution must prove that the accused is guilty beyond reasonable doubt and, if reasonable doubt remains, the accused must be acquitted. This is a legal right and an international human right under the UN's Universal Declaration of Human Rights, Article 11. In the case of your father, the accusations were not proven. Everything was based on opinion, and opinion is not what matters, but proof. Are you following me so far?'

From the way he spoke, I recognised him as an experienced and rigorous academic.

'Yes, I follow.'

'If you want to understand what happened in Equatorial Guinea and to your father, I would strongly suggest you study a Master's in a subject such as international law, the history of the UN or African politics, where you can explore colonialism and post-colonialism. I will also give you some books that will help you. And one more piece of advice from this old man: if you want to make a serious analysis of these events, you must put aside your emotions and feelings. Can you do that?'

'I can.'

'I thought so, but wanted to emphasise it. What happened in the Macias era is a consequence of events. So, lest the same events happen again, we must know the cause. There are two main factors to bear in mind: first, the process by which Equatorial Guinea achieved independence; and second, tendencies in African politics during and after decolonisation.'

I hung on his every word, hypnotised by his intellect and professorial manner.

'Regarding Guinea's path to independence, you need to understand the power dynamics before, during and after decolonisation. You also need to know the real problem posed by the decolonisation of Guinea, both in the international context of Afro-Asiatic countries and Spanish colonialism. Only within this context, and from a political-economic perspective, can the drama that Guinea suffered, which it *continues* to suffer, be fully understood.'

Don Antonio took from his shelves a book he had published – entitled *The Whole Truth: My Intervention in Guinea* (*Toda la verdad: mi intervención en Guinea*) – and referred to certain pages as he spoke.

He listed the names of several key figures on both the Spanish and Guinean sides, as well as some non-political figures who blackened the name of the new republic in order to disguise their commercial ambitions.

'Do you mind if I take notes?'

'Of course not. Go on. To understand the second factor, you need to study African politics.'

'Yes, I will,' I answered determinedly.

'May I come in?' It was his South American housekeeper. 'Lunch is ready, sir.'

'Thank you, Claudia,' he said, before turning to me. 'You are going to stay and have lunch with us.'

I had completely lost track of time.

He led me to the dining room, where a long table was already set for two. We sat down, Don Antonio at the head of the table and I next to him.

'That is enough for today. We will have these sessions twice a week and by the end you will have a clearer picture, not only of who your father was but also of Guinean-Spanish relations. But, for now, I want you to know that your father wasn't a killer. I knew him very well.

'Your father was in "the group of twenty-four", which fought for Guinean independence. I paid for them to go to Madrid and stay at a hotel. Your father was the only one who refused the money. He said he had saved money for the trip and would pay his own expenses, while some of the others abused my generosity by bringing prostitutes to their rooms, ordering expensive drinks and making long international calls. As you can imagine, the bill was very high. Your father was different. He was serious and had moral integrity.'

'Is that why you decided to advise him?'

'Yes, in part. But not only because of him. I wanted to help an African state achieve independence and political freedom. I saw in him the charisma of a leader. However, I stopped advising him in legal and political matters when he asked me to draft a law that would allow him to be president for life. I told him that this was precisely what I was fighting against in Spain with Franco and that it would be hypocritical. He told me that in the African context it was the best way to govern the country. I told him he was wrong and I stopped giving him advice. He later asked a Cuban lawyer to draft the law under which he became president for life.

'Although we disagreed on that matter, he managed to get me out of prison when Manuel Fraga, the founder of the *Partido Popular*, sent me away because of my political activism against Franco. Your father persuaded other African presidents and the African Union, the Organisation of African Unity [OAU] back then, to put pressure on the Spanish government, saying if I was not freed within twenty-four hours, they would break diplomatic ties with Spain. I was freed.'

I breathed a sigh of relief. My father was not a killer but a person with moral integrity, though I was disappointed he had not followed Don Antonio's political advice.

'Now, tell me about you. So, you grew up in North Korea? What did you study?'

I began to tell my story.

Are We from the Same World?

As time went on, I became more and more a citizen of Madrid. I was able to give directions to foreign tourists when walking the streets. I met Don Antonio regularly for our sessions and to visit archives. After work, I would sit in the Plaza de Cataluña in Torrejón de Ardoz feeding the pigeons, and on weekends, I'd roam the nooks and crannies of the city centre with no particular aim. I had been thinking only of work and earning a living from the moment I left Pyongyang and now, for the first time, I had some time for myself.

On one of these aimless days, I was passing a pavement cafe, Damasco, in the centre of Madrid when I happened to see a sign that read: 'Belly dancer wanted'. My curiosity aroused, I strode boldly inside.

'It says you're looking for a dancer,' I said to the waiter who came to take my order. Soon after, the friendly looking owner came up to me.

'Are you a professional dancer?'

'No.'

'We need a professional dancer who can dance for about an hour in the evening at weekends.'

In that moment I was overcome with memories of dancing on the eighteenth floor of the Ch'anggwangsan Hotel as a student. From the second my Syrian friend Al Waleed showed me a videotape of belly dancing, the 'dancer's instinct' that had been sleeping within me awoke. When I danced, all my worries would disappear, and I felt an indescribable joy.

'I was asking because I just want to dance, it's not for the money.'

At that, the cafe owner smiled and put on some music. A cheerful Middle Eastern rhythm started to play, and the man started to dance. He held his hand out and beckoned me to join him. The next moment we had mounted a small stage and were dancing.

Something Sŏn Hwa had said long ago came back to me: 'Monica, it's like you were born with a sense of rhythm. I think you have some Spanish Gypsy blood in you.' I danced like mad. It was the same as on the Ch'anggwangsan Hotel dance floor. As long as I kept dancing, I could forget all of my problems.

I danced ecstatically until the second song finished, and the waiter and some customers clapped their hands, shouting 'Bravo!' I felt a different kind of joy from the sense of achievement I had from working at Leroy Merlin. And I was amazed that people could live this cheerfully.

'Monica, why don't you start this week?'

I gladly shook on the deal with my new boss.

It felt like fortune was smiling on me after having turned its back on me for so long. From then on, I was a workaholic from Monday to Friday, and on Saturdays I would race to Damasco to dance the stress away. Around that time, I became close to a young woman my age named Amelie. Until then, there had been nobody I could call a friend in Madrid, though I had many acquaintances. Becoming friends with someone means getting to know each other well, and for a long time I didn't feel up to it. I had always tried to keep a certain distance from others to avoid them knowing about my past or my family.

Amelie was a bank teller near my workplace. On payday when I'd go to the bank, I often happened to end up standing at her counter. After a few encounters we naturally became friendlier and eventually started going for tea at a cafe after work, or having breakfast together.

Having dinner with my friend Amelie at her home in Madrid

One day, Amelie and I were at an outdoor cafe in front of the bank having coffee, when someone waved at us and called out a cheerful '*Hola!*'

'Fernando! Get over here!' Amclie beamed at him.

He strode towards us and flopped down in the chair next to mine. In that instant, my heart began pounding.

Amelie introduced us. I was very attracted to his well-built physique, his light brown hair and his smiling face. I glanced briefly at his eyes. I'd never seen eyes that colour before; they were mysterious, resembling the emerald green of the Mediterranean. Every time the sun moved, the colour of his eyes changed with the shifting light and shade. My senses were working overtime to capture his every peculiarity in one look.

After that, I went to that cafe terrace in front of the bank every day without fail, and the three of us became teatime buddies. Before I knew it, the whole day long, I looked forward only to having tea with Fernando in the afternoon. As time went on, we would go for lunch or he would come to watch me dance at Damasco at the weekends.

One day Fernando carefully asked me, 'Monica, your last name is Macias… Would I be right in saying…?'

He had connected my birthplace and surname. This is it, I thought. I looked him in the eyes and replied, 'It's true.' Fernando and Amelie were shocked, and in no small way. Now they too had come to know that I was the daughter of Equatorial Guinea's former president, with his reputation preceding me. I looked from Fernando to Amelie and back, and then averted my gaze. It was a critical moment. If these friends disliked my identity and rejected it, then this was the end of our relationship. In my heart I prepared myself. Then Fernando put his hand lightly on mine and said, 'Monica, how hard has it been for you all this time?'

Amelie, too, slowly stroked my shoulder. I gained such courage from their warm-hearted reaction that I blurted out the rest of my life story. I told them about my fifteen years in Pyongyang. When I had finished, the two of them gazed at my face, expressionless. I felt catharsis. We stayed up late, drinking wine, laughing and talking.

But after that, our meetings became noticeably fewer. And then it happened that I was more often sitting by myself at our regular cafe.

So, it was a mistake to tell them, after all. I was filled with regret for having shared so much about myself. I had not committed any sin, but my fate weighed more upon me than any sin ever could. And people were uncomfortable with and alienated by this weight.

For a short while, my life had felt refreshingly light, flying above the clouds, but suddenly I had fallen back to earth. Dancing at Damasco was no longer a joyful release but had become a gesture of lamentation. I felt I needed to give it up.

One Saturday, I was dancing on the stage, sensing that it was my last time. Near the end of my performance, I spotted Fernando in the audience. He was sitting perfectly still, like a stone statue, staring at me. After hurriedly finishing my routine, I got changed and went to his table. He poured me a drink and said abruptly, 'I have two daughters.'

Fernando had not said a word about his own life story before, but now he began to share. He had been married, and after his divorce he saw his daughters twice a month. He said that after failing at marriage once, he couldn't conceive of the idea of loving again, and had no intention of ever remarrying. And, looking at me, he said, 'Can I still love you anyway?'

I was confused but happy. And then out of my mouth came these words: 'Fernando, are we from the same world?'

He laughed.

'Until now our worlds might have been different, and in the future they might be again, but at this moment, right now, aren't we living in the same world?'

That was how our love began. That evening he invited me to his house for the first time. Books were scattered on his living room and dining table. They were mostly related to the history of Equatorial Guinea, Southeast Asia and Korea.

'I've been doing some studying. Because I wanted to know you,' Fernando said, laughing.

From that day on, we spent almost all our time together. I had thought that I had more or less adjusted to life in Spain, but with Fernando it was like starting over again from the beginning. He taught me everything anew, down to the smallest detail: European restaurant etiquette, the art of conversation, the Spanish sense of humour, and so much more.

He was my lover and my teacher in all areas of life. Then one day, I raised a subject that I had needed to ask him about but had been putting off for a long time: my father, President Macias, and President Kim Il Sung.

'What do you think of those two men, Fernando?'

He spoke calmly and cautiously, like someone who had long been preparing an answer.

'Monica, as you know, all I have is an indirect impression informed by the records known to the world. When I was young, I tended to believe everything that was in the newspapers or on television without question. But not any more. The world has two faces, one of truth and one of lies. That's especially the case in the world of politics, where lies often pretend to be the truth.

To be honest, I've decided not to judge hastily anything that I haven't experienced directly. Because most of what is recorded in history was not written from the perspective of the losers, but from that of the victors.

'It's the same with your father and Kim Il Sung. If your father had prioritised the interests of the Spanish government above those of the people of Equatorial Guinea, maybe things wouldn't have turned out so tragically for him. If America weren't a superpower, maybe the world's judgement of North Korea would be very different. Monica, I worry about you because you have no choice but to live in the world of truth and lies and bear its weight on your own shoulders. That's something that nobody can help you with. All a person can do is lend you their shoulder when you get exhausted.'

As I listened to his words, I was giving thanks to that 'invisible power' that had made it possible for me to meet Fernando. He was a deep thinker who took time to reflect and didn't act in haste. But more than that, he was a person I could trust.

'Monica, if you want to be the owner of your life, you have to shake off these biases that the world has made. If you want to pick out only the facts in this dizzying world of truths mixed with lies, you have to seek them out and confront them for yourself.'

Thanks to him, I was at last able to make peace with the confused and traumatised girl from Pyongyang I had been. I began to mature, and to become a woman who knew how to take ownership of her life.

For the rest of the time that I lived in Madrid, I loved Fernando truly. But neither of us thought of marriage. The pain he had experienced from his divorce was too great, and I was still a traveller with a long journey ahead of me. We were simply lovers and friends, and comrades who came running whenever and wherever the other called. Once I sang a song from Pyongyang that expressed my feelings for him.

'Fernando,' I explained, 'this is a song that young men and women in North Korea sing when they confess their love.'

A flower that blooms secretly on the edge of an unknown field,
Do you know this nameless flower?
Atop a rocky path, radiating its fragrance
Please know, this is my heart.

When the song had finished, Fernando looked tenderly at me for a while and then asked, 'Monica, do you miss Pyongyang that much?'

Visiting Pyongyang After Ten Years

In early 2004, I sent an email to a man named Agapito, who I had come across on the internet. Agapito, who lived in Barcelona, ran an organisation called the Korean Friendship Association and had a relationship with the North Korean government. I asked him to help me to get a visa to visit, though I stressed I was not interested in joining a group tour. A week later came the reply: there would be no problem securing me a visa.

Excitedly I asked my company for time off and began preparing for my visit to Pyongyang with a nervous heart. Fernando kissed me on the forehead and blessed my trip. Ten years earlier, when I first arrived in Spain, I had tossed and turned every night, missing Pyongyang. All the time I worked and studied, getting gradually used to living in this new country, the homesickness was hidden deep inside. As I boarded the plane to Beijing on the first leg of the journey, the accumulated longing burst forth at once.

After disembarking at Beijing airport, I arrived at the appointed time in the hotel lobby where we were to meet, only to discover that, against my wishes, I would have to join a group tour. I had thought I would be able to get a visa and move around by myself, but Agapito had already advertised the tour with the headline that I, the daughter of the former president of Equatorial Guinea, would be taking part. He did this despite my request that he not reveal my identity. I felt betrayed.

Sightseeing at the Forbidden City in Beijing

The group included an American, and other people of various nationalities and occupations, among them a couple of journalists. From the start of the tour, the journalists kept badgering me for an interview. They asked: 'What was it like growing up in Pyongyang?', 'How do you feel coming back?' and so on.

I firmly rejected their requests. 'Please just leave me alone.'

In front of the Temple of Heaven, Beijing, with my friends Sel Da Ming and Guo Xu Gun

The plane left Beijing airport and within an hour it was flying over Pyongyang. The instant I saw the cityscape through the aeroplane window, tears started streaming down my cheeks. When I had first arrived at Sunan airport, it was crowded with people waving flowers to welcome our happy family. Now I was coming back as an adult, alone, with tears in my eyes.

Malcolm, an American sitting next to me, kept looking at me with concern etched on his face. Avoiding his gaze, I kept my eyes fixed on the view out of the window. Not a single person in that group could possibly understand what I was feeling.

Sunan airport had not changed a bit. The portrait of Kim Il Sung still hung on the second floor of the airport terminal. Our group of fourteen disembarked the plane and, while we were taking a commemorative photo, I had to keep wiping tears from my eyes with a handkerchief.

A group of English and French interpreters descended upon us. Since I knew the North Korean system well, I was not surprised, but the other members in the group were taken aback by the way so many strangers suddenly attached themselves to us. When I went through immigration, the officer in military uniform inspecting my passport lifted her head and said, 'Monica Macias? You're Fran's little sister?'

'Yes, that's right.'

'Wow, Comrade Monica, nice to see you. I was in the same class as Fran.'

I was so happy to hear that. It had been so long since I had been addressed as 'comrade' that I could not help feeling a surge of affection.

Outside the airport we got on a bus, and all the way to the Chongryŏn Hotel I sat at the very back and gazed out of the window at the landscape. The blue sky, the fresh breeze, the green stalks of rice growing lushly in the paddies… I was starting to tear up again when a North Korean interpreter of French came and sat down next to me.

'I heard that you lived in Pyongyang. What's it like to come back after ten years?' she asked.

I didn't know how to answer so I hesitated a moment. The

bus had left the city of Sunan and was entering Pyongyang. The interpreter asked another question: 'Hasn't it developed a lot?'

'Yes, it's true. As they say, in ten years even rivers and mountains change.'

But that was a lie. The cityscape of Pyongyang that I saw as we drove by had not changed much at all. The buildings looked a little older, but the streets were still as clean now as they had been then, and people's clothing was not much different from a decade ago. My way of life and thinking had altered radically, but Pyongyang was the same as the day I had left it.

The bus traversed the centre of Pyongyang and came into Mangyŏngdae district, finally arriving at Chongryŏn Hotel. Agapito quickly gathered the group together and began to give us some precautionary details.

'When you leave the hotel, you must leave with an interpreter. After seven p.m., please refrain from going outside. When you take pictures, don't take any with a statue or portrait of President Kim Il Sung in the background.' That was almost true. You could take a picture with Kim Il Sung in the background as long as you did not cut across him or include only part of him in the image. It was cultural; purely a matter of showing respect to authority.

While Agapito was speaking, I glanced around the hotel to see if I could see any familiar faces. But the people at the hotel shop, bar and restaurant were all new to me. Feeling lonely, I looked at the tour schedule. We would begin with the Kim Il Sung statue, and go to the Sinchŏn province to the Sinchŏn Museum of American War Atrocities. There was nothing new for me there, and the itinerary bored me. I went to the representative from the foreign ministry.

'My name is Monica Macias. When I was younger, I lived here for many years, attended the Mangyŏngdae Revolutionary Boarding School, and graduated from the Pyongyang University of Light Industry. Because this is like a hometown visit, the group tour's itinerary isn't very suitable for me. I'd like to request to go alone to the Haebangsan Hotel where I used to live, or my old school.'

The representative smiled and said, 'I'll talk to my superiors.'

I wanted to bump into an old friend, even just one. To have a chance of that, I would have to visit the hotel where I once lodged, the school I went to, and my old haunt of Changgwang Street.

I sat alone in my hotel room and pondered. What had become of Sŏn Hwa? I hoped she was happily married, and her child was well. I wondered if Yun Mi still lived in Pyongyang. Would my old teachers still be at the school? I was a rare black student, so surely they would remember me.

I suddenly realised it was dinner time. At the restaurant a big banquet had been laid on for our delegation. Sticky rice, *kimchi*, chicken and cucumber salad, seasoned octopus… I choked up at the sight of Pyongyang food after so many years.

A little later, one of the waitresses picked up a microphone and began singing. The tourists from America and Europe gawped at this novelty, while with every bar of music I recalled the school lawn, the forsythias that adorned the Chŏnsŏk restaurant and the charming footpaths that clung to the skirts of the Taedong river. As the song came to an end, a waitress approached me and without warning handed me the microphone.

'Would you please sing us a song, as you're back for the first time in a long while?'

'Oh, it's been so long, I'm not sure if I—'

'Hey, don't be like that. Just sing. I'll sing with you.'

I was dragged out by the comrade waitresses and had no choice but to begin singing in Korean:

Pleased to meet you, nice to see you
Fellow Korean brothers and sisters
It's wonderful to meet you here today.
Embracing each other we smile,
Hugging each other we are happy.

At first, I was embarrassed and I stumbled over the lyrics that had gone unsung for so long, but in spite of myself the song kept coming out. The tourists, kitchen staff and waitresses who had been serving all stood dumbstruck, staring at me. When the song was finished, the journalist and reporters from Spain and the UK crowded around.

'You really speak Korean very well! Studying an Asian language is difficult for a foreigner. Oh, sorry, I'm from ABC News, in the USA.'

'Nice to meet you. I came here from Spain, but I grew up in Pyongyang.'

'What an unusual situation. Then you know Pyongyang well?'

'Yes!'

The other foreigners at the same table listened to our conversation keenly. I became their interviewee, a subject for interrogation. I understood their curiosity, but I was really tired of it. My visit to Pyongyang had a different meaning to theirs. They were visiting a strange, new land, while I was visiting my hometown.

After dinner, I went looking for familiar faces. I met some *ŏnni*, older 'sisters', who used to work at Haebangsan Hotel and had been transferred to Chongryŏn Hotel.

'Wow, you look prettier, but your body shape is still the same,' said one of them, catching hold of my hands in hers. It was Cho *ŏnni*. She was one of the wait staff back when we lived at the Haebangsan Hotel.

'How are you, *ŏnni*?' I asked warmly. 'You also look beautiful.'

'I am old now. What about Maribel and Fran, are they OK? Have all of you got married?'

'Fran and Maribel are married and have children. I am still single.'

'I can't understand that. You are very beautiful. Are your eyes gazing too high?* How old are you now?'

'This year I will be thirty-four in Korean age.'

'See! If you keep going along those lines, you won't get married and you'll end up alone. There is nothing sadder than being alone. Think carefully – seduce a rich man and live well. If it doesn't work, get pregnant, then you will see how he will come to you. Understand?'

Cho *ŏnni* was her usual confident, outspoken self. Wrong or right, I did not want to argue; I just smiled and enjoyed the moment.

'Oh! Do you remember the former director of the Haebangsan Hotel, Director Kim? She has been transferred here. Shall we go to see her?'

'Yes! Where's her office? Let's go together.'

Cho *ŏnni* took me to the office. She knocked on the door. A

---

* A Korean expression which suggests excessive pickiness when selecting a partner.

familiar voice from the office said, 'Come in.' I bowed when I saw Director Kim. She recognised me immediately, stood up and walked towards me with open arms. I remembered her as a dependable, warm person, who did not waste words unnecessarily. She hugged me fondly.

'Gracious me! Ten years and you haven't changed at all. Married?'

'No, she is still single and is thirty-four this year.' Cho *ŏnni* answered for me.

'What are you waiting for? Get married quickly. Time flies!'

I'm definitely back in Korea, I thought. Every *ŏnni* I met would ask if I had married and had children, usually followed by 'you should lose some weight' or 'you look beautiful', and so on. Unlike in much of Europe, in Korea women start to come under intense social pressure to marry and have children when they are only twenty-four or twenty-five. In some cases, mothers-in-law have even pressured their daughters-in-law to produce a baby boy followed by a baby girl, despite massive educational campaigns against this patriarchal mindset via movies in the 1980s.

Director Kim and I spent about half an hour catching up.

'Remind me when are you leaving?' she asked.

'Next Monday.'

'Why so soon? Anyway, eat anything you like while here. I will ask them to make your favourite foods: *songp'yŏn* (Korean rice cakes with red bean), grilled red bean buns, steamed red bean buns. And you don't need to worry about the bill.'

'Thank you! I can eat all the other Korean dishes now as well – except *kimchi*! The chefs don't have to suffer because of me any more.'

With Cho ŏnni (left) and Director Kim (right)

On the second day, the representative from the Ministry of Foreign Affairs got back to me. 'On Wednesday, Thursday and Saturday only, you may undertake personal travel. Ten years is not a short time; almost all the people you knew back then probably won't be here now. But I hope you won't feel too lonely.'

Just as he warned, the teachers and cooks I found at the boarding school were all unfamiliar faces. Only the buildings were the same. I sat down in the school campus and called to mind all the old friends I used to play with, one by one.

From across the campus, I heard the sound of children singing. It was lunchtime and they were marching to the cafeteria in orderly lines. I watched them for a while and recalled the faces of Sŏn Hwa and my other friends.

The next day I went to my old university and met a few of my former teachers as well as Ri Kyŏng *Ŭn*, a former classmate who had become a teacher in the faculty. Kyŏng *Ŭn* had been the first to have an operation to create a crease in the upper eyelid – so-called 'double eyelid' surgery – which became a huge trend in Pyongyang and across the Korean peninsula in the 1980s. After Kyŏng *Ŭn*, everyone in our class had had the surgery. Her eyelids were still doubled. We hugged each other for a while.

'I thought I would never see you again.'

'See, I came back. I was missing you all.'

We spent more than an hour chatting. According to Kyŏng *Ŭn*, Sŏn Hwa had given birth to a beautiful baby girl, married her boyfriend and was living in Kaesŏng. Everybody was married, including Kyŏng *Ŭn* herself.

On the Friday, I went with the tour group to the truce village of Panmunjom, just north of the *de facto* border between the Koreas, a relic of thc Cold War. When I lived in Pyongyang, I visited Panmunjom three times but felt nothing. This time it was different. Seen from Panmunjom, the sky to the south made my heart weep. I was also reminded of conversations with friends at university.

'Girls, why do you think people say "southern boys, northern girls"?* Does it mean that South Korean guys are hot? I must meet a man from South Korea, fall in love and get married! Bring on Korean unification!' Those friends who used to chatter away like that were now somebody's wife or mum.

Next stop with the tour group was the Sariwŏn History Museum. That provoked a little discomfort. When we emerged from the museum after seeing the terrible photographs of

* A reference to an aphorism suggesting that the most handsome men are to be found in the south of the peninsula, while the most beautiful women are in the north.

slaughter committed by the American army during the Korean War, our guides stood in the middle of our group and asked the Americans: 'How did you feel seeing that?' The Americans did not know what to say and looked away. These Americans who had taken the trouble to visit Pyongyang had a more neutral and sober view of history than many of their countrymen. Maybe that is why I felt sorry for them.

The next day was Saturday, and finally I went to visit the Haebangsan Hotel, where I had lived, as well as Changgwangwŏn health complex and Rakwŏn department store, places I used to frequent. At the Haebangsan, I met many of my old *ŏnni* who still worked there, cleaning the guest rooms and in the kitchen. It was like reuniting with long-lost family members: we hugged and cried tears of gladness. When we parted once again, they gave me a package of the rice cakes they knew I loved. They waved me off with tears in their eyes.

Changgwangwŏn seemed much quieter than in my university days, when we international students hung out there almost every Saturday. Now there was nobody, just a sad silence that hung in the air. On the off-chance, I opened the door to the hairdresser and said, 'Hello. I'm here to have my hair done.' But there were no familiar faces among the hairdressers, who were rather startled to see me.

'Huh? You can speak our language? But how…?'

Then someone appeared from a far corner.

'Goodness, it's Monica, isn't it? How many years has it been?'

It was Mrs Kim, the one person who could handle my hair when I lived in Pyongyang.

'Mrs Kim, you haven't changed a bit!'

'Right. Are you married now?'

'Um, I will be soon!'

To commemorate our reunion, Mrs Kim did my hair as she had in the old days. To be honest, she gave me the exact same hairstyle I had had at university ten years earlier, and by now my tastes had moved on. But the instant I looked at that old-fashioned hairdo in the mirror, I was again on the verge of tears, remembering my time as a student. During ten years living in Spain and going through so many emotional ups and downs, I had become more mature. I was no longer that Monica who at college replicated Lim Su Kyung's hunger strike for Korean unification – though in my case, for the more trivial goal of losing weight.

With Mrs Kim the hairdresser, after my haircut

After saying goodbye to Mrs Kim, I went to the Rakwŏn department store, five minutes away, where once all the goods bore labels saying, 'Made in Japan'. Now everything was 'Made in China'. And then I headed to the Koryŏ Hotel, about half an hour further on. As I walked, a sorrowful nostalgia pervaded me. Ten years had gone by but Pyongyang was like a city suspended in time, a little more worn but still the same. The last place I visited was the Kimchi Bar.

I pushed open the door with a nervous heart. The Kimchi Bar of my memory was always bustling with foreign students. But on this day, there were just two or three customers quietly sipping tea. It had become a forlorn place. After a cursory bow to a server, I took a seat in my old spot at the table where we had carved our names with knives, the lines now faint. One by one, I traced our names with my finger: Ali, Fran, Herve, Montan… and then the words: 'Let's meet again'. There was no doubt that it was Azar who had carved the words. It might have been the day before Herve and Montan left Pyongyang for good. Ali always stood out, whatever he did. When he first learned Korean, I remembered, the teacher asked him one day to prepare a short sentence using the word 'gallantly'. He stayed up all night wrestling with the dictionary, and in the next morning's lesson swaggered up to the blackboard and wrote: 'I will gallantly take her virginity!'

Shocked, the teacher hurriedly erased the chalk, prompting the other international students to ask 'What? What did it say?' That was the kind of spontaneous, uninhibited person that Ali was. Despite living hemmed in by Pyongyang's restrictions, our schooldays were as exhilarating as anybody's because he was there. Now, more than ten years later, the old tables and chairs of the Kimchi Bar stood empty, as if tired of waiting. In my ear I could still clearly hear the noisy music and the awkward conversations of the tenderfoot youths. Suddenly a waitress appeared.

'What would you like to drink?'

'Um, could I have a glass of blueberry liquor?'

As I spoke, her face lit up with the usual surprised expression at my fluent Korean. Actually, I had never enjoyed blueberry liquor. Fran, Herve and Azar drank the stuff like it was water. I hated it. But it had suddenly come to mind. I poured the liquor into a glass and drank it in one go. Inside me, it felt like a fire had started.

That night I wanted to shake off my depressed mood, so I went to the Taedonggang Diplomatic Club and sang karaoke with the rest of the tour group.

'I never imagined that I'd be drinking alcohol with Americans in Pyongyang. It's so weird,' I said in English.

One of the Americans – Peter, a medical doctor – said, 'Actually, North Koreans are just as ignorant of America as Americans are of North Korea. How well do you know America, Monica?'

I shook my head and said, 'You're right, I don't know a thing. People of both countries don't know anything about each other but have this belief that the other is evil. But because of that hatred it's only the people who lose. We don't know what we hate and detest. As long as we don't choose to find out, the hatred will continue.'

Despite the malaise I had felt during the trip, on the plane back to Spain I felt somehow refreshed. For ten years I had been saying to myself 'I have to go, I must go' and I had planned this trip over and over. Now it was done, my mind felt supremely calm. And it occurred to me that one day I would return again. Visiting Pyongyang, something that for so long had felt like a burden, now became another kind of hope.

Adios Madrid, Hello New York

In the ten years I had spent living in Spain, I had got to know Spanish culture and a bit of Equatorial Guinean culture, and learned a whole lot about my father's political life. Now I felt that I needed to go to America, North Korea's enemy number one, to understand the antagonism between these two countries.

I started the process of applying for a visa for the USA. I had Spanish residency with a Guinean passport, and was still waiting to hear the outcome of my application for Spanish nationality. It wasn't a given that I would be granted a US visa, but I decided to give it a go nevertheless. I found a two-week intensive English course at a language academy in New York City and applied, paying the required fee. They provided a document required for the US visa application. After a while, I was granted a two-week student visa. I quit my job at Leroy Merlin, and said goodbye to my Spanish friends and mentors, the supporters of my emotional struggle: Silvia, Amelie, Benito and Don Antonio. But our friendship would remain despite the distance. I spent my last night in Madrid with Fernando, who understood me so well.

'Go, Monica. I know you won't settle down until you achieve your goals. You are a free spirit, beautiful inside and outside. I love you and precisely because of that, I let you go.' I could only kiss him.

In December 2004 I took off from Madrid's snowy Barajas international airport and flew to Newark, New Jersey, via Schiphol in the Netherlands.

I passed through immigration without incident and hung around in the arrivals hall waiting for Peter, the doctor I had befriended in Pyongyang, who had offered to pick me up. All the signage was in English, but the first language that hit my ears was Korean, followed by other Asian languages and Spanish. There were a lot of Koreans, Chinese and Japanese, and many others from different cultures. I could not be happier to hear my language in this new land.

Peter appeared. 'Monica! I'm sorry – there was a lot of traffic! How was your flight?'

'That's fine. It was a really long flight but I am OK.'

'Welcome to the US! Your language school is about forty minutes from here. Let's drop your luggage at your dormitory, then we can go for dinner. Sound good?'

'Yes, perfect!'

To my surprise, he had booked a table at a Korean restaurant in Korea town. When the waitress came to take our order, he greeted her in Korean: '*Annyŏnghasimnikka*.' The waitress smiled and said 'Hello' in English.

'She is Korean like you, you know?' said Peter proudly, nodding towards me. The waitress looked at us both and laughed. 'I'm serious! She is Korean. Monica, come on, say something to prove it, please. Do it for me!'

'*Annyŏnghaseyo*.'

'Oh my! Your pronunciation is perfect!' said the waitress, surprised.

'See, I told you she is Korean.'

I ordered in Korean for both of us. The waitress could not work out how I was able to speak her language so flawlessly. 'How come you speak my language? Did you grow up in Seoul?' she asked. I answered somewhat evasively.

Peter and I enjoyed recalling our shared trip to Pyongyang. Thanks to him, I felt at home on my first night in 'enemy territory'.

The next day I called my cousin Lino, the former Guinean ambassador to Beijing who was now its envoy to the UN, headquartered in New York, and arranged to see him that weekend.

My busy life in New York started the very next day. In the morning I went to the language school for a two-hour English class, and in the afternoon I explored the city, as well as looking for a job and ways to extend my visa. I came across people from all around the world. Many immigrants were, like me, trying to extend their student visas or to convert them to work visas, and others were working, legally or illegally. I encountered many Mexicans in low-wage jobs, working hard to send money to their families back home. There were Eastern Europeans, Italians, Spanish, Africans, Arabs, Koreans, and so on, all looking for new or better opportunities to make money. Everyone was busy pursuing their goals; I had never seen such a nonstop city, and one so young, multicultural and dynamic.

I felt my New York life should be about meeting people from other cultures, and learning what they thought and felt, so I tried to meet as many people as possible and spent hours talking to them. I went to a lot of parties. The city truly had a vibrant party culture,

On Times Square

and there is no better place for talking to all kinds of people from all over the world than at a party. Those conversations helped me understand what New York was to those who lived there, and gave me a sense of America as a whole, albeit an indistinct one.

The people I trusted most and felt safest with were my Korean friends, especially Lee Seung Hyeon, a South Korean woman I had befriended at the language school. They gave me the practical information that I needed to make it in New York, and through Seung Hyeon I found a part-time job in a kindergarten near my neighbourhood that was owned by one of her compatriots. But it was also through these friends that I was able to better understand the spirit of South Korea, a place I had grown up so close to but never visited.

Lino threw a party and invited me, and there I met some Equatorial Guineans who were living in New York. Even though we were people from the same country, the fact that we had grown up in such different cultures made it very difficult for me to fit in. There was fatty meat, loud music and songs with lyrics I could not understand.

The American friends I had met on my trip to Pyongyang made my adjustment to the US easier. One of them, Curtis, lived in Washington DC, so we could not meet that often. One weekend, Seung Hyeon and I went to visit him.

Having drinks with Curtis (centre) and his friend in Washington DC after a city tour

He showed us around his city and introduced us to his friends, acting as our own personal tour guide and host. We visited the Lincoln Memorial, the Capitol and Chinatown, among the other attractions of the city. Unlike New York, with its endless skyscrapers, Washington DC reminded me of a European city with its massive, squat buildings exuding power.

* * *

The months passed and, around the time the Tribeca Film Festival was in full swing, I got a phone call from Curtis. He said that one of his friends, a British documentary filmmaker, was in New York for the festival, and asked me how I felt about meeting him? I had no reason to refuse. Meeting and getting to know Westerners was, after all, what I had come to do – especially people from cultures and professions I did not know much about.

John and I met, and I learned that he had already made a few documentary films about North Korea, and had even been invited to South Korea's famed Busan Film Festival. Maybe that is why, even though he was a Westerner, he seemed well-versed in Asian etiquette.

John said he had heard a lot about me. He was putting together a documentary film about Pyongyang and wanted me in it. His abrupt invitation left me at a loss.

'I don't think I can give you an answer right now. I need to think about it.'

'Of course. I completely understand.'

I mulled over his request as I trudged home. If I appeared in John's documentary, people from all over the world, including South Korea and possibly even North Korea, would end up seeing it. Regardless of the quality of the film, it would be accepted as 'fact'. Even if the film tried to avoid embellishment, it was inevitable that particular opinions or positions, as well as the director's own vision, would be conveyed. Even if I gave genuinely truthful responses to his questions, my story would still be framed in the wider context of the film as a whole. Besides, who was I to presume I had something important to say? Of course, no matter how much I wanted to become ordinary, my past experiences would never allow it; that was my destiny. That might sound proud or arrogant, but it was an undeniable truth. When I thought about my father, who brought me into this world, and Kim Il Sung, who looked after me, there was no one else, apart from my siblings, who could understand what it all meant. Because of that, I could not act rashly.

I wrestled with this problem for a few days. It would not leave my thoughts: not at the kindergarten, not at the language school. Then suddenly a kind of answer occurred to me: *Monica, you are still not done with your journey.*

Since leaving Pyongyang I had been leading a nomadic existence, searching for my place in the world. It did not really matter what questions John asked when I did not yet know the answers myself. It would be impossible to appear in John's documentary and tell my story when I had not fully decided what that was. That evening, I sent him an apologetic email saying I wasn't ready yet.

A few days later, Jack, another European filmmaker came to see me. He made the same offer as John, and I had to give the same refusal. Jack told me that I should take my time and think about it carefully, and that his offer was always on the table.

Out of politeness, I agreed to meet with Jack all the same, along with Dmitry, another American from the Pyongyang trip. After dining together at a Korean restaurant, we walked the streets of New York, sharing stories about Pyongyang. Around that time, news was emerging that a rapidly growing number of people in North Korea were starving to death; I carried the private pain of this knowledge around with me like a stone. That was where I had grown up, and it was my friends and their families who were facing this tragedy. But Dmitry and Jack, who were walking ahead of me, laughed and joked as they talked about the famine: 'Dying of starvation in today's world, does that make sense? Well, they are communists after all!' Their mocking comments pierced my heart like a dagger. I stopped short and glared at the two of them.

'What's wrong, Monica?'

They both looked at me in puzzlement. Behind them stood the forest of Manhattan's skyscrapers and blinking neon signs. I struggled to control myself. 'People starving to death is funny? How can you laugh so easily at other people's pain?'

Communism and capitalism aside, I was dismayed to see starvation being joked about – and by people who said they wanted to make films to increase understanding of other societies. How could the lives of foreigners so easily become a joke, a conversational trinket?

I came across hostility whenever I told New Yorkers that I had grown up in Pyongyang and tried to answer their questions about North Korea from my perspective and experience. Whether they were language teachers at the school or strangers I met at parties, their facial expressions would harden and they would insist: 'North Korea is an evil country', 'North Korea is the axis of evil', 'I am glad you left that country and came here to embrace freedom', and so on. It was immensely difficult to engage in a constructive and rational discussion with them because they would immediately jump to conclusions: 'You are a communist', 'You are brainwashed!' or 'You shouldn't defend them. They are all evil.' When I asked whether they had been to North Korea or how they knew the things they were saying to be true, their answer was: 'I've never been there, and I don't want to' or 'I learned it from the news and from defectors.' A neighbour where I lived in Queens even went so far as to warn my South Korean friends that I was a North Korean spy trying to recruit them to espionage, adding that they should keep me at arm's length because I was a very dangerous person. Such comments left me speechless, though inwardly I thought that perhaps it was people like these who had been brainwashed.

On my first day working at the kindergarten, I had had an experience that had left me in shock, prompting me to reflect on how thought control begins – and to find an unexpected analogue between North Korea and the United States.

My co-worker gathered all the children, aged between four and six, and told them to stand in rows of three. On an old tape recorder, she put on the American national anthem, 'The Star-Spangled Banner'. She began singing it with her hand on her breast, ordering the kids to do the same. The kids followed the order like soldiers, mechanically miming her actions. At much the same age, I had been expected to unthinkingly follow suit in, for example, eulogising Kim Il Sung. The parallel was astonishing to me. Young minds are easily moulded. Small children are unable to question what they are asked to do, or to see how habitual actions could shape their adult lives.

That night, I could not sleep for thinking about what I had seen that day. I began to realise that in both societies, whose ideologies were so at odds, the means of controlling people's thoughts were different but the end was the same: to sway public opinion in favour of the prevailing ideology. In North Korean society, the means were somewhat coercive; in the US, diffuse and insidious. Why does public opinion matter? It constitutes one of the pillars of power that gives legitimacy to the actions of the powerful. The need to control citizens' thoughts surpasses ideological differences and is directly related to the domination of the weak by the powerful. Years later, during my Master's studies at the School of Oriental and African Studies (SOAS), I learned that the French philosopher Michel Foucault termed this phenomenon of internalised social control, this 'conduct of conduct', 'governmentality'. This orchestration of people's conduct by the powerful begins at kindergarten.

I recalled Ali telling me that my way of thinking was because of having grown up in Pyongyang. Like me at that time, these New Yorkers could not see the invisible fences that surrounded them and impeded them from thinking critically and analysing things beyond the obvious.

After leaving New York, I watched a documentary made by a white Western European filmmaker, and was pained once again. Around the time that the film was being completed, I had been asked to translate some of the Korean soundtrack into English subtitles. I gladly did so, but when I saw the finished product uploaded on social media, I was shocked. Not only was my translation not used, but the English subtitles completely twisted the meaning of what was being said.

The scene in question showed the director interviewing a North Korean official.

'Does he think that North Korea needs nuclear weapons to protect the country from the Americans?' the filmmaker asked through an interpreter.

'We are prepared to defend our country and ourselves while defending our right to exist and our sovereignty,' the official answered. But the translation on the screen read: 'We are ready to protect ourselves against an American attack. So if the USA attacks us, we will revenge it a thousand times, anytime.'

This was more like creative writing than translation. I was dumbfounded. If that was the intention, then he should simply have written the text he wanted from very beginning. Why ask me to translate at all? And why distort the truth? Was it to impose a negative impression of North Korea on the viewers?

That was when I realised how learned hatred can infect people's hearts. Through the 'frame' of its director, a documentary can manipulate the audience so that what they see or are told is taken as established fact. It was frightening. If the story of the world is told this way, then what on earth did it mean to live freely? Was the simple dichotomy I so frequently encountered in the West correct: that the people of North Korea are not free, while Westerners enjoy total freedom?

Americans' knowledge of North Korea mostly derives from narratives such as President George W. Bush's 2002 assertion that it was, along with Iran and Iraq, part of an 'axis of evil'. How can one say one is free or knows the truth when a puppet master grants this knowledge, this freedom? It reminded me of Plato's Allegory of the Cave, which Don Antonio had introduced me to in one of our sessions in Madrid, and which tells the story of people chained in a cave, unable to turn their heads. Behind them a puppeteer casts shadows with the help of a fire. All the chained people can see is the shadows; all they hear are echoes produced by the puppeteer. The prisoners spend their whole lives chained, mistaking what they experience for reality. They are entirely ignorant of the source of the shadows.

Likewise, people tend to confuse freedom with rights, such as the right to protest, right to free speech, human rights, and so on. However, laws created by lawmakers grant rights; and those rights can also be taken away by those same lawmakers. True freedom is different and not subject to laws. One can be incarcerated, denied freedom of movement and yet also in a sense be free, so long as one has the capacity to think critically.

The New York I experienced was a sort of Plato's cave, with immense wealth and many rights, rooted in liberalism that has individualism at its core. The cave in Pyongyang offers fewer material comforts and fewer rights, with a contrasting emphasis on collectivism, feudal customs, Confucianism and communism. But neither is truly free; people in both cities are subject to manipulation by unseen forces that, by different means, shape their thoughts – and therefore, their capacity for freedom.

Knowledge sets us free. I believe we are all capable of achieving that freedom through critical thinking, being honest to ourselves, gaining self-awareness and expanding our knowledge through empirical experience. It was true that I had been brainwashed; an invisible fence had been erected in my mind of which I was unaware until Ali came along and pointed it out. My path towards freedom began with the admission that there was indeed an invisible fence in my mind. This acceptance of my own internal barriers and my subsequent willingness to learn more pushed me to go beyond my comfort zone and change my perspective.

In New York City

Dreaming of Seoul

As 2006 dawned, change came into my life. My friend Lee Seung Hyeon had finished her studies and was returning to Seoul. She was sad but I remained composed.

'We're not saying goodbye for ever, are we?' I asked.

'We have to meet in Seoul, OK, *ŏnni*?'

We made a pinkie promise.

After Lee Seung Hyeon left, I moved to New Jersey, and around that time I was granted a new visa that would allow me to be in regular full-time employment, so I quit my job at the kindergarten. I submitted my CV to a jewellery company on 32nd Street close to Seventh Avenue, at the heart of the New York fashion industry. I was attracted to that place partly because it was fashion-related, and partly because it was a Korean company and all the staff were Korean. I caused surprise when I showed up to interview for the position.

'When we spoke on the phone, I thought you were Korean…'

'I am Korean.'

From that point on it was less of a job interview and more of a personal interrogation. I chatted with the woman interviewing me for quite a while and she hired me. I was starting to see how the unique advantage of being a black woman with a Korean soul could become one of my biggest strengths.

The main focus of my work was jewellery design. The idea that the items I made could end up all over America gave me a weird feeling, given that I had grown up hearing horrific Korean War stories that portrayed America as evil. I would never have predicted that I would find myself in the US, using skills learned in Pyongyang – but here I was, designing adornments for Americans. The months went by and my job satisfaction was almost total because the atmosphere was dominated by a Korean sensibility, which suited me just fine, especially as I had started to consider a move to Seoul to learn more about the other Korea, which I had heard so many unreliable things about for so many years. Ever since I left Pyongyang, I had known I had to get to Seoul, but I did not know when that part of my journey would come to pass. I had been waiting until my heart told me, of its own accord, *it's time.*

Now, after almost three years in New York, I couldn't deny the feeling that the moment had arrived: my time in America was drawing to an end.

I had learned so much in a short time. America was not the 'country of the enemy' that I had learned about since childhood. It was, however, very different from the hierarchical society I had grown up in.

New York City is the quintessence of capitalism, and I was shocked by how seemingly every facet of the human experience – eating, drinking, loving, breathing, giving birth – could be converted into a dollar value. Unlike anywhere else I had lived, even basic healthcare came with an itemised bill. To live in New York, you had to share the common dream of making money, and you had to strive with every fibre to achieve that. But I did not want those things. I wanted to continue learning and travelling while interacting with people from all over the world.

From the time I started mentally preparing to leave, without even meaning to I developed a new habit of walking everywhere in New York. When I got off work, I would wander here and there, or sit at a cafe and listen in on people's conversations; sometimes I would just zone out and gaze into space or watch the people passing by. Every country, every city has its own unique fragrance, its own atmosphere. That was true for Malabo, Zaragoza, Madrid and New York, whether I stayed in a place for years or only visited in transit. At this point in my journey, I really missed the fragrance and atmosphere of the Korean Peninsula. It was time to return.

I took courage from my conversations with Wang Tien Mou, the Chinese friend I had met as a student in Pyongyang. After gaining experience working for a Korean company in China, Tien Mou had finally moved to Seoul where she had started her own business and begun to get noticed by the fashion industry.

'I'm coming to Seoul,' I told her on the phone.

When Tien Mou got excited, she often switched into Chinese, and would then translate her own words into Korean. It was great news and she was happy to hear it! After she had quietened down a little, she asked, 'How long are you going to stay? Do you have enough money?'

'I'm saving hard at the moment. But I'll need to work to be able to live in Seoul.'

'What kind of work? You can't be vague about this. Seoul is a really tough city. You have to prepare meticulously.'

'Hey, since leaving Pyongyang I've survived on my own so far. If I have to do hard labour, I will.'

A short silence followed and then Tien Mou said, 'Are you sure? Can you even do hard labour? No matter how dirty and difficult?'

'Yes.'

Then she said, 'Come and work at our company. You'll see when you get here, Korean people work really hard. At our company you'd have to work even a little more than that. What do you say?'

'I'm already so grateful – yes!'

'Prepare yourself. I won't be able to bend the rules for you. You'll have to work your butt off just like the others. But you can stay at my house until you get settled.'

Inwardly, I screamed for joy. I had been worrying about finding accommodation and a job for a year, and now the problem was solved. Before hanging up, I asked Tien Mou, 'About Seoul… what's it like?'

'You have to come here and see for yourself.'

In my heart Seoul already felt a lot closer, but given my upbringing, I wondered whether I would be welcome.

Finally, in December 2007, I packed my bag again and headed for JFK airport. Before I reached Seoul, I had decided to pay a long visit to Madrid. More than anything, I very much wanted to see my sister Maribel, who had been living there with her young family for a few years.

At Madrid airport it was snowing again. For a place where it does not snow very much, it was strange that it always seemed to

With Wang Tien Mou on a visit to Tokyo

be snowing when I passed through. The airport looked exactly the same as it had when I had left for New York nearly three years earlier. It was as if I had woken from a long restorative dream. I felt I had thrown off a huge weight in New York and come back unburdened. I had grown to like the 'country of the enemy'. In my years there, I had come to realise that the enemy of freedom was hatred, but I still had a lot more baggage to throw off before I could feel free from my past. Perhaps life is above all a process of shedding burdens of the heart?

The second I got off the plane I raced to Maribel's house. After finishing at Pyongyang Medical University, Maribel had interned at a hospital in China. Then she went to Malabo where she worked as a gynaecologist, before coming to Madrid. Absurdly, she was not able to perform official medical work in Madrid because her qualifications from Pyongyang were not valid in Spain. Twelve years of uninterrupted study seemed to count for nothing. But my sister was surprisingly serene about it. In Madrid she looked after elderly people, working in places like geriatric care facilities and nursing homes. 'After all, the job of a doctor is helping people,' she would say.

'How was New York?' she asked enviously when I arrived.

Maribel was actually more curious about the world than me. But she had acted as a guardian to Fran and me since she was young, so had become practised at self-denial. Maribel had to fulfil all her desires that she could not outwardly express through books and movies. That is why she knew so much more than I did about not only New York, but America's history and culture. She just had not been able to experience them in person.

'New York was… very different from Pyongyang.'

'Sure, it would be.'

'Rather than me telling you everything, it would be better for you to go there and see it for yourself.'

'Right, because seeing is believing.' Maribel chuckled to herself. 'Monica, are you really going to Seoul?' She said that she still could not believe it and wondered where we had lived in our past lives. I replied that maybe we were Koreans in a previous incarnation. We looked at each other and laughed.

When it was time to go, Maribel said, 'I don't know when you'll stop all this travelling.'

'I'll keep travelling until the day I die. I'm going to see the North Pole and the South Pole with my own eyes. I kept my heart locked up for so long that now I'm going to roam around with it open for ever.'

I would leave Madrid and go to Seoul as a blank sheet of paper once again. During my upbringing in Pyongyang, I had been taught not to feel hatred for the South (as was the case for the US) but rather a kind of compassion, and so this trip would in some ways be an easier one than my years in New York.

The day I left Madrid, sure enough, it snowed again. Now I cannot even imagine Barajas Airport without snow. I got up at dawn, took my single bag and boarded a plane for Seoul. My heart was thudding so wildly I could hardly breathe.

The Two Cities Furthest Apart in the World

Seoul is less than 200 kilometres from Pyongyang, but during my fifteen years in Pyongyang it had been utterly out of reach. Back then, it seemed to be in a different universe. During the time that I lived in Seoul, I would sometimes wander the streets and suddenly stop and look around me. It felt bizarre that I was now living and working not only in Seoul, but in the famously upmarket district of Apgujeong. There were days when I would stand on the banks of the Han river and gaze blankly at the water flowing by, taking in the breeze. Whenever I detected the scent of Pyongyang in the air, I pined for it with all my heart. To me, Seoul and Pyongyang were not such different places. The eastern watchtower of the old palace that I saw on the road from Gwanghwamun to Insa-dong was the same as the one I used to see on Mount Taesŏng in Pyongyang. Just as Seoul had Namdaemun and Dongdaemun, the old city gates, Pyongyang had Taedongmun. But sometimes I felt bleak because of the unfathomable emotional distance between Pyongyang and Seoul.

When a shop owner asked me, 'How come you speak Korean so well?' and I replied, 'I used to live in Pyongyang,' he immediately retorted: 'Pyongyang? That's not our country.'

Hearing those words, I answered irritably: 'Then in which country is Pyongyang? China? Japan?'

On days like that I was melancholy. Most Seoulites I met had no idea how similar they were to Pyongyangites; perhaps they hoped there was no comparison. To me, the differences were not just superficial accents and fashions; their way of thinking, their demeanour and even their emotions were more alike than they were different. If I shared this observation with Seoulites they looked uncomfortable.

'Of course we look the same. We come from the same ancestors. But how can you say that Seoulites and Pyongyangites are similar otherwise?'

Most people emphasised not only the distinct political ideologies but also the economic and cultural contrasts between Seoul and Pyongyang. They pointed out North Korea's economic weakness and said the two cities were incomparable in terms of individual freedoms. Even young people, or those who took pride in appearing more enlightened, thought that way. Though I could see only the points in common between the two cities, it seemed others could see only the gaps.

Sometimes I would drink wine and chat with my female colleagues at the fashion design company. During these conversations, I was struck by the free and easy way they reached an opinion, by their speed in forming a forcefully held belief. When they talked, they flitted like leaves in the wind from this topic to that – movies, music, the fashion style of a soap opera star or trivial internet news. This easy way of speaking, this collective intimacy brought back memories of my student days in Pyongyang and a longing welled up inside me.

A meal with friends and colleagues in Seoul

One time in Pyongyang, the movie *Girls in my Hometown* was screened at the cinema. As always, after watching it together, my fellow students and I sat around on the campus lawn and talked about it.

In the film, a young woman moves from Pyongyang to the countryside for work. Meanwhile, a soldier loses the sight in both eyes while serving in the army and when he returns home, his girlfriend leaves him. But at the end, the girl from Pyongyang falls in love with him and true love blossoms.

The storyline idealises youthful virtue and modesty, underwritten by a didactic message. The young woman chooses to make a home with an honourable soldier who has lost his eyesight in the sacred fight for homeland prosperity and his compatriots' happiness, while the film also encourages young people to move back to the countryside, counter to the trend of moving to big cities.

But after the movie there was a robust debate between the male and female students in my class. The men said: 'You girls are all the same. You promise you'll love a man for ever and then when things change you end up betraying him. If you love somebody, shouldn't you love them through thick and thin?'

But Yun Mi retorted, 'How are women all the same? The one who married that man in the end was a woman, wasn't she?'

'That's because in movies you have to depict devoted women characters. But in real life how many women like that are out there?'

Back then we would have been a little over twenty years old. What would our peers in another country have been talking about? Thinking about it now, it feels as if we were having such innocent conversations.

That evening, Yun Mi asked me, 'Monica, what about you? What if a man you loved lost his eyes?'

Suk I, who was sitting next to me, said flatly: 'I couldn't stay with him.' Her reasoning was that even the noblest purpose fades through the difficulties of life, and that it was no wonder that a declaration of love would lose its potency over time.

I thought about it for a while before answering, 'I would never leave him. And I wouldn't value people according to whether they were disabled or not. I would fall in love with someone with whom I felt a strong affinity, regardless of whether they were blind.'

Back then, most of us were at the age when we wanted to deny that time changes even the most virtuous heart. Did our contemporaries in the West, and in South Korea and Japan, think the same as we did as they were growing up?

With a woman in traditional Japanese costume on a visit to Japan

They were probably worried about much more complicated and varied issues than we were. But Pyongyang, cut off from contact with the outside world, seemed like a hermetically sealed, uncontaminated room, and our debates revolved around loyalty, sacrifice, and rewarding virtue while punishing vice.

Twenty years had since passed and now I was in a pub in Seoul's Apgujeong, talking about light, frivolous things that brought to mind my school days, now so distant. Just then, someone in the group asked an unexpected question.

'Monica *ŏnni*, can young people in Pyongyang sit around and chat freely like we do here? Or is it impossible?'

And somebody else chimed in, 'Come on, those people are limited as to what kind of happiness they can enjoy.'

The conversation began like that and got more and more provocative as we drank. We got onto human rights issues. Someone mentioned the *oho tamdangje* system – the North Korean system of neighbourhood vigilance – and the great famine. I had grumbled about the food in Pyongyang in the 1980s, but the North Korean economic situation then was not nearly as bad as it was as we spoke. Back then, rice and other staples were still regularly provided by the state, so North Koreans tended to be relatively well-off. I could even remember the country sending aid (rice and other resources) to South Korea when it suffered bad floods. And after the Korean War, the North was one of the Northeast Asian countries whose economies boomed. However, these youngsters seemed fixated on the present moment, ignorant of historical events.

It was painful to read about the many people who died in the great famine that struck North Korea after the calamitous flooding of 1995. A sense of guilt bubbled up whenever I thought back to the time I clandestinely emptied a dish of tofu behind a flowerpot, and the times when I could not stomach the rice and vegetables I had been given and so spat them out in the toilet. Would Sŏn Hwa be all right? Would Yun Mi, Su Jŏng and Suk I be safe? Every time the faces of my friends came to mind it distressed me.

The Pyongyang my South Korean friends were conjuring was gruesome enough to remind me of Picasso's Spanish Civil War painting *Guernica*. Its surrealist shapes, suggesting atrocities, chaos, violence and sadness, elicited in me dark, fearful and obscure feelings. With increasing frustration, I listened until I could hear no more and then I opened my mouth.

'It's not like that. Do you really think North Korea is an "axis of evil" like Bush says? Think about it: how could such a society keep going? The people there are living their lives and pursuing their happiness every day, just like we do.'

I told them about everyday life in North Korea, and the peaceful times when people walked up Pyongyang's Mount Taesŏng with their families and talked and laughed and watched the sunset together. And I told them to let go of this premise that Pyongyang and Seoul were all that different.

'Think about East and West Germany. They were separated politically, but the people didn't think they were from separate cultures. The people up in the North are not born with preconceptions about the people of South Korea. It's the politicians who create this feeling of diplomatic enmity. Normal people aren't like that. They're just like us. The more you think they're different the further away they become.'

They were too young to understand, and not having lived on the other side of the peninsula, it was to be expected that they could not see the commonality of the Koreas. Their country's economic superiority made them proud and apt to judge others by harsh standards.

While living in Seoul I met people who hoped for Korean unification and people who opposed it. There were people who hated North Korea, and people who believed they ought to help their neighbour. I neither agreed nor disagreed with their views. I only felt sorry that all these opinions were coming from a very limited base of knowledge about North Korea. Just as Northerners did not know about the South, Southerners did not know about the North. They had been cut off from each other for several generations and the emotional distance between them grew wider with every passing year. When people fight, dialogue can help allay the anger, but the political chasm between our two countries prevented that opportunity. If I could take Sŏn Hwa, Yun Mi and Su Jŏng from their homes in North Korea to that bar in Apgujeong and let them mingle with their South Korean peers, within an hour they would have developed close bonds, and be calling each other *ŏnni*. After that idea occurred to me, whenever I walked the streets of Seoul, I would imagine that I was walking along with my friends from Pyongyang.

Seoul became my second hometown after Pyongyang; I made good friends there and could always come back. I stayed about two years before, once again, the time came to move on.

With Lee Seung Hyoun in Seoul

Fangpañol

After Seoul, I went to Shenzhen and Shanghai. Following commercial success in her Seoul office, Tien Mou had opened new design offices in those two Chinese megacities, which were then growing at breakneck speed. China was becoming increasingly important in all fields, even in the fashion industry. Most European luxury brands were producing their designs in China. So I asked for a transfer to the Shenzhen design office, and then to Shanghai. Once again, I immersed myself in learning the language and culture. I found that, by comparison to both the Koreas, China had a hint of individualism within a broadly collectivist society. Also, while Korean society is male-centred and patriarchal (though there is a bit of a challenge to this tradition coming from younger generations), China seemed female-centred. In Korea, men do not even set foot in the kitchen, while in China I came across many men who cooked and washed the dishes. And China impressed me with its power and permanence, spanning centuries from the ancient marvels of the Forbidden City and Temple of Heaven in Beijing to the modern

Sightseeing in Shenzhen

With my friend Guo Xu Gun in Shanghai

global financial hub of Shanghai and futuristic Shenzhen, China's own Silicon Valley.

After about two-and-a-half years in China I felt it was at last time: I was ready to go to Equatorial Guinea.

I had developed the emotional maturity I needed to persevere on my journey of inquiry into my African and European genetic heritage (I say genetic as culturally I had always viewed myself as Asian). I decided the moment had come to shift my focus to Equatorial Guinea, and so I found myself embarking once again for Malabo.

My two brothers, Fran and Teo, were my main reference points as I began the slow process of acclimatising to my Guinean surroundings and way of life. They introduced me to my large family; we had so many cousins it was virtually impossible to know all of them. The potential for misunderstanding was almost limitless.

I was alone at Fran's house. Fran had gone to work, and I was reading a book when the doorbell interrupted me. I opened the door.

'*Mbolo*?' said the man standing in front of me. I knew that meant 'hello' in Fang.

'*Mbolo*.'

The man continued to speak in Fang, assuming I understood him.

'I'm sorry,' I said in Spanish, 'I don't speak Fang, but I am learning it. Do you mind repeating it in Spanish, please?'

The man was outraged. 'What! How come a Fang doesn't speak her own language?'

'It's a very long story. As I said, I'm learning. How can I help you?'

'I am looking for Paquito,' he said, referring to Fran.

'My brother is not at home.'

'*Akieeeee*!' the man shouted excitedly in *Fangpañol,* the mixture of Fang and Spanish commonplace in Guinea. 'You are Paquito's younger sister who I heard came back to Guinea? *Akieeee*! I am your father, you know?'

'What do you mean, you are my father? My father was assassinated in 1979. Did you come here to make some kind of nasty joke? My brother is not at home. Please leave!' I instructed him coldly and shut the door.

When Fran returned home, I told him what had happened. 'There was a man who came to see you while you were at work. He claimed he was our father. I don't like that kind of joke. I asked him to leave and shut the door on him.'

Fran seemed to find the episode amusing.

'You are so Korean! OK, listen: in Guinean culture, when a couple have a child, they like to give the baby the name of one of their parents, a member of the family they admire. It is a way of demonstrating respect, love or affection. I am named Francisco after our father, and you are named Monica after Mama. You will see that in many Guinean households, names are repeated, although it's now a bit old-fashioned and is changing with the younger generation. I don't know exactly who that man was as you didn't give him a chance to give you his details. But I guess he would be a member of our extended family and his parents named him after our father. So he wasn't playing some kind of nasty trick on you. He was probably excited to see the daughter of the person he was named after. It's just the culture. In future you'll meet a lot of people telling you the same thing. Just don't be rude to them. They don't understand the world in the way we do, and that is their custom. We just need to be aware of it and respect it. Got it?'

Two days later I received a call from Luisa, Fran's ex-wife.

'Hi Luisa, how are you?'

'I am OK, thank you. Listen, I am calling you to tell you that your cousin Nsue VI has died. Many of your family members are in his house where his body is. Fran is already there, busy with funeral preparations, and I don't think he's had time to tell you. I thought I should let you know, especially given the language barrier.'

'Oh, thank you very much for calling me. No, Fran didn't tell me. I want to go, but I don't know how to get there.'

'Don't worry. I will take you there. But I won't stay long.'

We took a taxi; it was smelly, but I had known worse.

Luisa gave the driver directions in Fang. When the asphalt road ran out, the driver took a muddy track into a shanty town with no electricity or running water. It was the first time I had seen the reality of life in a poor area within an oil-rich country. It was heartbreaking to see kids playing in a rubbish-strewn ditch. Some houses had no proper roof, and I dreaded to think what they were like during the wet season. This is not living, I thought to myself. How do people survive under these conditions? This is inhuman! There is no reason for this when the country is the third largest oil producer in Africa!

Luisa paid the driver 500 Central African francs, a little under one US dollar. No matter what distance you went, you always paid the same amount.

'My condolences!' said Luisa, using the traditional greeting for such occasions, as we entered the house.

'My condolences,' I repeated. There were a lot of people around.

'These are all your cousins,' Luisa explained. I recognised some of them – Aulowo, Andem.

Fran appeared. 'Thank you for bringing her, Luisa. I wasn't sure whether she should come as she's still in culture shock. And a funeral is quite a big thing.'

'She is strong, and sooner or later she needs to learn about our culture, doesn't she? You can't protect her for ever.'

They were speaking about me as if I were not there.

'OK, must go now. I have things to do,' said Luisa.

'Thank you again, Luisa,' I said, kissing her cheeks.

'How did it happen?' I asked my brother under my breath in Korean. Nsue VI had not been an old man.

'I don't know. Everyone gives a different version of events. There's no serious organisation that investigates and gives the cause of death, so everyone is free to explain it as they choose. It's chaos!' explained Fran, signalling for me to sit in a chair next to some of our cousins. The wake was being held prior to the burial.

'Come with me to express your condolences to our uncle. He's the half-brother of our father. He's inside the house where the body is. Do you think you can?'

'Yes.'

I said yes, but I felt unsure about seeing a dead body for the first time. I held my brother's hand and followed him inside the shack.

A strong smell hit my nose. I could not breathe properly and thought I might pass out. A body was lying on the concrete floor. It looked like he was in a deep sleep. Next to the body there was a man who looked exactly like me but with a darker skin tone. It must be my uncle. I approached him.

'My condolences, Uncle.'

'Thank you, my daughter! I heard you came back, but we haven't had a chance to meet.'

'Nice to meet you.' I did not know what else to say. I felt warmth towards this man who looked exactly like my father, but the circumstances in which we were meeting prevented me from saying so.

Instead, I managed: 'I will come to visit you on a different occasion.'

I walked out to the courtyard where another cousin was sitting. 'Hi, Juan. Do you know how it happened?' I asked.

'Nsue VI died practising occultism,' said Juan. He stood up and went into the house. I was not convinced. In hope of a more coherent explanation, I asked another cousin, Carmen, the same question.

'He died from *Kwong*,' she said.

'What's *Kwong*?'

'It's a kind of witchcraft thing. A ghost appears and kills people in a zombie state.'

'I'm not sure if I understand what you are saying. A ghost that no one saw killed him? Come on, that's nonsense! There must be a logical explanation.'

'That's the most logical answer in our society. It's happened many times,' she said earnestly.

I really did not expect that answer from Carmen, who had studied to become a nurse in Cuba.

'I don't think so. And you guys don't do autopsies to find out the cause of death. That would give us a logical answer.'

'Do you think this is Korea or Spain? This is Africa, my dear.'

'And you really believe this *Kwong* thing?'

'Yes, I do. My sister and I had those experiences, but we survived thanks to an antidote they gave us.'

Another cousin started describing his experience with that alleged invisible killer called *Kwong*. He began in Spanish and then swiftly switched to Fang, and I lost the thread.

I sat in silence, thinking. How could a person who studied medicine believe in such a thing? Then I remembered what my sister Maribel had once told me. After her long medical training in Pyongyang, she had gone back to Guinea and worked as a gynaecologist in Loeri Comba hospital in Malabo, alongside some Cuban doctors.

'I often felt powerless against these beliefs and practices of witchcraft. Ninety per cent of our patients came to us in hospital in the last stage of their disease, giving us very little time to save their lives. First, they went to sorcerers and only when that didn't work did they come to us. Often by then it was too late. Do you know what it is like to lose patients every single day because of these beliefs? And when it's an expectant mother it's heart-breaking. I studied medicine because I wanted to save lives, but I was failing. I tried every which way to persuade them but it was as if I were fighting an enormous invisible army. I didn't know what to do and I was getting so stressed and frustrated that, when I became pregnant with Cristina, I left the country.'

I mused on this as I sat at Nsue VI's wake. Education might help to eradicate these notions. It might not work with adults whose beliefs were fixed, but perhaps if children were educated differently, change was possible? Witchcraft had existed in all societies since ancient times, but most mature societies had overcome this problem, I thought.

As the days passed, I spent my time getting to know Guinean society, and continued on my quest to find out more about my father by interviewing people who had been around at the time of his rule. Most were afraid to talk openly but some were not.

With Fran and Herve in Malabo

The Guinea I encountered approximated the 'state of nature' that Thomas Hobbes, the English political philosopher, articulated in his 1651 masterpiece *Leviathan,* which Don Antonio and I had discussed in Madrid. In the Hobbesian state of nature there is no civil state, no set of laws, no government, and so on. I say 'approximated' because in Guinea there did exist a dysfunctional nominal government, laws and civil society, albeit with a broken structure.

In the Hobbesian state of nature, people live in constant fear of each other as they compete for the resources necessary to secure their survival. Social life is virtually non-existent, due to the fear and uncertainty experienced by individuals. Whenever I interacted with Guineans, I could immediately sense fear, insecurity, jealousy and suspicion of each other. Everyone was against everyone else.

When a society is in a state of nature, industrialisation and development cannot take place because their fruits would be seized by the most powerful. As a result, no culture can emerge; there is no nation building; there is nothing but fear and violence, and nobody but the solitary, poor and nasty. The Guineans termed this state *Guineologia*, and seemed to think it was a unique phenomenon, although the Global North, Asian and other industrialised nations had had similar experiences in the distant past before reaching a social contract.

I remembered what Don Antonio had said about putting everything in context. The Guinea which my father attempted to lead was in a Hobbesian state of nature – and it remains so today.

I could not stop wondering: can a tribal society with a background of colonial oppression, finding itself now in a state of nature, leapfrog to democracy? Can a baby skip learning to walk and start running like an adult?

Dr Pipa

'I will pick you up at 8.15 p.m. Be ready and I will introduce you to the doctor.'

It was a message from Terrence, an Australian with Angolan and Portuguese heritage who had been living in Malabo for about three years, working for an English oil company. I had met him at a private party that Fran had taken me to.

At the agreed time, the doorbell rang and I rushed to open the door.

'I'm ready!'

'OK, let's go,' said Terrence. 'Dr Pipa is waiting for us.'

Dr Pipa was a Catalonian doctor who had been working in Guinea since before independence. He had a clinic in Malabo.

I jumped in Terrence's 4x4.

'You look down, Terrence. What's wrong?'

'A relative died two days ago in Angola, and family members living abroad asked me for money for flights to attend the funeral. I told the person who takes care of my bank account to allow money for flights for seven people to be withdrawn. Do you know what they did? They withdrew 17,000 euros and bought business-class flights. You give a hand and they take your arm.'

I recalled another similar incident Terrence had told me about before. He had bought a plough and a tractor for family living in Angola. He put one of his cousins in charge of working the land so they could make some money with the harvest. Six months later, Terrence travelled to Angola from Australia to check how things were going. People in the town told him his cousin had sold the machinery and used the money to fly to Brazil. He never returned.

Terrence had also contributed funds towards a new school in the Guinean port city of Bata. In an effort to change his mood, I asked him about it.

'How did it go in Bata?'

'Well, it's been a year already since our company opened that school, so I went to see how things were going. It's not my job but I felt I should follow it up. Like always in Africa, half the materials that we bought have been stolen and there has been zero maintenance of the schoolyard. They did absolutely nothing. I had told them to cut the grass, but it was still overgrown. It is something that could be done in one day with a machete. It's so difficult to work with Africans. They don't cooperate. Their own unwillingness to make their lives better is sometimes discouraging, honestly.'

I saw the frustration in his eyes.

'And that's not the end of my problems this week. Before I arrived in Bata, I sent some money to a guy to rent me a car. Guess what! He rented his friend's car. The day we took the car to visit the school we got stuck in the middle of the road. The school is on the outskirts of the city. We got a puncture and he didn't have a spare tyre. I decided to go back into the city and get a car in good condition. I got very upset, not because he rented from his friend but because when you rent a car from an individual instead of a professional company this is the kind of thing that happens. And his friend wanted me to pay him full price!'

I spent the trip listening to his stories and by the time we reached the restaurant he was calmer.

'Thank you for listening. It helps a lot. Equatorial Guinea and Africa in general are difficult. You can go mad even if you are a strong person.'

'It's my pleasure.' I knew this was only one side of the story of Guinea but there was a grain of truth in his generalisations. I was on a journey of learning about the problems of everyday life in Guinea, and apparently in the continent as a whole.

The restaurant had round tables covered in crisp white tablecloths and set with silver cutlery, and it was decorated with a fusion of African and Spanish art. It was an era of booming oil prices in Guinea, and the room was full of businessmen, both white and black. At one of the tables sat an old white man with grey hair, the old-fashioned tobacco pipe for which he was nicknamed before him.

'How are you, Dr Pipa?' called out Terrence. 'This is Monica Macias, who I told you about. Thank you again for agreeing to meet her – I know you are the busiest doctor in Malabo.'

'He is exaggerating!' said Dr Pipa. I was struck by his voice, which was strong and firm for an elderly man.

I felt emotion welling up in me. I had wanted to meet this man for some time. He had lived in Guinea during and after the colonial period and had witnessed independence. He was a learned man, and I was keen to hear his view of what had taken place.

Dr Pipa scanned my face keenly.

'You look like him. I knew your father before and after he became president. He used to come to my clinic and he was courteous and kind.'

'I wanted to ask you how you survived his era, you being a Spaniard. The Spanish government say that my father hated Spaniards and expelled them all.'

'That's not true! Political lies!' he protested forcefully as I finished speaking.

'He did not expel us. They – the Spanish – left the country voluntarily. They behaved hysterically after independence. Many Spaniards were arrogant. They did not like mixing with Guineans and acted like their superiors because of their white skin.

'After independence, there was a ceremony in Malabo where the Spanish flag was lowered, and the Guinean flag was raised. Then there was a magnificent parade from Plaza Mayor to the Women's Plaza. And you know what? The only white people watching were my wife, the military chief and me. The other Spaniards despised the indigenous Guineans and did not show up. Shame on them!'

While listening, I thought of how indigenous Guineans lived during colonialism.

Dr Pipa was clearly a strong character, but he modulated his tone of voice according to what he was saying. Now, he took on a softer tone. 'I still remember what your father said to me as though it were yesterday. "Doctor, independence has come but you and I are going to eat fried chicken."' He smiled.

'When he was in his black Mercedes and saw a Spaniard, he used to stop the car and greet them and ask whether everything was OK, whether the natives were treating them well. His enemies have invented lies and people who never knew him at all talk about it as if they were there. The victor writes history and they won't say what really happened or give a complete version of events. Come to see me at my clinic and we can talk at our leisure.'

I nodded.

'Where did you grow up?' he asked with interest.

'In North Korea.'

'So, you are Korean. And when did you arrive back in this country?'

'A few months ago – this is my second visit. I am trying to find out who my father was and learn about where I come from.'

'Very good. Do not forget your roots. But I see you are mixed race. What is your other half?'

'My mother's father is from the Basque Country.'

'Ah, a good mixture! And do you know which part of the Basque Country?'

'Not yet, but I'm planning to learn about that too.'

'You will have to adapt to this place, step by step. I've been to some Asian countries and am quite familiar with their cultures. Asia is completely different from Guinea. For instance, here on Bioko Island, it is a matriarchal society, while on the mainland they are patriarchal.'

'Really? I didn't know that.'

'Yes, yes. Here, women have power,' he said with a grin. 'I have been living in this country a very long time and I know the culture very well. You will be fine. Like I said, come to see me at my clinic and we will talk.'

The First Coup d'État

It was midnight and I could not sleep. My mind was busy with questions that I wanted to put to my mother. Since meeting Don Antonio and Dr Pipa, I had gradually gained the confidence and emotional resilience to talk about my father. It was time. My mother did not like talking about what happened as it caused her so much pain, but for me, it was important.

I went to her room and knocked on the door.

'May I come in, Mama?'

'Yes, come in.'

'Mama, please, will you tell me about Atanasio Ndong's attempted coup?' I had heard about this Spanish agent who had tried to overthrow my father and it was playing on my mind.

She sighed and sat up in her bed. I sat beside her, all my attention on her. I knew how difficult it was for her to talk about my father, but it was necessary.

'You weren't born yet. Teo was about five, Maribel two and a half, and Paco [Fran] was a baby. We were in our house in

Bata.* Your father never liked living in the presidential palace, which he used as an office. It began on the night of 4 March 1969, just five months after he became the first legitimate president of Equatorial Guinea. I noticed that our bodyguards were nervous.

'Early in the morning I told Teo and Maribel to stay indoors. But while I was with the baby, your sister took her bicycle and went out for a ride in the courtyard. I was watching her from the window when I saw a man in uniform calling to her. I didn't recognise him, and I started shouting, "No, Maribel! Do not go to him!" I ran out as quickly as I could, alerting the bodyguards. Luckily, I caught Maribel in time. The guards captured the man. "Who are you?" I asked him. "Why were you calling my daughter? What do you want?" He said he had been sent by Atanasio Ndong to kidnap one of my children as a hostage.

'Your father had been locked away in his study since he came back from Mbini, a town in Rio Muni. He rushed out angrily and told me to take the children and keep them inside. I did as he said. Your father was a strong character and very upset that day. He did not think twice before leaving the house with his followers. He walked with them towards the palace. He was shouting: "Atanasio, wait for me there, traitor! You coward, face me! Who do you think you are?" He was so angry it was as if the earth was shaking. More people were joining him in the streets. I saw that with my own eyes. What happened in the palace I learned later from the bodyguards and your father. Members of

* The seat of government moved at intervals between the capital Malabo, on the island of Bioko, and Bata on the mainland.

the Ntobo-Esangui had summoned him, your father, there the night before.'

'Wait, Mama. Who are the Ntobo-Esangui?'

'It is a branch of the Esangui tribe, of Fang ethnicity, living in Ntobo, a region in Mbini, in Bata. You know your father was Esangui, right?'

'Yes! Go on, Mama.'

'They sent someone to call your father to Mbini. They told your father what was about to happen: a coup d'état against him orchestrated by Spain, with a Spanish military ship supporting Atanasio. During the night, Atanasio rounded up your father's ministers and jailed them. His forces were also killing people, saying it was on the president's orders. Atanasio managed to get into your father's office in the palace. There he sent a telegram to Madrid, reading "Mission accomplished". Your father had spent the night in his study agonising over what to do until the attempted kidnap of your sister. Once he got to the palace with his followers, he shouted, "I am the president. Where are you, traitor? Face me, coward!" as he climbed the stairs towards his office. Before he reached the room, Atanasio jumped out of the window.'

'But Mama, some people say that Papa killed him.'

'That's not true. He never even touched him. Atanasio was a coward. He couldn't face your father and jumped.* Everyone who was there with your father witnessed it. Your father never ordered that anyone be killed – it was his enemies who were killing people, saying that it was by presidential order. When they

* Atanasio suffered a broken leg during the fall and was sent to hospital by Macias. He later died in prison in unexplained circumstances.

caught Bonifacio Ondo Edu, the former ruler of Guinea under Spanish rule, your father ordered that he be placed under house arrest, but they killed him. It was the first time I ever saw your father cry – for a week, he didn't even eat. You cannot imagine the atmosphere in which he was trying to govern the country, and he had so little support – internal or external. Even his own family used his position to underwrite their actions, saying "my uncle is the president". It was a chaotic country where your father tried to implement order, but no one obeyed. They would say "Yes, Mr President", but then go off and commit atrocities. There were too many things going on behind his back. Many killings happened that way. And by the time he knew, it was too late.'

Listening to my mother, I recalled a passage from Machiavelli's *The Prince*, another foundational political treatise which I had looked at with Don Antonio: 'Because this is to be asserted in general of men, that they are ungrateful, fickle, false, cowardly, covetous, and as long as you succeed they are yours entirely; they will offer you their blood, property, life and children… when the need is far distant; but when it approaches they turn against you.'

My mother went on: 'He used to say to me, "I don't want any of my children to be politicians in this country. It is hell."'

'Who accused him of the killings, Mama?'

'Many military men, double-dealers surrounding him, even his own family. Many of them are still alive. Hypocrites! That's what happened that day. That's life. Your father was honest and worked hard for his country. He never stole the country's money. Just look at us! We don't have money. How many African former presidents can say that? And yet his enemies invented the rumour that we had an account in Switzerland.* If that had been the case, I wouldn't have had to sell plantain on the streets when I returned to Guinea from Pyongyang. I started over from scratch.'

'Are you upset that Papa did not leave us any money?'

'No, my love. On the contrary, I am proud of him because he didn't steal a penny. And I don't care what his enemies say about him. It's not true. So many people talk about your father and yet they didn't even know him.'

'So why don't you speak up to defend his honour? You are the former first lady. You have a powerful voice and you are the one who can dispel those lies. Mama, please speak up.'

'I can't.' She was adamant. 'They already tried to murder Paco,** and Teo in the aftermath of the coup that killed your father. They came to our house, they kidnapped Teo, who was a young man back then, blindfolded him and took him somewhere to be executed. I was helpless. He was shot but they failed to kill him. When they were about to take a second shot, a man rushed up in his Jeep and saved Teo's life. Several times since then, Teo and Fran have been locked up in Black Beach jail. I've already lost my husband and I don't want to lose my children too. I won't speak up. Don't ask it of me.'

'But Mama, by speaking up you can save far more lives than just those of your own children. Look at the state Guinea is in.

---

* In a 1978 Spanish newspaper article, Jesus de las Heras reported claims that my father had funds in Switzerland. 'La esposa del presidente Macías puede estar en España', *El País*, 31 January 1978.

** The Bubi are the second largest ethnic group in Equatorial Guinea and aborigines of Bioko Island. In the 1990s some people of this ethnicity instigated a protest, in the course of which the armed forces, ostensibly there to shut down the protest, attempted to kill Fran in his home.

How many more must die, disappear in the night, and suffer every violation of their human rights? Your silence might save us, but what about other people's children?'

'I don't expect you to understand because you are not a mother.'

While living in Spain in the 2000s, my mother had received many interview requests from independent reporters, but never agreed to talk about what happened or about my father. Protecting her children was more important to her than anything else.

There was no point continuing to argue because I knew she would never risk sacrificing us, so I didn't pursue the subject. But I could not help but think that her silence had led to the continuation of bloodshed in our country.

Could I have convinced her? Could I have impressed upon her that by exposing what was really going on, she might have lost a son or a daughter but she would have begun a process of rescuing an entire nation? How could I tell her that she might not succeed but might plant a seed of change?

If some of us are not free, none of us is truly free.

Despite Guinea's enormous natural resources, the majority of its population are struggling and suffering. The wealth of the country is unevenly distributed. Esangui, the Fang clan I belong to, is the most powerful. My close and distant relatives were and are deeply implicated in the economic and political corruption that ripped apart our country. I know I am not directly responsible for the malady that afflicts Guinea, which is in need of a genuine and serious national reconciliation. However, as the daughter of the former president, whose clan and relatives continue to steal from the National Wealth Fund and destroy our country, I feel a strong need to ask forgiveness from all Guineans: Fang, Bubi, Bisio, Kombe and Annobones.

Two Sides of the Same Coin

The more time I spent in Guinea, with every personal interaction I had and every investigatory interview I conducted, the more I learned about my homeland. My confidence grew day by day. I visited Mongomo, a region on the eastern border with Gabon where my family and clan are from. Connecting with my ancestry gave me a clearer idea of who I was, and this in turn gave me the courage to share my story and experiences with others.

The idea of publishing my diaries had first occurred to me while I was living in New York. Everywhere I went, everyone I met – especially Koreans – asked me the same questions: *How come you speak Korean so well? Why did you grow up in Pyongyang? Why did your father leave you there? Was he a diplomat? Are you some kind of African princess?* I grew tired of giving the same answers all the time, so I considered writing an account of my story. But back then I realised I was not yet ready to share it; I needed to learn more and travel more. My time in Guinea had fulfilled that need.

Writing a diary, putting my thoughts and feelings on paper, was a habit that had been instilled at boarding school. As an adult, I wrote only when the need arose: when an external event affected me; when I needed to reflect; or when I was sad or happy.

After carefully selecting the stories and reflections from my diaries, I sent a Korean manuscript to a South Korean publisher. The Korean version of my autobiography was published in summer 2013.

I decided to wrap up my time in Guinea and went back to Seoul to promote the book. I had no inkling of the magnitude of interest that my story would elicit among journalists, filmmakers and academics. Some were simply interested in hearing my story, but others, I came to realise, wanted to exploit it for their own political purposes.

For instance, the BBC's Dan Damon, BBC Korea's Kim Hyo Jung and Seo Myung Jean and Ree Dae Wook from Korea's SBS channel all demonstrated outstanding professionalism, reporting my story accurately and fairly. Their work was rewarded by positive responses to my interview from the public on social media.

Thanks to Monica, I have realised our [the two Koreas'] homogeneity and that we need to work to restore our nation.

Monica, you are cool. Our nation is one.

So emotional. We must live without prejudice.

I am surprised. Your demeanour and expression are just like ours. We can learn the truth when we look for it ourselves. Thank you, Monica, for expressing our nation's sincerity.

You just showed us that by eliminating prejudices we – the two Koreas –
can quickly be one.

We humans are all the same.

But others had more sinister motives for their interest in my story.

One day, when I was busy giving interviews to Korean TV channels and newspapers, I received a phone call from Gasol, a Spanish friend who taught Spanish at Seoul University.

'I wanted to ask if you would be interested in meeting a woman called Mrs Park,' he said. 'She's a professor here at Seoul University and speaks Spanish as well. I told her about you and she said she is really interested in meeting you.'

'No problem, I'll meet her,' I agreed.

The next day, I took the subway to Mrs Park's office in Youngdeungpo district. A strange feeling came over me as I looked at her face. She was smiling, but her eyes were shifty, flicking from side to side. They say the eyes are the windows to the soul, but she was unable to hold my gaze and her friendliness seemed to be a mask. All the same, I decided to stay and hear what she had to say. She introduced herself.

'I run an organisation that works for North Korean defectors. We deal with their human rights issues and give assistance to defectors in South Korea.'

A noble cause, I thought, wondering if I had misjudged her.

'Since you grew up in North Korea, I'd like you to take part in our conference. I have written a speech for you to read.'

I agreed to look at the two-page speech in Korean. I could not believe what I was reading. She wanted me to claim Kim Il Sung had taught me to hate South Koreans.

'I thought you wanted to get to know me!' I said, aghast. I dropped the papers and walked out of the room. She shouted after me but I kept walking and left the building. I took a breath of fresh air and looked up at the sky. What had just happened? I could not believe it. Lying for political purposes – was that not what South Koreans frequently accused North Koreans of doing?

Kim Il Sung never talked to my siblings and me about politics. How could this woman make up such blatant falsehoods while working on human rights issues? How many more ulterior motives were out there masquerading as noble causes? I was not here to get caught up in politics, but other people were keen to entangle me in their prejudice.

The most egregious example came a few years later in 2017, when a South Korean documentary filmmaker, Cha Ha In, contacted me because he wanted to make a documentary about my life. I was interested – I could use the money to support an idea I had been dabbling with. A few days later, I received an email explaining the concept. After we negotiated terms and conditions – making clear that the documentary should not serve political purposes or misrepresent my story – I signed a contract for a one-off presentation at the Art Sonje Center in Seoul.

But when I read the script Mr Cha sent, I was perplexed. According to his version, Kim Il Sung had asked me to leave the country once I finished my studies – whereas the truth was that he gave me the choice to leave or stay. Disappointed,

I immediately emailed back a correction, reminding Mr Cha of his contractual obligations. Nonetheless, he continued along these deceitful lines. He took my pictures from online without my permission and used them to promote the film. I only found out because my friend Lee Seung Hyeon, who was suspicious of this man from the start, did some research. Then, during filming in Seoul, someone whom Mr Cha referred to as *hyŏngnim* ('older brother') took photos of me without my permission until I angrily told him to stop. That seemed to upset Mr Cha, who bowed and scraped to placate him. When Lee Seung Hyeon told me that the *hyŏngnim* was a famous South Korean film director, I understood why.

The worst of it was when Mr Cha started to promote the documentary at several film festivals in South Korea without my permission, despite our contractual agreement. The festival organisers cancelled the screenings and gave profuse apologies once they learned about Mr Cha's duplicity, and I emailed all film organisations in South Korea to warn them off.

About a year later I received a message from Valerie, a filmmaker from Berlin:

> *I just watched a short documentary called* Utopia *in a small gallery in Berlin. You appear in it. My associate Elsa found out about it while we were researching you on the internet, and we went to watch it. It's a short documentary made by a South Korean director, Cha.*

Was this some kind of joke? What was wrong with this man? It turned out that Mr Cha had made another documentary, once again using interview footage and images without my approval.

He had presented it at one of the largest film festivals in South Korea, the Busan International Film Festival, prompting the German gallery curator to contact him.

This time I emailed all the organisations that had funded the documentary, warning them that Mr Cha had used my images illegally and that I was seeking legal advice on the matter.

Not long after that, I was contacted by a French filmmaker, Jean, who was making a documentary about North Korea and wanted me to feature in it. This time I consulted a lawyer before signing an agreement with the producer, but once again things did not go according to plan.

Our interview took place in a flat in Madrid I was staying in. We began filming, but it quickly became clear that the director wasn't happy with my answers. Visibly upset, he started raising his voice to insult me, calling me a 'dictator'. I could not work out what was happening at first and I tried to respond. Then I realised he was not reasoning with me but trying to provoke me into anger. He wanted me to discredit myself on camera.

'I am not going to get involved in this stupid discussion. Please leave my flat,' I told him.

Jean left the room, fuming.

The next day I sent an email to the production company's lawyer about the underhand conduct of the crew, outlining my disappointment not only with the interview itself but with their double-dealing over other issues. And as I reflected on these incidents, I wondered how many interviewers insult or coerce their subjects because they do not like their answers or are in pursuit of sensational headlines. When somebody invents lies about your life story, or takes photos of you without permission and uses them repeatedly for whatever purpose they please, it strips you of your dignity; you feel violated. The English philosopher Bertrand Russell said, 'When you are studying any matter, or considering any philosophy, ask yourself only what are the facts and what is the truth that the facts bear out. Never let yourself be diverted, either by what you wish to believe, or by what you think would have beneficent social effects if it were believed, but look only and solely at what are the facts.' Life was complex, and critical thinking was required to get at the truth. Even well-intentioned individuals could be deeply confused and irrational. My experiences showed how important it was to distinguish the professionals from the pseuds.

Promoting the Korean version of my memoirs in Seoul

The Money

While promoting my book in Seoul, I had the chance to meet some defectors from North Korea. It was a great opportunity to learn about their experiences of living in the South.

I met the three defectors at a traditional Korean restaurant in the centre of Seoul with a Western friend. We sat on the floor, at a low table in the traditional way, with a variety of food in bite-sized pieces before us. As happened so often in Seoul, I was reminded strongly of Pyongyang. It was a strange feeling to meet someone from my city in Seoul. To break the ice, I said in Korean: 'Judging from your accent, I would say you are from Pyongyang.'

'Yes, we are all from Pyongyang,' one of the men replied. He was middle-aged.

'Then we are all from the same place. Glad to meet you! It's like a meeting of hometown friends!' I said.

In Korean culture, when people from the same hometown meet, or find that they are from a similar age group, it creates familiarity and eases the conversation.

'Between us, tell me, was Pyongyang that bad for you? And what do you think of Seoul?' I asked.

After a few moments, looking straight into my eyes, he answered.

'Seoul is OK, but it is difficult to make money, and it is a city where you need money to live. If Pyongyang had the same resources it did in the sixties, seventies or early eighties, I would go back.'

I deeply appreciated his candour. He reinforced an idea that had been forming in my mind – that often, people do care about human rights but they care more about financial security and a strong economy. Economic opportunities allow people to bring bread or rice to the table to feed their family, and it is these prospects that prompt them to migrate from one place to another. This seemed to be his motivation for defecting to South Korea.

Communist ideology was appealing to the people of North Korea because of the economic success they experienced until the collapse of the Soviet Union. In the 1990s, many North Koreans then defected to the South where the economy was picking up quickly. However, in recent years an increasing number of defectors had been returning to the North. 'Send me back to the North,' one defector stated in a documentary of the same title made by Newstapa, an independent South Korean news agency. (Newstapa also reported that a North Korean defector organisation in South Korea misused a South Korean government subsidy while disseminating fake news about the North Korean government.) The key factors encouraging such defectors to return were a lack of income-generating opportunities in the South, discrimination against them as second-class citizens, and public suspicion of them.

Defectors Kim Ryon Hee and Kwon Chol Nam have publicly said they regret their decision to travel to the South to earn money, as reported in the *Guardian*.* Since being arrested in a dispute over wage discrimination with his boss, Kwon said his 'will to go back to the North has never changed. In the North, no one treated me like that. When I arrived [in South Korea] I was told I would be treated equally but that was bullshit.'

South Korea hosts about 30,000 North Korean defectors and about half of them report facing similar discrimination. Yet many fear speaking up publicly to raise awareness of their situation.

In the same week I met the North Korean defectors, I was invited to lunch with a Japanese-Korean man, who worked at NHK (Japan Broadcasting Corporation) in Seoul but regularly visited his family in Pyongyang. He spoke Korean with a Japanese accent and sometimes needed help with Korean words. We got on well from the start.

During lunch, he said that he liked my book because I was honest in describing Pyongyang just as it was and I was balanced in my presentation of facts, which was rare as few people were willing to analyse Pyongyang without politicising it.

Koreans use the term *Konanŭi haenggun* – the Arduous March – to refer to the period from mid-1994 to 1999 when famine plagued North Korea. The *Konanŭi haenggun* had a devastating impact on North Korea's economy. I remember in early 1994, before I left, there were people who used to approach the back door of the Haebangsan Hotel asking for food, and the hotel chef would give them some. This stuck in my mind as I had never seen it before. Until that point, the North Korean society

---

* '"Forever strangers": the North Korean defectors who want to go back', *Guardian*, 26 April 2018.

in which I grew up was modest in the supply of material goods but had enough resources to feed people.

The man said that when he visited family living in Pyongyang once *Konanŭi haenggun* was over, he saw improvements in the economy. Social change was also underway; his nephew was 'freely singing a South Korean song'. Private markets were permitted, giving women greater responsibility and the opportunity to earn their own money for their family – an important shift in gender roles in a patriarchal society such as Korea. Additionally, China supported the North Korean economy greatly, according to a Chinese friend who was working as a director of Bank of China in Seoul.

From the outside, these changes might seem small, but for North Korean society they represent a huge stride on the path towards opening up.

These phenomena also prompted a steady increase in the number of returning defectors. I could not help but compare the Korean situation to what I had seen while I was living in Madrid.

Madrid has the biggest Equatorial Guinean diaspora community – so big that in 2002, *El Pais* published an article with the title *Malabo queda al Sur de Madrid* ('Malabo is located in the South of Madrid').

When my father was president, the era was characterised by human rights violations and poverty that triggered a mass migration of Guineans to Spain. The regime of Teodoro Obiang, which replaced my father's, increased attacks both against civilians and against the Guinean diaspora abroad, particularly in Madrid. While I was there, I interviewed Guineans who had left the country to escape persecution and kidnappings and lived in

Madrid anonymously. One such interviewee was Daniel Mba Oyono, my father's former secretary, now a political dissident, who allowed me to name him in this book. He had gone into exile only to survive an assassination attempt, when he came face to face with his would-be killer in a Madrid restaurant. The assassin, who did not recognise Mba Oyono, sat at the same table and revealed his mission in conversation, not realising that he was talking to his target.

But following the discovery of oil in Guinea in 1995, the economy boomed. From 1997 to 2001, Guinea is said to have had the fastest-growing economy in the world. This led many Guineans in Spain and beyond to return to their country despite the worsening human rights issues.

According to organisations such as Human Rights Watch, both Equatorial Guinea and North Korea score very poorly in terms of human rights. And yet in both cases, when the economy started to pick up, expatriates returned home regardless. While for some people human rights are a key driver of migration, for others the ability to earn a living overrides everything else.

Part 3
Consolidation

In London, near Tower Bridge

London Calling

'Omission is the most powerful source of distortion'

Nick Davies

Promoting my book in Seoul, with all the interactions with new people that it entailed, was a rich experience. I made a lot of new friends in the South, and many were very similar in demeanour to my classmates and friends in the North. I fervently wished that one day I could introduce them to each other and we could spend a joyful day eating Korean barbecue and drinking *sochu* while singing 'Arirang'.* I even found the red bean buns of my Pyongyang past in a bakery in Dongdaemun market, Seoul.

In Seoul, the sensation of being back in my hometown once again washed over me as I looked back on the long journey I had undertaken. I was no longer that young girl who had run away when she met an American in Beijing for the first time, I was no longer the girl who left the Korean peninsula searching for her own

* The Korean peninsula's best-known folk song and unofficial unity national anthem.

identity, I was no longer the scared girl who confined herself to her room for months in Spain. I was now a woman with my own identity: I had published my memoirs, I spoke a number of languages and I had travelled the world. I had learned about who my father truly was from the people who knew him. Up to this point, I had avoided questions about my identity by using my Basque family name, Monica Dorronsoro, but now I had the confidence to say my full name publicly: Monica-Mening Macias-Bindang, the daughter of Francisco Macias and adoptive daughter of Kim Il Sung.

Multiple interview requests rained in following the publication of my diaries in Korean. After thinking carefully, I gave one interview in Korean, which received a good response from South Korean audiences. Following that success, I accepted another request, this time a radio interview for a world-renowned broadcaster in English. A few weeks later, when I heard the edited interview, I could not believe how the interviewer, Sarah, described me in her introduction. She claimed that I was 'struggling to condemn' – could not bring myself to condemn – the atrocities committed by my two fathers. In other words, she attributed my prudence and caution in casting judgement to my reluctance to condemn atrocities, even though I had explained that I was in the middle of investigating my father's presidency and was making my own independent effort to establish the facts. Once established, I would be the first to condemn atrocities – whoever is responsible – but I believe one must be one hundred per cent sure of the claim before making that condemnation. There I was, being interviewed on my story, ready to answer the questions, but it felt as if I was not heard; for this journalist, it seemed, the file had already been closed before I even walked in the door.

The irony was that, after the interview, I had asked Sarah and her producer, Philip, 'Winston Churchill, hero or villain?' Churchill was at the time the subject of fierce public debate, his status as heroic wartime leader coming under challenge from those who depicted him as a racist whose policies had directly contributed to the deaths of millions of Bengalis in the famine of 1943.* Without hesitation, Philip said 'Villain!' while Sarah said, 'Well…' unable to articulate a coherent answer. She too, it turned out, was reluctant to cast judgement.

This faith in unsubstantiated allegations, without consideration of the reliability of the sources of the information, is something I come across frequently when it comes to coverage of my father. It seems to be symptomatic of a wider problem in the age of the internet and 'fake news', when claims are recycled from site to site with little regard for the robustness of the original source, particularly when it comes to marginal and little scrutinised histories such as that of Equatorial Guinea. It is a tendency that is ever more present in the world's newsrooms, as news organisations reduce the numbers of journalists out in the field in favour of churning out content based on ever scanter sources from their offices, a phenomenon dubbed 'churnalism' and analysed by Nick Davies in his book, *Flat Earth News*:

> This is churnalism. This is journalists failing to perform the simple basic functions of their profession; quite unable to tell their readers the truth about what is happening on their patch. This is journalists who are no longer out

* See, for instance, 'Churchill's policies contributed to 1943 Bengal famine – study', *Guardian*, 29 March 2019.

> gathering news but who are reduced instead to passive processors of whatever material comes their way, churning out stories, whether real event or PR artifice, important or trivial, true or false ... This is the heart of modern journalism, the rapid repackaging of largely unchecked second-hand material, much of it designed to service the political or commercial interests of those who provide it ... Ignorance is the root of media failure. Most of the time, most journalists don't know what they are talking about ... They work in structures which positively prevent them discovering the truth ... It is endemic. The ethic of honesty has been overwhelmed by the mass production of ignorance. The whole story of media failure is complicated ... But the story begins with journalists who tell you the Earth is flat, because genuinely they think it might be.*

I came across a similar lack of rigour in academic circles. I was invited to a webinar presentation of a book, *Red Burdel*, by Juan Tomás Ávila Laurel, a Guinean author. I accepted the invitation gladly given the scant international support for Guinean authors. The panel consisted of academics from Hofstra University in New York, Harvard University, the University of Maroua in Cameroon and the University of Wuppertal in Germany.

The author was from Annobón, an island that is part of Guinea but whose people are of a distinct ethnicity. Before the author spoke, the panellists gave their own introductions to his book. I listened patiently, taking particular note of the scholar from Germany, who

* Nick Davies, *Flat Earth News* (London: Chatto & Windus, 2008), pp. 28, 59–60.

claimed energetically and adamantly that Macias had refused to send vaccines to Annobón in the 1970s when a pandemic hit the island.

During the Q&A, I wrote a question for the German scholar asking for proof of her claim. However, for some reason my question was passed over. I later contacted her privately to request the evidence. To my surprise, she politely responded:

I did not specifically mention (at least consciously ☺) the topic of vaccines. Rather, that in general the [Macias] government refused to offer aid to the island of Annobón during the epidemic of 1973 when the island requested it. I don't know the details, and I know more about testimonies than about 'proof'.

And she forwarded me some journal articles that again lacked verifiable evidence instead of sharing primary sources, such as, for instance, documents signed by Macias ordering the government not to send vaccines to Annobón.

In my reply, I thanked her for her honesty in acknowledging that she did not 'know the details'. I said I had thoroughly investigated and researched Macias and his rule, and my investigation revealed a different story.

The American scholar Randall Fegley has even claimed in his book *Equatorial Guinea: An African Tragedy* that my father was impotent and that I am not his daughter – without any proof of this claim and despite our clear physical resemblance.*

In South Korea, another scholar has claimed that the first, failed coup d'état against Macias was staged and planned by

* Randall Fegley, *Equatorial Guinea: An African Tragedy* (New York: Peter Lang, 1989).

Macias himself, again without any first-hand evidence to corroborate such claims.* It seems the practice of 'churnalism' has overtaken some scholars in the academic world, who are able to make dramatic assertions without reference to basic norms of verification. If the journalist's and the scholar's duty is to tell the truth, fact-checking is their tool to accomplish that duty.

I have long reflected on this phenomenon. Do these people know the pain of a mother who fears losing one or all of her children if she speaks out to correct the false narrative they lightly peddle? Have they been to Equatorial Guinea and spoken to people with different opinions to ascertain the facts of what happened in the Macias era?

Are they aware that, wherever there are asymmetric power dynamics, the victor's version of events is accepted as the truth, creating a warped narrative of historical events?

Do these people understand the heartbreaking pain of having brothers whose lives were nearly taken unjustly, solely because they are the sons of the former president? Do they understand the fear of having your brothers incarcerated several times, and at a moment's notice, in the brutal Black Beach jail – without the power to do anything to save them? Do they know or understand the fear of receiving a phone call in the middle of the night to tell you that your brothers have been assassinated?

Do these people understand African politics at all? Do they know that in politics, things happen behind the scenes and that what they see is merely the distorted shadow cast by real events? Is it acceptable that the powerful, white West so

---

* https://youtu.be/5ZnY4r-u0hY

frequently misrepresents and defames the weaker, non-white Global South?

I grew up in Pyongyang with a half-baked narrative about the West, especially when it came to the US. However, once I left Pyongyang, I decided not only to travel to but to live in the US, South Korea, Equatorial Guinea, Spain and the UK, and to interact with the people of those societies to better understand their culture and ways of thinking. Yet I do not dare to claim that my experience or knowledge obtained during that journey is the absolute truth. What I encountered was just a tiny part of the big and complex world, a fragment of the complicated stories of their societies. I have long wondered whether any nation has earned the moral authority to lecture others on human rights issues; I have found none. World history teaches us that bloodshed was an intrinsic part of the origin story of the dominant powers. Instead of joining resources to fight injustice where we find it, many seem to use human rights as a pretext to demonise their opponents.

In Madrid, back in the early 2000s, Don Antonio had urged me to study for a Master's degree related to international and African politics. I realised the time had come to back up my personal experiences with rigorous academic study in order to analyse the role of geopolitics, colonisation, decolonisation and international law in understanding my father and what happened in Guinea.

After considering various options, I finally decided to study in London because it was relatively close to Madrid and had some of the best tertiary education institutions in the world. London would be my next stop.

* * *

My first impressions of London were of its similarities to New York. It is a big city with a diverse culture, which I loved. I did not feel different from the other inhabitants. Growing up in Pyongyang, I had always been noticeably different, despite my efforts to blend in. But in London, like in New York, I felt marvellously inconspicuous. As I walked down the street, I heard many languages, including Arabic, Korean and Chinese, as well as a range of English accents. This experience is so rich and nourishing; it enables us to appreciate what is distinctive and special about our identities and cultures. But many people take it for granted until they arrive in places like Korea, where the culture is more homogeneous.

While Londoners possess a strong individualistic mindset, much like I observed in New York, it also seemed that the British took politeness to the next level. Customer service was excellent (by stark contrast to what I had experienced in other cities), and in social exchanges, people seldom asked me where I was from, which helped to eliminate divisions between immigrants and locals. Regardless of your ethnic appearance, if you were

Outside the Houses of Parliament

born and raised in the UK, you were considered British. In the job applications I completed, an applicant could identify as 'Black British'. That might not strike native inhabitants as unusual, but it was both revolutionary and pleasing to me; I had never seen this on Spanish job application forms. I also observed diverse people in important positions in society, serving as police, lawyers, politicians or professors. It seemed you could succeed in London no matter your origins. I came to learn that there was a long history of black representation in Parliament. Of course, behind these achievements there had been a long, hard struggle against racism, for dignity and for human rights for black, brown and yellow people.

During my time in Spain, it was very rare to see the second generation of immigrants, who had been born in Spain and had the same upbringing as their white fellow Spaniards, in important roles. There was no Spanish Diane Abbott in parliament representing the interests of the black community in Spain. Even if a person was born and

My nieces Cristina, Fatima and Isabel (left to right)

raised in Spain, like my lovely nieces Cristina and Isabel, Spaniards would consider them Guinean, and would say something like, 'Ah, not that kind of Spanish'. They would imply that the second or third generation of immigrants born in Spain were not 'real' Spaniards, drawing a line between them and white natives and treating them as second-class citizens. If you told them you were Spanish, they would usually insist on knowing your ancestry or country of origin.

As I made my way around London, observing this majestic city where modern architecture grafts onto old, I could see the expression of wealth and power. The evidence of one of the most powerful empires in world history is embedded in each historical monument, and in buildings such as the British Museum. And yet I could not help but think about how the wealth and power had been acquired: through colonisation.

London, my new home. It seemed a fitting place for me to investigate the fundamental role of colonialism – in my father's story, in my own unusual identity, and in tearing my family apart.

Anguish

My first impressions of London were broadly positive, but my first experience of working in the city revealed its darker underbelly, where racism, classism and discrimination were still rife, where bullying of the weak and vulnerable occurred. I managed to find a job as a room attendant at a hotel on Park Lane. This was a job that attracted many new immigrants to the UK as their first opportunity, opening the door to other work. It was physically demanding, but I thought it was a great chance to learn about society from a working-class level.

This job is one of the most undervalued there is. Too often, the arduous work done by amazing, strong women is dismissed and patronised, as I found out. I serviced eleven rooms, spending forty-five minutes on each, which filled my day from eight a.m. to four p.m.. You had to move fast if you wanted to finish on time and go home, but my supervisor Doloris was a hard taskmaster and would often force me to reclean rooms I had already finished over again. I wrote a letter complaining about it to the housekeeping manager, Eliana.

She said, 'Monica. You didn't write this letter but you presented it as your own.'

'No, I wrote it,' I replied.

'No, this letter was written by someone with a high-level education. The letter is well structured and coherent. It is not written by someone who works as a room attendant.'

'You are judging a book by its cover.'

It was true that I had not listed all my education on my CV when I applied because I did not want to appear overqualified, so she was not wrong to think that I had not completed any higher education. But instead of addressing my complaint, Eliana dismissed it, and Doloris continued to give me a hard time, so I took the issue to the next level. I wrote another letter, complaining this time about both Doloris and Eliana, and sent it to the director of Human Resources. This infuriated Eliana, who from that moment started to make my life miserable – as did Doloris. I felt frustrated and alone in this struggle. My co-workers – who also complained about Doloris and Eliana behind their backs – did nothing to support me when I tried to stand up for myself. I was getting more stressed and depressed; my hair started to fall out. The hotel became an unpleasant place to be. I was constantly wondering what they would come up with next. Because nothing was changing, I wrote to the general manager and I also went to see a solicitor in the union representing hotel employees.

The solicitor said, 'Rule number one: do not mess with your managers because they always win. Rule two: you are black and an immigrant. Unless you have a watertight case, nothing is going to change. A remote possibility would be if you have the support of all your colleagues – as many as possible – who have gone through a similar unfair experience and are willing to speak up.'

In the end, the legal advice came down to: 'Just try to be nice to her if you want to survive. Don't fight a battle that you cannot win.'

I left the office more frustrated than before. It felt as if the solicitor had poured a bucket of cold water on me. *What are unions for if they do not defend employees? What must happen to change this horrible situation, which is slowly consuming me like a cancer?* I became more and more depressed. It seriously affected my work, health and quality of life. I could not sleep and sometimes I could not breathe properly from the anxiety of it all. My skin colour and origins determined my social status – and whether I could win a legal case or not. My colleagues were also filled with fear, expressing their true feelings in private but not daring to take action, especially after what they saw happening to me.

Bullying is a serious human rights issue that entails mental and physical harm to an individual where the perpetrator holds the real or perceived power. I wondered who would defend my human rights and where were they when I needed them most.

Despite the situation, I had to continue to work at the hotel while I figured out what to do to overcome it.

One evening, my mother rang and asked me to visit. I flew to Madrid to see her. Sitting together in her living room, our conversation alighted again, as it often did, on the unresolved and complicated nature of our relationship.

'Mama, all I needed back then was you,' I said. 'I missed you so much. You suddenly disappeared from my life and when you came back to visit us the first time, you said I didn't want to speak Spanish on purpose.'

She took it the wrong way and the discussion started to become heated.

'You hate me because you think I abandoned you.'

'No, Mama. That's not true!' I was adamant that I needed to prove my point. I forgot that she suffered from high blood pressure.

'You wouldn't understand me because you are not a mother. You don't understand the pain of a mother leaving her own children behind to save another one in danger. I had to leave you with Kim Il Sung because it was your father's will. Pyongyang was the safest place for all of you and I couldn't risk losing you. Teo was alone and in danger. I had to make a rational decision. And it wasn't an easy decision to make.'

'Mama, I understand all that now, but I want you to see it from my perspective as well.'

Since we were not getting anywhere, I decided to go to sleep at my friend Amelie's place to calm down.

'Mama, I will spend the night at my friend's place. And tomorrow I fly back to London.'

'No, no, no. Please, please, daughter, don't leave me alone. Please, please,' she begged with tears in her eyes, but I left anyway, slamming the door on my way out.

A few weeks later, as I was on the number 36 bus home after a very hard day at work, my phone pinged.

'Aunty, Grandma is not OK.' It was a message from my niece Fatima, my sister Maribel's oldest daughter. She had been living with my mother in Madrid since she left Malabo in 1998.

'You know Grandma sometimes exaggerates things, looking for attention. Just hug her and she will calm down,' I replied.

'No, Aunty, this time it's serious. I was at my boyfriend's when she called me asking when I was going to come back. She said she was feeling unwell. And suddenly her voice was gone. I rushed home and when I arrived, there were police and an ambulance already there. Apparently, before calling me, Grandma knocked on the neighbour's door for help. They came back to check on her but she wouldn't open the door. So they called the police. They broke the door down and found her on the floor, unconscious. Then they called the ambulance and took her to the hospital. She is in a coma now.'

The bus continued on its way, but I was stunned, utterly at a loss, rolling along through the streets of London, so very far away from Madrid.

My god! What I am going to do? I yelled inwardly.

My last conversation with my mum had been an argument.

An image of her with tears in her eyes was lodged in my mind and I could not help feeling guilty. *I should have stayed. I should have at least tried to put myself in her shoes, not insisted on asking her to see things from my perspective. I feel horrible! I provoked this situation. My sister always warned me to be careful with her because she has been suffering from high blood pressure for so long and arguments could have fatal consequences. But I was so adamant, I forgot my sister's warnings.*

I booked a flight to Madrid early the next morning and asked Fernando to pick me up at the airport. He immediately agreed. 'We are friends. I will be there for you.'

I could not sleep the whole night.

* * *

As I came out of arrivals, I ran to Fernando. For a long moment, we embraced.

'I am afraid, Fernando. I don't know what to do,' I whispered in his ear, my voice breaking.

'Try to stay calm. Let's get to the car.'

'It's my fault that she is in a coma.'

'How do you mean?'

'Do you remember a few weeks ago I came to see her?'

'Yes.'

'We had a huge row.' As I spoke, I tried to dry my eyes.

'Honestly, I don't think you provoked the situation. The argument happened a few weeks before,' said Fernando as we drove to the Hospital de la Princesa in the centre of Madrid. 'I understand your pain. I know what it feels like to lose a parent. My father passed away a couple of years ago. Don't blame yourself – you did not cause her stroke. She has been ill for a very long time.'

We arrived at the hospital, but visiting hours didn't start until five p.m. and it was still early. We decided to have lunch, and I began receiving calls from concerned friends – first Amelie, who said she would come to the hospital after work, and then Don Antonio, who insisted I go to his place in Somosaguas after lunch.

When I got there, Don Antonio eased himself to standing and said, 'Come here!' as he threw open his arms.

'Cry, cry and let it all out!' He hugged me for a long minute. 'I will go to the hospital with you. Have your brothers arrived in Madrid?'

'Not yet. Teo and Fran are trying to get a flight from Malabo to Madrid. Maribel is arriving tonight from Germany.'

'I do not have to remind you that my home is your home!' he exclaimed.

I smiled and said, 'I know! Thank you.'

As visiting hours approached, we took a taxi to the hospital, where we arrived to find Fernando waiting for us. I introduced him to Don Antonio and they shook hands. We took the lift to the intensive care unit where my mother was.

My angst had been soothed by the warmth of Don Antonio, Fernando and Amelie, and by encouraging messages from friends around the world – South Korea, the US, UK, other parts of Spain and Equatorial Guinea, and Syrian friends living in the UEA, Jordan and China. But as the lift ascended, my heart started to pound.

'Don't be afraid. I am here with you,' murmured Don Antonio, holding my hand. As the lift doors opened, I saw visitors of different races and nationalities from Spain's former colonies gathered in the waiting area. As a rule, the black folk were wailing while the white people sobbed. The anguish made me feel worse, because I was already overwhelmed by emotion. Only the doctors and nurses were composed.

Two big doors swung open and a nurse came out. As she called patients' names, relatives entered. When it was our turn, I walked in cautiously, Don Antonio leaning on me while keeping my hand firmly in his.

As we proceeded down the corridor, doctors and nurses running past, a doctor approached us holding some papers.

'Hello, you are here to visit Mrs Macias, right?'

'Yes, that is her mother,' said Don Antonio. 'Where is she?'

'Can you follow me, please?'

The doctor led us to a small room with a desk and asked us to take a seat.

'Tell us, doctor, how is she? Tell us the situation as it is,' said Don Antonio as he lowered himself into a chair.

'She is in a very bad way. Her organs are very damaged.'

'How long?' I blurted out, my eyes filling with tears.

'We think about a month,' the doctor said gravely. Then she led us to my mother, who was lying unconscious on a hospital bed.

She was alone in the room. Tubes ran into her mouth and hand, and she looked puffy. It was heartbreaking to see her in that state. I burst into tears.

'Talk to her,' said Don Antonio. 'She can hear us and might respond to your voice.'

'Mama, forgive me. I am very sorry for being such a difficult child.'

'Very good. Keep talking to her.'

But it felt like something in my throat was blocking my breathing; I could only weep.

Don Antonio interjected, 'I have vivid memories of her. On one of my visits to Guinea, she was wearing a long white dress for a banquet. She was so elegant and beautiful.'

Don Antonio stayed for about an hour. The news that my mother was in a coma had already reached the Guinean community in Spain, and Guineans began to arrive. Daniel Mba Oyono, with whom I had spoken about my father's presidency some years earlier, was one of them. Fernando stayed with me until Amelie arrived, and she and I went in to see my mother.

'Hi Monica, I am Amelie, your daughter's friend,' she said, addressing my mother.

Amelie is a sweet person who has always been there for me. But I was surprised by her forthrightness in addressing my mother's silent form directly.

'Speak to her, Monique,' said Amelie, using her preferred form of my name. 'Don't cry. She can feel and hear us.'

'Mama, I love you!'

As I said it, Mama moved the fingers of her right hand.

'She moved her fingers!'

'No, it's your mind playing tricks on you,' said a doctor who came in response to my cry. 'She can't move.'

After a week in Madrid, I had to come back to London and return to work at the hotel. Teo stayed in Madrid with Mum. Although physically I was in London, my mind and heart were in the hospital with my mother. I found it difficult to concentrate; I suffered from insomnia worse than ever and felt emotionally very fragile. Everything was happening at the same time: the bullying at work and my mum's illness.

My sister insisted I attend counselling sessions. I was reluctant because I did not really believe counselling had value. I always thought that I was strong enough to overcome all the difficulties that life had presented me with; that life itself was the best teacher and I the star pupil. For me, the best therapy was sharing my experiences with the friends who knew me best, not a psychotherapy professional who did not know me at all. Besides, I grew up in a society where counselling as such did not exist – apart from the psychiatrists and psychologists at the psychiatric hospital in Pyongyang known as number 49 hospital, where my sister had done a rotation during her medical studies at Pyongyang Medical University.

Maribel persuaded me by explaining that a professional could help me to address my problems at their root: the trauma I had experienced as a young girl and carried throughout my life. She said that my painful relationship with our mother and the guilt I felt over our heated last exchange would inevitably be contributing factors to the problems I was facing – my difficulty in concentrating and the insomnia.

It was as if Dr Maribel had emerged to treat patient Monica. I was hesitant, but in the end, I followed her advice and began counselling.

I cried the entire first session. I had never cried like that before; tears fell like a waterfall, leaving me short of breath. It was as if I had a wellspring inside of me and the counsellor had turned on the tap.

A few sessions later, I felt better. It was not that all my pain disappeared with counselling; that pain will be with me for ever. Instead, what I learned was to understand, to be aware of the pain and the emotion, and not to ignore them. I also learned to forgive and make peace. Anger is not a good feeling, especially when we do not know when the person at whom the anger is directed will depart this life.

I also acknowledged that I was not the emotionally strongest person on Earth as I had believed, but that we were all vulnerable in the face of life's difficulties. The therapy helped me to appreciate how not dealing with our emotions or traumas could not only negatively impact quality of life but could ultimately result in serious consequences: debilitating depression or even suicide.

The Funeral

At eight p.m. on 28 February 2017, after six weeks in a coma, my mother passed away in Madrid's Hospital de la Princesa. I had officially and definitively lost both my parents.

My mother always wanted to be buried in Mongomo, my father's hometown in Equatorial Guinea. My sister and I flew to Malabo and, after completing the paperwork, Teo and Fran followed a day later with my mother's coffin.

I was flooded with contradictory emotions, too many to hope to process. We had had a very complicated mother–daughter relationship. We shared the same goal: love and reconciliation with what life had offered us. But our standpoints were poles apart. I guess there were many factors in this: cultural, generational, personality type, not to mention the enforced break of several years in our relationship as I was growing up.

The wake took place at Fran's house in Malabo. I was expecting a quiet, intimate family affair. But it seemed that this was not allowed in Equatorial Guinea. In the tiny country where news spread like wildfire, everyone seemed to know my mother had passed away and there was a crowd waiting to view her body. The whole of Malabo, including, to my surprise, representatives of the incumbent government – still led by Obiang – came to pay their respects.

'My condolences!' they said, as they approached the four of us.

'Thank you,' I said, attempting to paste a smile on my face. After about two hours standing in line to receive all of these people, I found a space among others on a sofa in Fran's large house. Most of the conversation was about my mother and, somewhat surprisingly to me, harsh complaints about the state of Equatorial Guinea.

'She was a great woman and the best first lady that this country has ever had. I mean, just compare her with the current first lady, who has stolen all the country's oil wealth,' said one woman.

'There is no comparison!' rejoined another. 'Monica carried her status with dignity. We all know who the real *chorizos*[*] are in this country: the incumbent president and his family. They think this country is their backyard – they think every business and all the land belongs to them.' And a third jumped in. 'They're not only *chorizos*, they are assassins. The people are starting to wake up and they are losing their fear. The other day there was a protest against the social problems; it is small but it is a start.'

Their chatter reminded me of an incident I had been told about that took place in Malabo in broad daylight. According to Amal, a Guinean I knew living abroad, a driver had gone through a red traffic light and failed to obey orders from traffic police to stop. The traffic police proceeded to shoot and kill the driver. The incident triggered protests on the streets and vocal demands for justice – but the driver's family received none.

---

* Spanish slang for thieves.

The conversation meandered on along the same lines. A fifth voice addressed me: 'You must be proud of having such a brave, strong woman as your mother.' I could only nod my head. I did not have the strength to speak. 'All these people are here not only for your mother but also your father,' they went on.

When the coffin arrived at Fran's house, a choir began to sing and dance.

I wondered what on earth was happening, and went to ask my sister.

'Why are these people singing and dancing? They came to express their condolences, but they seem happy that Mama is dead! The words of the song are "joy, joy, joy"! I don't get it!'

'No, they are not happy because Mama is dead. In Guinean culture, when someone dies, they sing and dance during the wake and funeral. The idea is to let the late person's spirit go with joy and good wishes. It's not like the solemn Korean funerals that we're familiar with. Why don't you go upstairs and have a rest? Teo, Fran and I will attend to people.'

I obeyed and went to my room, where I fell onto the bed. I tried to sleep, but I couldn't. I was so tired, but I couldn't stop thinking about Mama.

This was the woman who had refused the safety and comfort of the life that Kim Il Sung had offered her in the 1980s, and went back to the peril of Equatorial Guinea to protect my adolescent brother Teo.

This was the woman who went through the humiliating process of *akus* while mourning her husband.

This was the woman who had started over from scratch,

selling fried plantain in the streets to survive and using the money she earned to visit us in Pyongyang.

This was the woman who had survived a physical attack in the streets from my father's enemies in Malabo in the aftermath of the coup d'état.

This was the woman who had cooked and delivered meals to my brothers every time they were incarcerated unjustly in Black Beach jail under inhuman conditions.

This was the woman who had remained silent and ignored public opinion in order to protect her children's lives.

This was the woman who carried her legacy as Equatorial Guinea's first lady with dignity.

I love you, Mama! Thank you for giving me life. I am proud to be your daughter! Why did you have to die for me to say this? Why didn't I say it while you were alive?

I spent the night thinking of her, accompanied by the singing of the choir in the courtyard. I took a photograph of the choir to remember that day. In the early morning, at about six a.m., we flew to Mongomo with the coffin for the funeral. At my father's house there was another wake. Again, it attracted crowds, again the city authorities came to express their condolences, and again there was singing and dancing. I gathered my strength and stood in front of the crowd. I thanked the crowds in Fang: '*Akiba*!' Then I continued in Spanish.

'Thank you all for coming to my mother's funeral.' Applause erupted, giving me a few moments to try to quell my tears.

'I am very sorry that I cannot speak Fang yet.'

A voice cried out, 'It doesn't matter. We love you, daughter!'

'My mother loved our country and its people. You have

showed us that her love was reciprocated. My brothers and sister and I thank you again! Please enjoy the food we offer you.'

Traditional funeral rites for my mother in Malabo

My mother's wake in Mongomo

SOAS

'In politics, what is not being said is often more important than what is being said.'

Dan Plesch, former director of the Centre for International Studies and Diplomacy, SOAS

I finally resigned from my hotel job as the start date of my Master's course approached. Over the summer, I was required to take a pre-sessional course to improve my academic English and introduce me to the British academic system. I was looking forward to it, despite my generally low spirits.

On 31 July 2017, I woke up at five a.m. as usual, eager to begin my studies, and took the bus to the main campus of SOAS in Russell Square. The school is located in the heart of Bloomsbury, a block away from the British Museum. It is a leading institution for the study of the Global South, particularly Asia, Africa and the Middle East. Ironically, SOAS was established by the British Empire to provide training to its colonial administrators in the indigenous languages of the colonies. The campus includes four main buildings: the Philips Building, also known as Main building, Brunei Gallery, Faber Building and Senate House.

I was the first to arrive in the classroom. About twenty minutes later, other students started to enter the room along with our teacher. Most of the students in our class were Chinese. There was also one student from Japan, one from Italy and one from Turkey. I wondered how we would all cope with studying in another language and culture; I was determined to withstand the academic culture shock and not drop out of the course.

'Hello, everyone.' Our lecturer introduced himself, saying he would be our teacher for the eight-week course. He explained that the course would familiarise us with the British system of higher education ahead of the academic year that would start in September. Also, we would learn how to write an essay in English, its structure and rhetoric, and how to analyse texts. He then strongly encouraged us to read the reading materials. After a short introduction of each student, we got into the subject of the day.

Later on, at home, I reflected on my impressions of the first class. Unlike the academic culture in North Korea, the teaching style promoted critical thinking and evaluation, and academic freedom with a strong individualistic identity. The relationship between the lecturer and students was much more equal and there seemed to be a student-centred pedagogy.

By contrast, in North Korea, my classmates and I had been taught to respect the lecturer as he or she is considered to be the authority in the classroom, which created more distance and esteem. We also tended to put our learning responsibility on our teachers – we expected instruction from them – thereby creating a teacher-centred approach to learning, which was also significantly informed by a collectivist world-view.

I found these cultural differences very important. The culture shock I experienced in my new class could impact the outcome of my learning. Culture shock begins with a 'honeymoon' period followed by an 'argh' or frustration period, then

With my friend and collaborator Becky Branford, whose family I got to know during my time at SOAS

an 'adjust' period and finally an 'acceptance' period. The honeymoon period is incredibly positive: meeting new people, making new friends and sharing experiences. Then, the 'argh' period surfaces when language barriers, misunderstandings and miscommunications take over. This is the most difficult period, which can last a long time depending on the individual. However, after a somewhat stressful period you can see a light at the end of the tunnel triggered by the adjustment period. This is when you start to understand and feel familiar with your new environment.

You have successfully overcome the emotional struggle and now you are set to enter into the acceptance period, where you realise that we are just different in the way we do things and no one way is better than another: you accept our idiosyncrasies and move on.

There were students who had not been able to get past the 'argh' period and dropped out of their programmes. But I was determined to overcome all those academic cultural shocks.

Since I had been resident in London for three years, I was eligible to apply for a student loan, which covered a significant part of my postgraduate course fees. However, there was a balance left over that I had to pay myself. Having been awarded the student loan and completed the summer course, on 25 September 2017, I officially started my Master's degree in International Studies and Diplomacy at SOAS. I was very excited, but at the same time still worried about whether I could make it. My first degree was in a completely different discipline, textiles and fashion, and besides, I was coming back to rigorous academic study after more than twenty years of being out in the world of work. Furthermore, I was challenging myself to do it in my third language. The excitement and fear grew simultaneously.

My thoughts flipped back and forth between the two. *Am I going to be able to do this? All my classmates are young. Their brains are still young. Besides, most of them are native speakers, with only a few who speak English as a second language. I can do it. No matter how hard, I will manage and learn a lot. Besides, age is not a problem, but an excuse. Look at Don Antonio, he is almost ninety and he has more lucidity and quicker wits than many young people. It seems his brain doesn't match his age and he is still a practising lawyer. So, I can do it!*

On the morning of the first lecture for my Foundation of International Law module, I sat at the desk closest to the lecturer's desk, as I did not want to miss a single word. I didn't really know any of the handfuls of other students already seated at their desks since we had only met briefly at the orientation lecture.

I had chosen modules that were relevant to my objective, which was to use the Master's course to gain a deeper understanding of the political context of my father's leadership and assassination – and therefore of my own story – and secondly, to analyse my personal experiences in an academic context. I would study modules including Foundation of International Law, General Diplomatic Studies, General Diplomatic Practice, International Relations 1, International Relations 2, The History and Future of the UN, and Government and Politics in Africa, alongside a written dissertation.

Our law lecturer introduced herself as Catriona Drew. In a friendly and somewhat light-hearted tone, she said that she was going to teach us how to talk and understand law, so that when we read about international affairs in the news, we would understand what was going on.

Having been educated in North Korea, where we were expected to treat teachers as an unassailable authority in the classroom, it was hard for me to adjust to engaging with my teachers as peers or in an informal manner. SOAS practised student-led pedagogy, which would have been unheard of in Pyongyang. Catriona was very friendly and to the point, and skilled at creating a relaxed atmosphere in her class. She had the ability to explain complicated legal terminology and jurisprudence in simple plain English, including funny empirical examples that lodged in your brain as anecdotes. One time as we chatted after class, she said she admired some of the foreign students in the class who decided to take the law module, as she didn't feel she would be able to take a law module in Korean or Chinese.

Afterwards, at about six p.m., I headed over to the Wolfson lecture theatre in Senate House to attend my first lecture in International Relations. I was very much looking forward to it. Facing the lecturer's podium, there was one long, semi-circular desk, and along the side of the hall, stepped bleachers that reminded me of a Roman amphitheatre.

A man entered the room and walked towards the lecturer's desk. He had a kind face with large blue eyes, pale skin and collar-length light brown hair.

He checked the monitors on his desk and, with a smile for the assembled students, began to speak, introducing himself as Dr Hanns Kendel and then opening the floor for a young Middle Eastern-looking man, Omid Nouri. Omid was a teaching fellow and our tutor for International Relations, and every other week, he would lead a seminar on the topics raised in Dr Kendel's lectures.

To my great surprise, this, my first lecture in International Relations 1: Foundations of World Politics, was about North Korea in international relations. *Well, here we go. Yet again, the North Koreans will be depicted as the bad guys and Westerners as the good guys! Now he will start off by skinning North Korea, like most people in the West. A shallow analysis. How boring is this going to be?!* Disillusioned, I closed my notebook and glanced at my watch, wondering how long the lecture would take.

Dr Kendel was showing a PowerPoint presentation on one of the large screens behind the podium, featuring the typical images that outsiders use when they talk about North Korea. Then he proceeded to explain the so-called 'Western' perspective on North Korea, but always detached himself from the narrative. He would preface remarks by saying 'According to the mainstream media...' or make it clear that he was paraphrasing the media's opinions. He spent about twenty minutes speaking in this way, and then he said, 'Now, I want you to listen to another perspective.'

As soon as I heard the words 'another perspective' I felt myself become instantly alert and engaged. This time the perspective was from within Pyongyang. He used the same tactic: he detached himself from the narrative, offered no personal opinion, and spent another twenty minutes explaining matters from the North Korean side. Then he posed a challenge to the class that I never thought I would hear from a Westerner. He wanted us to go away and reflect on the evening's lecture, giving critical consideration to whether North Korea's behaviour was irrational or rational. Clearly, he was encouraging students to think for themselves and analyse events from all perspectives.

Wow! This is it! I said to myself.

This analytical challenge meant a lot to me. It embedded what I had been doing and saying ever since I left Pyongyang, particularly in discussions with Westerners. Yet few people were capable of understanding my motivations. Most would say I was a communist as a consequence of growing up in North Korea, but that was not the case. In order to be a communist, a socialist, a conservative or a supporter of any other ideology, one must understand, believe in and agree with the ideology in question. Furthermore, precisely because I had experienced a communist society first hand, in my mind communism is a utopian ideology. My connection to the society I grew up in is partly emotional, but I do have the capacity for dispassionate logical analysis. The moment that emotion interferes with analysis, the analysis can become sloppy. But what Dr Kendel was doing made so much sense to me – subtracting emotions and opinions in order to look at a bilateral relationship from many sides.

I loved this methodology and I loved this learning environment. I recalled a seminar about North Korea that I had been invited to attend a couple of months earlier at the University of West Bohemia in Pilsen, Czech Republic. I was on the panel with, among others, a British man who introduced himself as a former diplomat. My expectations had been high. He began his speech by saying 'I don't like North Korea…' I was profoundly disappointed by this unashamed confession of his pre-existing bias and lack of critical analysis.

Then, during the Q&A, a young Czech student asked if the diplomat thought he could only see the Western point of view, and said that North Korea might not see the world from that perspective, although she was not defending its actions.

How brilliant, I thought. How intelligent is this young woman! She is able to question things and analyse critically. I approached the student after the panel, and we had an in-depth conversation.

Now, there I was in my first International Relations lecture as our professor used the same methodology to encourage students to think critically. I knew I had made a good choice to study there. I felt I had a place at SOAS!

I finished writing my Master's thesis on 28 September 2019, and the only things left to do were inserting a cover page, numbering the pages, creating a table of contents and proofreading it again. I went to bed quite confident, thinking nearly everything was done and that I was very happy with the thesis. The next morning, I sat down in front of my very old MacBook Pro laptop and turned it on. I was excited; in completing my MA, I had achieved one of my lifetime ambitions. I proofread calmly, then inserted page numbers. I created a cover page with the title: 'Can subaltern* leaders be heard and taken seriously?' followed by my name and the word count.

I found a fancy cover template that allowed me to insert the SOAS logo. It looked very nice. I saved and scrolled down to see the overall look. Then it happened!

Starting from page one, all the letters had become numbers – a string of 1s! I started panicking. My mind went blank. I did not know what to do. I had only one day to submit the thesis. I

* In Postcolonial and International studies, the term 'subaltern' refers to people or populations of lower social rank and/or from the Global South whose voices and actions are ignored, misappropriated or rendered inoperative.

had to rewrite the work of my life from the beginning, recalling everything, in twenty-four hours. It felt like an impossible mission. I wanted to cry and scream, but there was no time. I must not fail.

I started to write the abstract again from memory.

Abstract

Traditionally, the study of subaltern leaders has meant analysis through the lens of the powerful while ignoring their version of historical events. My research has shown that power influences the creation of stereotypes and the incomplete narratives that enjoy the status of the only truth. Having been born as a daughter of Francisco Macias, a subaltern leader, and drawing on personal empirical stories, I ask: Can subaltern leaders be heard and taken seriously? In this paper I am aiming to demonstrate that when the political social climate is characterised by an asymmetric power dynamic, it is the narratives of the powerful that prevail. Michel Foucault's power-knowledge and 'The Order of Discourse' in conjunction with *Orientalism* by Edward Said set the theories to examine these phenomena while exhaustive interviews were carried out with certain limitations. The result shows that power does have an impact on narratives and political discourse. On this basis, it is recommended that Western scholars and institutions analyse subaltern leaders thoroughly, objectively and individually rather than collectively as one category of dictators while rejecting single narratives.

I spent the whole night rewriting the thesis.

* * *

On 30 September 1979, my father was assassinated by his enemies. On the same day forty years later, after three years of challenging and illuminating study in London, I submitted my Master's thesis. Drawing on political theory, research in Madrid's archives, investigation on the ground in Equatorial Guinea and personal testimony from those who were there, I proposed that my father was not guilty of the heinous crimes of which he was accused: of mass murder; the orchestration of massacres, including at Black Beach jail; arbitrary detention and torture; forced labour; deliberate burning of villages; and embezzlement of public funds; among other charges. Instead, I argued that he was the victim of powerful enemies who elaborated a meticulous plan to eliminate him from the Guinean political scene. I had spent half my life investigating him and finally had come to London to pursue an MA to prove it academically.

A few months later, I officially completed my MA. I had learned about international relations and African politics, colonisation, diplomacy, international law and the history of the UN – all relevant to understanding what happened in Equatorial Guinea during my father's mandate.

Having spent my early childhood living under the conditions of decolonisation, my adolescence in the shadow of the Cold War and my adulthood in the post-Cold War period, the process of writing my thesis gave me an opportunity to examine how those historical forces affected my life in particular, while also enabling me to put them in an academic context.

During almost two hundred years of colonial rule in Equatorial Guinea, from 1777 to 1968, Spain implemented apartheid and systematically decimated Guinea of its people,

Francisco Macias alongside Spanish officials at the signing of Equatorial Guinea's declaration of independence, October 1968

wealth and religion for its own benefit. But, as I learned and documented, its attempts to intervene did not cease when my father signed the independence agreement for Guinea on 12 October 1968. When the Francoist Spanish government of that era realised that the legitimately and democratically elected new leader of its only colony in sub-Saharan Africa would not be its puppet, it turned vindictive. Spain withdrew overnight, leaving behind a political vacuum in the country which resulted in a Hobbesian state of nature, which my father's enemies turned to their own advantage and used as a weapon against him. Guinea's new currency could only be exchanged for Spanish pesetas, so Spain still held the purse strings. As relations worsened, Spain slammed the door in the face of our fledgling nation, withholding finance and obstructing imports. This campaign of strangulation led to the country's ruin, and Macias's advisers urged him to seek support elsewhere. The communist nations were in the neighbourhood, courting newly independent African nations. Russia and China were offering alternative assistance, as was North Korea, which had enjoyed an industrial and economic resurgence from the ashes of its pulverisation in the Korean War. Flushed with success, motivated by rivalry with its southern counterpart, North Korea was on a drive to restore diplomatic relations with countries outside the communist bloc. They were reaching out to my father with a lifeline, and he grasped it with both hands.

I also learned that there was a pattern of elimination of African nationalist leaders by their former colonial masters in the aftermath of decolonisation – the assassinations of Thomas Sankara in Burkina Faso and Patrice Lumumba in the Republic of the Congo being two examples.

My schoolfriends Montan and Herve Kerekou told me that France had tried several times to assassinate their father, Mathieu Kerekou, the former president of Benin.

'In 1977, France sent Bob Denard, the famous mercenary known for his "jobs" on behalf of the French government in FrancAfrique [France's former colonies in Africa] to kill my father. He orchestrated the failed Operation Shrimp. My father survived all those assassination attempts,' said Montan.

Herve, who after graduating from Kim Il Sung Military University in Pyongyang had served in the intelligence service of Benin's Republican Guard during his father's second term of office, continued the story, explaining the famous failed Operation Shrimp in more detail: 'It was seven a.m. on 16 January 1977 when Bob Denard and his henchmen landed at the international airport in Cotonou, Benin's second city.

Without an invitation, of course. When they landed, they took control of the airport. They managed to approach the presidential palace and started shooting, only to find themselves meeting the resistance of the presidential guards. The huge surprise to Denard was that Papa had contracted North Korean commanders to train our presidential guards and expand them into a full battalion. You know how serious North Koreans are! They were not shy at all in responding to the attack, along with their Beninese trainees. The mercenaries failed in their mission to kill Papa and rushed to escape, leaving behind all their documentation, which included receipts and details of the planning of the operation, and thus proof of who supported and endorsed the coup d'état. Denard confessed that he was acting on behalf of the French government to kill Papa. Maurice Delauney, a French ambassador to a country in Africa, corroborated Denard's confession, saying that President Valéry Giscard d'Estaing had approved Denard's plan.'

It was under these circumstances that my father decided to send us to study in North Korea, under Kim Il Sung's care. For me, decolonisation meant being torn from my roots, culture and family in early childhood and growing up in a continent far from that of my birth. I became an African-European and an Asian, a Korean soul who embraced all three cultures.

What if colonisation had happened the other way round? If the peoples of Africa, Asia and the Americas were the colonisers, and Europe the colonised? I believe a similar pattern would have emerged, whereby the colonisers acquired as much power as possible in order to control the subordinate parties. It is ultimately a relationship of power, regardless of skin colour.

Decolonisation coincided with the Cold War, which ended with the dissolution of the USSR and the Warsaw Pact in 1991, just as I was coming of age. This period deeply influenced my world-view, particularly in creating a skewed picture of the US and South Korea. Cold War thinking even infiltrated the American and Soviet films I used to watch as a teenager in Pyongyang, like the *Rocky* series, which tells the story of Rocky Balboa's rags-to-riches pursuit of the American dream. In *Rocky IV*, his rival is a Soviet Russian boxer, Ivan Vasilyevich Drago, a robotic character who lacks the ability to smile. In the Soviet films I saw, meanwhile, Americans were depicted as the stupidest human beings on earth; many ended up captivated by the beauty and intelligence of Soviet women.

In November 1989, when the Berlin Wall came down, I became an adult of the post-Cold War period, and embarked on my long journey towards understanding and intellectual and mental freedom.

After submitting my thesis and gaining my Master's, my sense of achievement was underscored when I received recognition from an expert scholar with particular knowledge of Equatorial Guinea.

Benita Sampedro Vizcaya is professor of Spanish Colonial Studies at Hofstra University in New York and a former Associate Director of the Center for 'Race', Culture and Social Justice. In an email to me, she summed up the point that I had been arguing for so long:

The topic that you present is relevant, there is no doubt that your father was the victim of a political plot, and that the era between

1968 and 1979 has been little studied and badly is also an irrefutable fact.

Many more studies and archival documentation are needed, as well as oral testimony.

Reading that email made me feel like I was harvesting a bumper crop in autumn after a year of back-breaking labour.

Forgiveness

'I read the draft article you sent us. Wow! That's amazing! I never knew anyone who lived in North Korea,' said Marisa from the other side of Atlantic, via Zoom.

I am contributing a piece to a new edited volume entitled *Radical Review*, an essay series created by an organisation called Collaborative Social Change, founded by my SOAS tutor, Sara, and her collaborator, Marisa.* It focuses on social causes of violence in modern-day society and explores unconventional ways to address them.

The title of my article is 'Following South Korea: Collectivism versus Individualism in COVID-19 Response'. I base my analysis on my own experiences of growing up in North Korea and living in South Korea – both collectivist societies.

'Yes, I grew up in Pyongyang. I had the same education as a North Korean. So I grew up thinking that the US was an evil

* Monica Macias, 'Following South Korea: Collectivism versus Individualism in COVID-19 Response', *Radical Review* 1 (online/Canada: 2021).

country. But then I decided to go to the US to find out for myself. Which part of the US are you from?' I asked.

'From New York,' she responded.

'Oh, I lived in New York for about three years.' I was happy to speak to someone from the city I once lived in. 'I used to live in Queens.'

'Really? So, was the US an evil country, as you thought?' she asked.

'My personal experience and my Master's studies revealed to me that there is no such thing as an "evil" or a "good" society,' I said. 'States function in accordance with what they believe to be their national interests. Besides, international society is anarchic. States fight to survive because there isn't a "Godfather" or global government to look after them. Also, states never trust each other and are suspicious of others' intentions, always reacting to perceived threats. So, every state wants to be powerful and dominant and their behaviours are the result of these perceptions and national interests. There is no exception here, be it the US, North or South Korea, Spain or Equatorial Guinea. They are all just rivals.'

After the call ended, I continued reflecting on my life's journey. My experience of living in societies with contrasting ideologies and cultures had also revealed to me that when people talk about other societies with differing world-views, they often refer to them as 'evil' or in negative terms, while referring to their own beliefs as 'good'. For many North Koreans, the US is an evil country and vice versa. In general, people tend to see the world through a binary – 'us' versus 'them'.

But finding forgiveness was perhaps the most valuable lesson of my physical and psychological journey.

When I first learned about the assassination of my father, while I was in Pyongyang, I was in shock, angry, confused about family members killing one another for power. I did not know how to deal with those feelings in the beginning. Back then, the only feeling growing inside of me was hate.

Just as with culture shock, I went through different stages of feeling. First, I was stunned and speechless. I spent two days in that state. From that stage I passed to the next: anger and hatred. This period lasted nearly half my adulthood. During this period, I also struggled to understand *why* my father had been assassinated.

Hatred is a mighty emotion that poisons one's soul slowly, like a cancer. In the holder, it can incubate further negative states – chronic anger, depression, anxiety and suicidal behaviour. It is self-destructive and can drive criminal or otherwise damaging behaviours. Blame is at the heart of hatred. As I grew up, I became mature and was ready to accept things as they were and not how I wished them to be. I was even able to step back and analyse the event from different perspectives. I began to comprehend and accept the facts about my father. Hatred would not bring my father back; I could not reverse time. The only thing I gained by hating my father's killer was bitterness. All I could do was to forgive, and by doing so, my feelings of hatred started to fade.

This process was another long psychological journey of reflection, reading and learning about the philosophy of life as formulated by Buddha and Confucius. There is a quote, attributed to Buddha, that resonates when I think about these feelings: 'Holding on to anger is like grasping a hot coal with the intent of throwing it at someone else; you are the one who gets burned.'

The environment in which I grew up also played an important role. Though at the time I railed against its extreme regimentation, Mangyŏngdae Revolutionary Boarding School instilled in me priceless life values which were rooted in Confucianism. *Yi*, probably the core value, refers to goodness and an intuitive moral sense of what is right and wrong. Now, as an adult, I understand why I was sent to Mangyŏngdae, where I was required to adhere to such rigorous discipline. The regimentation and Confucian ideas I absorbed there are now an intrinsic part of who I am. They have helped me to overcome all the difficulties and trauma, both emotional and physical, that I have faced.

After long meditation, I was able finally to confront and dismantle the hatred I felt, its motivation and consequences. In other words, I chose to turn a negative emotion into a positive one: the constructive energy of forgiveness. I chose to forgive Obiang and his accomplices for killing my father. I freed myself from a lifelong burden. I chose not to grasp the hot coal that was burning me and took corrective action. It was primarily a change of my heart and emotions.

To me, forgiveness meant acknowledging that I had been wronged and choosing not to harbour resentment towards the person responsible for that deep hurt. Forgiveness does not cancel out the consequences of one's actions, nor invalidate justice.

Forgiveness and justice are twin components of reconciliation. The final stage, embracing forgiveness, coincided with my time in New York City. I had overcome hatred and won the negative emotional battle.

In 2005, I met with Obiang when he came to New York for a UN gathering. I had moved beyond the stage of needing to avoid him. The morning of the meeting, though, I was nevertheless nervous, and Lino accompanied me. The Obiang I met then seemed remorseful. He was kind, and asked about my sister.

Years later, in 2021, my sister met Obiang in Malabo. The man she met was old and frail, leaning on her to stand up. He told her, 'I have a moral obligation to all of you.' Once again, he showed remorse.

Insisting on retribution, an eye for an eye, destroys individuals, and in societies is a hallmark of a Hobbesian 'state of nature'. When I chose to forgive, I did not feel that it was a sign of weakness. Instead, forgiveness creates an opportunity to mend broken relationships and rebuild a society torn apart by hurt and injustice – something Guinean society desperately needs.

My experience of living in different societies, with both contrasting and similar ideologies and systems, had opened my mind and made me tolerant of others. I do not see someone who does not share my beliefs as an evil person, but as a person with a different viewpoint and understanding of life. Different does not mean wrong. Societies are like human beings. They go through infancy, adolescence and adulthood. A society in its infancy, in my view, struggles to deal with human rights issues effectively and efficiently. As it comes to terms with these issues, it becomes more mature. Some societies I lived in were in their infancy, some in adolescence and some in adulthood, and all faced problems according to their level of maturity. All I can do is to embrace the fact that we are all different but all human, be respectful and accepting, and not impose my views on others.

What do I want now?

I did not have time to love someone until now. Now I am ready. After my life's journeys, I want to love, to settle, and in my maturity I harbour a yearning to be a mother, a yearning that persists despite the obstacles of age and circumstance. For me, motherhood is the most rewarding and beautiful thing I could do as a woman. I want to tell my children my story. I want to tell them that I pushed beyond my boundaries and comfort zone to find the truth about my father. I want to tell them how I purposefully travelled and lived in contrasting societies in order to interact with people with different ideologies, religious beliefs and cultures, and learned a lot from them. I want to tell them that I realised that I am nobody and other people are important. I want to tell them that although my story might be a tragedy, there are thousands of people on this planet who have it worse than me. I want to teach them that, as the Korean saying goes, if they fall one hundred times, they must stand up one hundred and one times. I want to teach them to judge no one and to avoid jumping to conclusions. I want to teach them to appreciate what they have, no matter how small and insignificant it might seem. I want to teach them to understand other people's views, to put themselves in other people's shoes. I want to teach them to accept others as they are and respect them as such. I want to tell them that tolerance is maturity and intolerance is childish.

I want to tell them that I am proud of who I am, daughter of Francisco Macias, adopted daughter of Kim Il Sung, a mixed-race woman forged in three cultures: Asian, African and European.

And I want to tell them that, as Bertrand Russell said: **'LOVE IS WISE, HATRED IS FOOLISH.'**

Acknowledgements

As you can tell from what you have read, my life has had many ups and downs. Through each challenge on this journey, there have been people who stood by me and helped me become who I am today: my North Korean teachers, university lecturers, tutors, classmates, friends and everyone who looked after us during our stay; my South Korean friends Lee Seung Hyeon, DaeYong Park, SangPil Won, Ree Dae Wook, Seo Hyun Seon, Seung Un Lim, Ryu Moon; my Syrian friends Alwaleed Issa Al Abdullah and Waleed; my Spanish friends Amelia Lumbreras, Silvia Cupertino, Ric, Benito Arranz, Josema, Bruno Requena; my Chinese friends Wang Tien Mou, Guo Xu Gun, Yang Lu; my American friends Curtis and David; and my Irish friend Chad O'Carroll.

I am extremely grateful to Pete, Matt and Rowan from Duckworth Books who believed in me and patiently supported this project.

The process of writing this English edition was somewhat more challenging than writing in Korean, my first language. We formed a group of five people to work on this project: Becky Branford, my best friend and a journalist with knowledge of Korean affairs; Rowan

Cope, Danny Lyle, Pete Duncan and Matt Casbourne, excellent editors with my publishing house. Each of us had a different world-view, life experience and education. I first wrote the chapters in English, and Becky helped me to find the right words to express my emotions and reflections, while Matt and Rowan edited the text.

Thanks to my SOAS lecturers and my tutors – Phil Clark, Saghar Birjandian, Dr Catriona Drew, Professor Stephen Chan, Dr Ashley Cox, Dr Hanns Bjoern Kendel, Professor Dan Plesch, Dr Yanan Song and Omid Nouri – who contributed enormously to my academic achievements.

Thanks to everyone who funded my Master's degree through GoFundMe, supporting me in my most financially difficult moment. Without your support, I wouldn't have been able to make it.

I am indebted to Jacco Zwetsloot, who helped with the first translation, and the Society of Authors (SoA) for their support of authors like me.

I am also indebted to Don Antonio Garcia-Trevijano Forte, who contributed enormously to my research about Macias. Thank you to all the Guineans and Spaniards who kindly allowed me to interview them as part of that investigation.

Thank you, Becky, and thanks to your husband Owen Miller for cooking Korean dishes for me in the delightful company of you and your children, Raya and Ellis.

Sincerest thanks to Montan and Herve Kerekou for contributing to my research and allowing me to tell their father's story.

Thanks to my second mother, Maribel from Zaragoza, who always treats me as her second daughter – *gracias, Mama.*

Lastly, love and gratitude to my siblings, and my nieces Fatima, Cristina and Isabel.